Brutal Vows

M. A. Worrell

Also by M.A. Worrell

The Brutal Reckoning Syndicate Series

-Brutal Promise

-Brutal Vows

The Deserted Hearts Series

-Deserted Hearts Awakening

-Bloody's Fury

To my readers

Writing these stories and watching you fall in love with this family and the special ladies who keep the men in check has been such a blessing. You make me push myself to make each new story so much better.

Dedications

First, of all none of my writing would never have seen the light if not for my husband, Brad. Thank you, for pushing me to follow this crazy dream and never letting me give up. None of this would be possible without you. Love you to the moon times infinity.

Second, to my author besties who let me bounce ideas off them. Gave me the kick in the pants I needed when the doubts started to creep in. I really needed every single one of those, so thank you ladies. Special thanks to Becca, Shelby, and B for all the extra help. You made this story so much stronger.

Trigger Warnings

While I would love for everyone to read and adore my work, I'm aware that this Mafia romance while written as lit, has some dark themes and situations that may be triggering to some. Please proceed with caution and protect your mental health.

-PTSD Representation

-stalker

-grief

-DV (not between the main couple)

-mentions of physical/ mental abuse (not between the main couple)

-graphic violence

-weapons

-torture

-explicit language

-explicit adult content

Contents

Chapter 1
Vlad

"What would the two of you say about what is going on right now?" I say, sighing with a tired smile.

It's a wonder I haven't wiped the ink from the old image. I find myself pulling the old photo out, stroking the faces staring back at me more often as of late. Nevaeh and Anya on either side of a younger me, as they squish my cheeks, while Frankie dumps water over us. All of our eyes were bright with innocence before the darkness of the world invaded. The angels of a life I can never go back to, no matter how much I long for the simpler time.

The knock I've been expecting still has my shoulders jerking. "Come in," I call, sliding the old photo back into the desk and locking the hidden drawer. My stern Pakhan mask settles into place with practiced ease.

My brothers and Mikhail's team file through the door, for an uninterrupted meeting. From the looks on their faces, I'd *much* rather have the children in the house. Even just to hear their distant screams as they play through the halls.

The house no longer carries the heavy silence that has hung over it for the past ten years. My sister's children are now firmly stamped all over the place. Barely recognizable drawings, Josey spends every evening creating now hang from the fridge with hardly any space for more. Laughter echoes off the walls. The house is slowly becoming a home again, not just a place to stare at the darkness of my ceiling each night. Becoming what I always wanted the space to be.

Not even this office has been left untouched. The light grey walls and wooden floors are littered with every new drawing Josey makes. A rogue nerf dart peeks out from under a filing cabinet from Hunter's last war game. Even the hardened men are not spared, given the flashes of colorful beads on wrists. Every single one of them instantly drops what they are doing to give their attention to the kids. Given our work, most don't take the chance of having families of their own, so they will protect our children with their lives. They will kill to keep the kids innocence intact because they all need the reminder and distraction they bring.

My brother is one lucky bastard to have met his other half on a one-night stand, even if he didn't know it at the time. His decision to let her go after their first meeting, all to keep her safe was reasonable. I understand the fierce need he had to tie her to him after he saved her when his team was out on mission. He may have been in the right place at the right time, but Ember was already working to save herself. She took his help, but refused to let him treat her like a damsel in distress. He was right not to let her go a second time., thankfully. And, I must admit, seeing her put my brother in his place has been highly entertaining over the last several months.

"Have the Albanians come up from their little hole yet?" I ask, looking to Mikhail for answers. We've found a group that's connected to the traffickers we have been hunting, thanks to their attempt on my brother's family. We just haven't been able to burn them out of hiding yet.

"No," Mikhail says, shaking his head as he sits forward in the leather seat full of frustration. "I need to find them. I don't know how the hell they keep staying ahead of us!" His fist slams into the top of my desk, hard enough to rattle my pen laying on the open file.

"I hate to say it but there *has* to be a leak for them to keep getting away from us." Dimitri groans. "There's no way it's just luck on their part. It's happened too often to be anything else."

The thought of being unable to trust our men doesn't sit well with me, but how else could they always stay two steps ahead of us? Every time we think we have one of them, it ends up being some *unfortunate* soul they swindled into doing their dirty work.

"I need this dealt with for Ember's peace of mind before the baby comes," Mikhail growls, closing his eyes. "She won't say it but she's more watchful and cautious than ever."

Unfortunately, I can't tell him any differently. I've seen the signs in my sister. She's been more on edge and watchful, but so was mother at the end of her pregnancies with my brothers. I keep my voice calm as I try to soothe my brother. "We all want that Mikhail. There isn't much time left. How are Ember and the baby doing?"

"Ember hasn't been sleeping well this week, due to the baby's movements, meaning I haven't gotten much sleep either. Our little one doesn't want to settle her nightly tumbling practice long enough for us to get more than a handful of hours a night." His big body folds forward to pull at his loose hair in helplessness.

It hurts to see him at such a loss and not be able to help ease his fears. I've always had the answers to get us through until we could make things right. Even when father had his stroke it was nothing for me to step up and take control. Anya and Nevaeh would have known what to say to make things better.The ache of missing them rises with burning intensity and I ruthlessly shove it away. I don't have time to mourn right now. My family will not continue to suffer because of our continued failure.

"Ember is *strong*. Your *child* is strong. They will be alright." I reassure him knowing that she will be fine no matter how stressed the rest of us are.

Laughter bubbles out of his throat, allowing his blue eyes to clear. "That damn woman is stronger than any of us."

I join in because he's probably right. Aside from our mother, Anya, and Nevaeh, I have never met anyone who I admire more. I wish I could find ten men in our ranks that had her tenacity and grit. She is a rare gem, and Mikhail is lucky to have her.

"MIKHAIL!" Ember's scream has us lunging from our chairs and out the closed door. Five of our men burst out of the gaming room and follow us with pistols drawn. Ember isn't one to scream which puts all of us are on edge and ready to kill.

I make it to the staircase, taking them two at a time as my heart pounds in alarm as we race up the stairs. I manage to stay just behind my brother, with Maskin right on our tail. She stands hunched over gripping the wall. A low pain-filled moan sounds fills the air, as the three of us draw closer. Her face is white, tension flooding her strong body. She would be on the floor if he didn't take her in his arms.

"*Moye plamya,* what is wrong?" Unease is clearly written on the lines of his face as he tries to keep her on her feet.

"Baby." Her throat works rapidly as she pulls in deep breaths through her nose.

"What's happening? Is something wrong with her?" Horror stains his features because he has no way to help her or the little one.

Understanding rushes through me as I study her in time to watch her stomach spasm. The skirt she has been wearing lately is dark, with deep flecks of liquid running down her legs. Even knowing it's time, I can't get my voice above a whisper. "The baby is coming."

"Back to your work!" Maskin barks, pushing the gawking men back from his charge. The silent sniper gives her one last look before turning to follow the others. "You cannot help with anything here."

She sends the man a grateful smile before looking at her husband. "My water broke."

"What?!" Mikhail looks like he's about to pass out as he holds her closer. "You are not due for another two weeks." One of his hands drops to run over her swollen stomach, as if he can rub the discomfort away. Or, soothe the baby into waiting longer before making its entrance into the world.

She doubles over with a grunt and grips his forearm with more strength than she should be capable of, as another rush of fluid wets the floor beneath her. "Not what your *sweet* daughter is saying." She laughs breathlessly, straightening up as the pain subsides. "She's coming now."

"Holy shit! We need to get to the hospital." Letting go of her, he runs for their room but stops short as the next wave of pain brings another whimper to her lips. Rushing back, he holds her through the pain before kissing her hair and whispers, "I'll be right back *moya lyubov'*, just stay strong," before racing away again.

Another contraction has her stumbling. There isn't time for me to take a full step to reach her before one of her hands latches onto my fingers in a crushing grip. Bones grind painfully against each other. Biting back the grunt of surprise, I step forward and let her use me as she needs. If taking the pain out on me helps her manage it, I'll gladly stand for her with a smile. Pain is nothing new and something I can easily take on.

“Ember. Mladshaya sastra breathe. We’ll get you to the doctor quickly.” She lets me rub gently up and down her arm. My mind doesn’t know what else to do for her. It seems to help in some small way at least as she leans closer to me.

“Won’t make it.” She pants more sharply than when she first came home from the hospital after being shot and stubbornly wandered the house against Mikhail’s orders. Pain strains her face white as she works on breathing through each one. I do not like the emotion etched on her face.

“Don’t speak nonsense sastra. You are more than strong enough to get through this.” My voice is bitter to mask the unease curling sharply in my guts.

“I’m fine, it's this baby that isn’t going to wait,” she laughs through the pain to correct my thoughts. I’m not sure what she finds funny, but it is better than screaming and tears.

Mikahil races up with a bag over each shoulder. “Ember.” The bags thud to the floor as he pulls her close from my hold. “Ember?” Worry clouds his eyes heavily as he clocks the changes taking place with his wife.

“No time.” Her legs nearly buckle beneath her as the next contraction hits. "She’s coming....”

Her words end in a long keening cry that has my body next to them on instinct to help but not sure how.

My poor brother pales as he stammers, "this is too fast."

"Third kid Mikhail! Each one gets faster, and this one seems to have your patience."

Mikhail's string of curses doesn't begin to sum up the situation we find ourselves in. Mother and father haven't returned from Russia. All but the team staying at the house are busy, and the maid is out shopping. There are only men in the house and Ember says that my newest plemyannitsa will not wait for us to make it to the hospital.

His fingers bite into my arm as he rattles off an order too fast for her to understand with her limited grasp of our language. "Something isn't right. I don't think there should be this much blood."

"Mikhail!" Her body folds a fraction more.

Mikhail lifts his wife up, whispering soothing words as he turns away. "Call the doctor and get him here."

Pulling my phone out, I do what he says without question. Being in charge does have its advantages when something needs to be done immediately. My next call is to our parents to let them know things are moving ahead of schedule. A few quick words and I hurry into the room in time to watch as she cries out again.

In the short time it took me to call, they changed her into one of his button up shirts and her hair pulled back from her face. Instead of lying in bed, she's still on her feet and walking. Every few steps she stops, bending forward over his arm to endure another wave of contractions.

"You should lay down, sastra." I stand back by the door not sure what to do but unable to leave. All I can do is watch and feel useless.

"When you push a nine-pound mini *you* out of one of your holes, I'll take your advice into consideration. Until then, *respectfully*, shut the fuck up!" Hazel eyes burn my way for a second while she goes back to doing what she wants.

The venom in her voice has me wanting to step back but my bratva training won't allow me to show any weakness. Wisely, I keep my mouth shut. I still want to do something to help but I'm less helpful than my hovering brother. Each one of her steps has me wanting to pace with her. My fists clench as I struggle with what to do. Fuck, I hate being helpless!

After twenty minutes, she sinks to the edge of the bed. Unable to stay back another second, I move to kneel on the blood-speckled rug before her. "What do you need, sastra?"

A drawn-out moan escapes her. Drifting back, Ember leans against her husband for support. Her fingers gripping his hard enough that both are strained white from the pressure. She pants between groans. "She's coming!"

My eyes snap up to my brother's. As much as he wants to be the one to welcome his daughter into the world, Ember needs him where he is.

One deep breath in, and I steel myself for a view of my sister-in-law I never wanted to see. There are no words to describe the view without making myself ill. Which is ridiculous with our line of work, but no less true. Only focusing on the task of seeing our newest princess into the world keeps me moving forward.

"You are almost done." I work to keep my voice light with encouragement, so I don't betray how terrified I am that I am going to mess something up and hurt one of them. "I can see her head."

Not a single piece of my training could prepare me for the task at hand. Nor for the burst of protectiveness that overwhelms me as I help guide her into the world. Not even the way my heart stops when I shelter her against my chest as the doctor rushes into the room, our eyes meeting for the first time.

"She's perfect Mikhail," I whisper, utterly in love with her already.

I'd hold her forever if allowed, but her mother's eager fingers are restlessly reaching in demand. Each movement is calculated as I stand, moving to allow the doctor to take my place. Reluctantly I hand the whimpering dark haired child that's stolen my heart to her parents to fuss over when Mikhail holds them in his arms.

The doctor mutters a curse. Fingers assessing things I have no knowledge of. One hand raises to press on her stomach, and she can't hide the pain as she tries to shift away from it. His stern eyes meet mine before looking back at my brother.

"We are going to finish up here and then we are going to the hospital," he says, tone brokering no room for argument.

Fear grips my guts. I have to keep it together. "Is she in danger?"

"Calm yourself, she'll be just fine. There's a tear, but she'll be fine as soon as we get that taken care of. The hospital is just to make sure I haven't missed anything."

"Can't you do that here?" Ember shifts, turning pleading eyes to Mikhail.

"You're *going*," I order, butting in. I know that she hates hospitals, but their health is too important to let that fear rule her. "I will handle everything here till you are released."

"Shit," Mikhail shouts, looking down at Ember with horror. "Someone needs to get the kids."

Chapter 2
Nevaeh

Pull yourself together, Nevaeh. Pull yourself the hell together! I repeat the mantra in my head. I love my job.

How many times must I repeat the words to truly believe them today? The whole morning has been a nightmare. I should have turned around, put on my comfy clothes, and crawled straight back into bed. My pants tore when I tripped over myself on the stairs. In the time it took me to change, I nearly missed my train. New York foot traffic is always hell, but today feels so much worse. By the time I make it to my classroom I'm sticky with sweat, out of breath, and over the day before it truly started.

Three eight-year-old meltdowns, two broken clay projects later, and I am ready to run out the door screaming. Thankfully the clay was an easy clean up, and for once I don't leave a mess for the janitors. I just have to get through sending the kids off, and I can go home to hide under the covers. My bed is *screaming* my name. Why does the world hate me so much today?

Most of the children are gone when I spot Hunter pacing along the curb in agitation. He kicks a lone rock, staring down the street, clearly *not* happy. I've never seen him look this upset. His little sister sits on the cold wall, humming happily to herself. Mr. Johnson is on traffic duty, checking his watch with a frown as he monitors them.

"Do you have somewhere to be Mr. Johnson?" I ask, stepping up with a smile.

"Yes," he sighs. "I have to be at the doctor's office in twenty minutes. If their parents don't show up soon, I won't make it to my chemo."

"Why don't you go ahead? I can stay with the kids." I smile, setting my bag down.

He frowns unsure, "Will you be alright?"

"Of course, you've helped me make my own appointments several times already. Go take care of yourself." I go quiet and let him radio the office to let them know of the change.

"Thank you, Miss Hawkins." He smiles and rushes to get his things.

Chuckling to myself, I walk over to the kids with a tired smile. "Hunter, Josey? Have you been able to get a hold of your family?"

"No, they haven't called the office." He stops to face me for a second before glancing at his watch again. "Mikhail should be here by now. He's never late. One of our uncles should have been here when we walk out."

"Your dad may be stuck in traffic. I'm sure he'll be here soon." I put on a brave face, as I lean over him, trying to get his attention. "How you tried calling?"

His face goes red. Head bowing as he shakes his head and shoves his hands in his pockets as he mumbles, "I forgot to charge the phone last night."

I can't say anything on that. Mine's dead in my bag too. "Do you want to go back to the office and use the phone?"

He ignores me, glancing again at the watch- like it'll make time go faster. I try a new tactic. "How about we play a game until your dad shows up?"

He sighs, looking a bit guilty as he says, "he isn't our real dad."

"Oh," I mutter, blinking in an attempt to cover up the emotions of my own complicated past at his words. "Not all families share the same blood. I'm sure he loves you just as much as if you were his own."

"Kail is the best daddy in the world," Josey giggles happily from her seat.

"Yes ma'am, I know." His eyes flicker back to the street. "Being late isn't like them though."

“Okay,” I say, taken aback by his formal way of addressing me. Folding the long skirt of my dress under my legs, I sit on the pavement and pat the surface beside me. “Sit with me please? It’s been a long day for both of us.”

Indecision filters over his face before he drops beside me with a nod. “Why?” He doesn’t look at me right away, but I can tell I have his attention.

“Well to start, this skirt wasn’t what I left the house in.”

His sharp eyes sweep over me as if looking for injuries. “Did you have an accident?”

“I fell on the way to the subway and ripped the knees right out of my favorite pair of jeans.” I make my sigh as dramatic as possible to lighten his mood.

He turns to look at me with his mouth hanging open. It snaps it shut, and he starts to laugh. “You are very clumsy, Miss Hawkins. I'm surprised you don’t have paint in your hair today.”

“That’s not nice, young man.” I pat at my eyes trying to hide my smile. "I'm not that bad."

His hands fly to cover his mouth, as we lean in closer together and start giggling. After a few moments we calm down to sit in silence. “What are you worried about beside them being late little man?”

“My mom. The baby hasn’t let her sleep much this past week. I don’t know how to help her.” He looks to the road again, eyes filled with more worry than a child his age should hold, searching for his ride.

"Babies do that. Crying is the only way they have to let us know their needs."

"No baby yet. Mikhail said she has a few weeks to go till she comes."

"I'm gonna be a big sister, Miss Hawkins," Josey yells, jumping up to spin around in excited circles.

"A little sister, huh? Do they have a name for her yet?"

"No, mom said she won't decide until she's holding her," Hunter says, pulling Josey back down with the patience of someone used to wrangling the little hurricane.

"They're here," Josey squeals, pointing to the end of the block.

A dark Range Rover rolls around the corner, and they jump up before I can say anything else. They only stay back until it slows to roll closer to the curb in front of us. Well, that wasn't too much of a wait thankfully.

"See I told you he'd be here." Smiling, I stand and dust off the back of my skirt.

"That's Uncle Vlad." Hunter laughs, grinning at his sister. "He must have beat Dimitri out the door to get us."

"So, he's approved to pick you up?"

"Yes. Mom put all our uncles on the list."

Tires roll to a soft stop but the man behind the wheel isn't anyone I've seen get the kids before though something about him looks familiar. Worry grips my stomach as Hunter jumps to the door and pulls it open. They both obviously know and trust the man. Plus he's pasted the security check at the gate, so I can see them off and get home myself.

The man inside has me almost choking on my own spit, as my mouth drops open. Good lord, he is gorgeous with dark blue eyes, tall, styled hair, and a neatly trimmed black beard. The kind of man I would trip over myself for if I could bring myself to date someone again. Chris really messed me up all those years ago.

"Dyadya! Is mom ok?" Innocent eyes plead with the man.

"Da plemyannik, she is fine. Your sastra decided that she was ready to join the world early," he grumbles with humor.

His heavy Russian accent makes me pull in air sharply through my teeth. It has been a long time since I've heard any of that language. Not since my brother was still alive. Back when life wasn't so confusing.

"Really!" The boy is bouncing happily. A huge grin stretches across from ear to ear. "Why didn't one of you come get me so I could be there? Mikhail said he would."

"I'm sorry Hunter, but there was no time. She did not want to wait for anyone, not even the doctor. Come, everyone is waiting for you." The big man doesn't crack a smile the whole time but the warmth for his family seeps through every word he says.

"Hang one, Hunter. I still need to check his ID," I say, gently laying a hand on his shoulder to stop him.

"We told you he's our uncle," Hunter nearly whines at my words.

"It is fine Hunter. The school has rules for a reason." He turns to me with respect in his gaze as he hands me his identification. "It's rare that I finish work in time to retrieve the kids. I should have had everything out and ready for you."

Well, that was easy. I make the call on the walkie and he is quickly cleared. "Okay guys have a good day."

The man nods to me as the kids climb in the back seat talking a mile a minute about their new sibling. I smile and wave, before taking myself to collect my things so I can head home. Something as simple as sitting with the kids has lifted my mood far more than I would have thought. One of the perks of working with at the school.

I don't mind the rat race of the subway tonight as I make my way home. When I walk through the door, the familiar smells of the space helps to restore my peace of mind. After freshening up, I heat up my leftovers and pull up my latest show. It feels good to curl up on my bed and take a night off from my writing.

The voice of the man in the car plays over and over again in my mind. There is something oddly familiar about him that my mind won't let go of. It eats at my mind all the way home, a voice pushing for me to remember.

A warm laugh filters through my mind as images of my brother flash before me. His warm brown eyes closing in laughter, as he and his best friend wrestle for the tv remote. Friendly insults fly, Volodya laughing as the prize is tossed into my lap. He tells me to pick, and much to Frankie's disappointment, I put on another sappy romcom that has him groaning in elaborated disgust.

Shaking the memory from my head I blink the tears from my eyes. Why did the sound of Russian words bring that night back? I haven't thought of my childhood crush in a long time because every memory of him is woven with my brother. Those thoughts hurt too much after he abandoned me. I needed him to make everything right after the accident that took my brother, and he never showed up. Maybe he...

"No." There's no way I'm going to think about any of that tonight. I've had enough of the what ifs of that night to last a lifetime.

Getting up I plug my computer in to recharge and turn off the lights before climbing back in bed. Under the blankets I stare at the glowing stars that litter my ceiling to calm my mind enough to sleep. The darkness hasn't been my friend for a long time. It was always when Chris became the most unstable with his ways to keep me under his thumb. I haven't been able to sleep in a dark room in a long time. Volodya's face flashes over the ceiling with a little grin making my heart skip a beat and sadness engulfs me as I remember how frantically I tried to reach him then.

Tallie yowls as I pull the pillow from under him to put it over my head. The tips of his claws scratch over my shoulder before he rolls over to go back to sleep. The silky warm fuzz of his fur feels good as he curls up into the side of my neck.

"Thinking about it won't do me any good," I whisper into the night.

Shivers roll down my spine, and I let them for a moment. Maybe one of these days that night won't hold me in its grasp so strongly. But probably not. It was one of the worst times in my life, and when I needed him most... He was just *gone*. No call, no show for the first time in our lives.

Reaching toward the pillow, I grab Savy my stuffed tiger the boys won from me at a county fair shortly after we met to pull close. I bet he has a couple kids by now. Anya was excited to have kids, and he'd promised her they'd have as many as she wanted.

Wonder if I would recognize him on the street now? How would the years change him after over a decade? Was his laugh still the same or have the years dimmed his brightness? THe questions make my heart ache in the same old uncomfortable way.

"I still miss you, Volodya."

Chapter 3
Vlad

Katya's soft cries drift down the hall, but are quickly silenced by her parents before they can cause any of the sleeping members of the house to stir. Mikhail and Ember's soft whispers float to me as I sit at the top of the stairs, looking over the garden, thinking about the future I was never allowed to have. Mikhail's short chuckles drift to me as they talk, offering some peace to my dark mood.

Sitting here feeling sorry for myself isn't going to do me any favors. It never has, not once in the fourteen years I've followed the same destructive ritual. Too many shattered dreams fill my head every time I try to close my eyes. It's rare I fall asleep without half a bottle of the strongest Russian vodka I can find.

I can't sit here any longer. Rising to my feet, I silently make my way down to my office. I don't want my nightly dealings to keep my family from getting the rest that they need. The nightmare that plagues my mind will not cause anyone but myself to lose sleep.

Clear liquid splashes off the bottom of the crystal glass I flip over to fill. Leather creaks softly as I sink into the chair and lean back to stare at the alcohol. Why can it not hold the answers that I'm desperate to know? I lift the glass and restrain myself to a sip instead of swallowing it in one go.

My eyes fall shut, and the woman who sat with the kids flashes by in vivid detail. Long brown hair, held back in a flowery clip. Soft brown eyes filled with humor, as she watches Hunter jumping in over exaggerated excitement. Her face perfectly narrow, filled with so much life. Those features are so familiar, but I can't put my finger on it just yet. As we made our way home, Hunter told me her name is Miss Hawkins and that she is his art teacher. I've spent a large chunk of the night racking my brain for anyone I remember with that name. Not a single one comes to mind.

Damn it, this is driving me nuts! The glass smacks off the wood as I turn to the computer and fire up the search engine. Several seconds later she stares back at me from the school's website. Nevaeh Hawkins. The name buzzes like an annoying gnat at the back of my brain. A small barely there feature has my eyes narrowing to study it more closely.

"It can't be." My right-hand traces over the smiling face before I can stop myself. It's *her*. Her hair, no longer a mess of uncertain colors has settled into a rich blend of soft browns creating a warm nest of brunette curls. Braces no longer frame her teeth, and the freckles are gone. A different name but the same girl now turned into a woman. Time has filled her body into an artist's dream.

After all this time, she's been under my nose without me knowing it. "There you are moya milaya malen'kaya tigrovaya lilya. I found our girl, Frankie. Sorry it took me so long."

Frankie is probably rolling in his grave laughing at the fact I let his little sister evade me for so long. Some friend I turned out to be.

***

The ride to pick up the kids is filled with the various thoughts of the Cooper's siblings. Memories of times long ago when I wasn't the broken man I am now. A time when the horrors of my world weren't a black stain on my soul. Back when I believed all of us couldn't be any happier. Before dad's stroke, Frankie's death, Nevaeh's disappearance, and Anya. Before everything went wrong.

I could have left my brothers to handle the pickups over the past week, but I refused craving just the smallest sight of her. Each day that she isn't at the curb to see the kids off makes me madder than the last. My thoughts are becoming more unhinged without any sign of her. Damn it, I need her back in my life. I should never have let her out of my sight. Damn the demands of my family for taking me away when she needed me the most. I have to see with my own eyes that she is safe and happy.

Finally, I catch sight of the large unruly mass of curled hair bobbing through the sea of children as she helps them into their cars. The monster in me settles down to watch as the line creeps along. Forty feet. Thirty, twenty, ten.

Her hearty giggles fill the thick, suffocating air inside of the cab, as she pulls the door open to allow Hunter. He slides in without dropping the project in his arms. My favorite little ball of energy bounces in after him, full of smiles, as she jumps between the seats to give me a kiss. She's sitting before I can get my hug too.

Nevaeh gives them a smile and wave. "Have a good weekend, Hunter. Bye, Josey."

The kids buckle up and say their own farewell, "Bye, Miss Hawkins!"

Greedily, I take in the sight of her. The small space between the open door only gives me a tiny glimpse. I feel like a starving man, dying for the chance at his last meal. Fuck, she grew up. The years have been more than generous to her. Bright, fresh eyes, that remind me of her brother. She looks so much like my friend that I can't say anything. Not until the chance has passed and I have to move so I don't hold up the line.

The sight makes my heart ache. How long since I last thought of Frankie? Too fucking long. Old pains wrap around my heart as my door is shut, and she turns away. I don't want to lose sight of her but sitting here staring isn't going to do me any good. One of the cars honks behind me eager to get their child. Down the block, I pull into an ice cream shop and park just to stay closer to her for a few moments.

"What's going on Dyadya?" Hunter asks, cocking his head to watch me just like his mother does when she's trying to solve a problem.

I open my door, getting out after seeing the guards that always follow behind at a distance exit their vehicles. They sweep the area, eyes shrewdly paying attention to every tiny detail of our surroundings. "Starting your break off the right way," I say, winking at them as playfully, keeping my mask in place. Small smiles at home are one thing but I can't seem to allow myself to do so in public.

They don't need to be told twice. They jump out, and pull me into the shop with excited giggles. I let them choose what they want without complaint. These kids deserve to have the world handed to them, and I have the means to do so. I may not be able to run after them and play but they will have all that they want in life.

My sweet little Josey insists that I try some of her chocolate swirl with sprinkles. Knowing she won't let up until I agree, I easily give in. She giggles playfully, making a mess and smearing it all over my nose. The sound of her giggles never fails to lighten the black cloud that hangs over me. Mikhail and their mother can enjoy the sugar high the kids will be flying on, thanks to my little treat. I'm going to eat up each smile and giggle that comes out of these two.

These tiny moments are why our people will never stop hunting the human scum who think they can take precious family away from others. Those who treat other humans as if they are lower than cattle. We will stand firm. We will never give up. We will burn that trash from the world. For these kids and anyone too weak we will be their shield.

Once they are safely within the walls of our house again, I hole up in my office and stare at the file I put together on Nevaeh in the early hours of the morning. I could have handed the task to one of the men, but with everything going on she will remain entirely mine in every way, from here on out. If nothing else, I owe it to Frankie to keep her safe now that she's in my sights again.

A photo of her at the last birthday I was around for is pinned to one side. She sits with Anya, squished in a booth between her brother and I. The last time all of us were together. On the opposite side, is the employee photo of her from the beginning of the school year.

The records of the years following her seventeenth birthday are nearly bare. All except a restraining order against an old boyfriend. A man who is currently sitting in a small Tennessee prison. The information isn't much to go on as far as what happened, but my mind is more than capable of entertaining a *lot* of things. There are no pictures, and most of the statements are blacked out. That tells me plenty, and has the monster inside me waking to look for blood. I'm sure I could get someone in there to deal with him.

What made her run back to the city from a job that she always dreamed of? After her brother's death, I lost track of her. Why didn't she call me for help? Even if she thought I was married and happy, I should have been her first call. Did she think that Anya would have kept me away? Surely not, when she always looked at Nevaeh like a sister. Does she believe that I would not still burn down the world for her? That she is less important to me now than when we were kids. So many things have been left unanswered between us.

Leading our Bratva has trained me to be as ruthless as I need to be to get what I want. Aside from my family's safety, I want Nevaeh back by my side in whatever way she'll allow. Nothing is getting in the way of me bringing her into the family. Not any longer. Mikhail's children allow light into the darkness of my soul, but I crave more. I need Nevaeh's light to burn the darkness away completely. She will be safest with me, and God help anyone who tries to hurt her.

Chapter 4

Nevaeh

Unplugging the hot plate, my stomach growls in anticipation of the spaghetti that I only just finished filling my plate with. I'm hungry enough to eat most of the pot but I retrain myself to one plate. The savory smell of perfectly seasoned sauce has been making my mouth water for the past hour.

Before I can climb into bed to eat, three solid knocks sound from my door. Fear is quick to bubble up, but I swiftly push the feeling away. Someone coming to see me is rare but nothing to fear. This is not Rosin Tennessee, and I am not a victim. Setting my dinner on the counter I check the peep hole just to be sure it isn't Chris. I know it can't be but I still check before leaving the chain on and crack the heavy door open.

Hard blue grey eyes drift down to mine through the space I create. "Can I help you?"

"Nevaeh." The sound of my name, rumbling out in that heavy accent, sends shivers of confusion through my body. Why is the kids' uncle is standing in my hallway.

"Yes?"

"May I come in?"

"Uhm," I mutter, shifting back and forth on the balls of my feet. It's like I can't stop myself from moving under his eyes. I've never allowed a man to enter into my safe space. It's never felt right. I'm not sure about him but I'm also not afraid.

"It will only take a minute." His eyes soften just the slightest. "Please."

Chewing on my bottom lip is a nasty habit that likes to kick in when I'm nervous. *Is he someone that I can trust?* My mind runs with useless questions I already know the answer to just to have another moment. "You're Hunter's uncle?"

He gives a sharp nod but doesn't say anything more, shoulders relaxed, posture slightly shifting as he waits for me to make my own decision. Blowing out my breath as quietly as I can, I shut the door and let the chain fall freely. Slowly, I make room for him. He steps into my space, the action oddly respectful, as I hold the door open for him to come in. His eyes sweep over my private space, then he closes the door behind himself shutting us in.

Moving back, I let some distance gather between us, watching his every move. He takes in the multitude of canvases that cover every inch of drywall. I'll never admit to anyone that they're to cover up the dingy orange paint the landlord layered on the walls. The small single bed with my multicolored purple quilt. The four feet of cabinets, small fridge and coffee table littered with all the supplies for my writing. Jammed full bookcases that house my horde of well used novels. The plate of my uneaten food sitting on the counter.

Before I can become too uncomfortable, he returns his focus to me. "You look.... *well.*"

What an odd, but civil thing to say. Do I know him?I blink slowly, confusion swirling in my head. I'm not sure how to respond, so I nod and say, "what was it that you needed?"

The air seems to shimmer around him before he takes a step closer. Stormy grey eyes skim over each inch of me before he moves another foot in my direction. His focus is controlled, directly on me, and wholly unwavering. He takes another step closer, leaving very little space in my suddenly cramped home.

A small curl of his lip, his eyes soften to look at me like something he lost and found after many long years. "It has been far too long tigrovaya lilya."

All the air in my lungs leaves so fast I stumble back, gripping the doorframe to keep upright. Only one person *ever* used that nickname. Tears flow without permission as my hand covers my mouth.

"Volodya?" I can barely get the name out as I fight to keep enough air in me to breathe.

How is it possible? How is he here before me? I look closer, examining every inch of him. Suddenly, small details begin to connect in my brain. His eyes, though not as lighthearted as they used to be, pull me in just the same. His face is narrower and harder, as if he has seen and done things far too dark for a normal person to comprehend. That tall lanky body is now filled out with wide muscles. I suck in a sharp breath at the realization that hits me square in the chest like a lightning bolt. *He could probably snap me like a twig.*

His eyes soften, just a fraction, and the smile lifts both corners of his mouth.. "No one has called me that in a very long time. I think you are the only one who remembers it."

Stepping closerhe pushes wisps of stray hair from my face. The touch doesn't fully connect before I retreat a step and embarrassment floods me. He *isn't* Chris. *He's safe.* At least... he *used* to be. Taking a deep breath, I force myself to calm down and lift my gaze back to his in time to see the flash of hurt.

"What are you doing here?" It hurts to force myself to stay still, and my voice is shaky, but I stand firm.

"Making sure I wasn't losing my mind. You've grown so much since I last saw you."

An uncontrollable nervous giggle bursts out as I bite back the old tease and try to wrap my head around the fact he's standing before me after so long. "That tends to happen with time, but the little girl you knew was lost a long time ago. And you never had much in the way of brains."

A larger smile lifts the hard edges of his mouth, and he chuckles. "There is that sass I remember so well. It's good to see your claws are still sharp as ever."

Blushing, I turn to hide the redness flushing across my cheeks, taking in the craziness I created on the walls to catch my breath. He always did know how to trip me up. I never seemed to come out on top when we started going after each other. Frankie would always sit back and laugh as we went at it.

"How have you been?" I have to take us back to safe territory. When he left all those years ago, it was to meet the relatives of his fiancé's parents. He should be married. A quick glance at his fingers reveals nothing. No ring. Maybe he's one of those who doesn't like wearing one.

"Breathing."

"And Anya? How is she?" I ask, needing the answer as much as I'm dreading it.

The humor drains from his face as he gives me a sad smile. "She died years ago."

His calm answer has my jerking back to take in his features. Nothing shows on his face, but the spark I remember so well is nothing more than a dim light. Time, it appears, has not been kind to him. "What happened Vol?"

"Life." Unconsciously he reaches out to take my hand. His eyes dim as his thumb rubs over my knuckles, but he doesn't elaborate.

I allow him a few moments of comfort before pulling away. "How is the family?"

"Father had a stroke a year after Frankie's death, so I am now head of the family. He and Mother are doing well. They came back to the states to be closer now that Mikhail has a family."

Shock rolls through me as I remember the strong man who always welcomed me and my brother into his home. He always seemed larger than life, like a second father to my young mind. It's humbling to think that he could be struck down so harshly at such a young age given how fit he always was.

"I'm happy to hear that everyone is doing good. You look well," I shyly add as I take in the impressive figure he has grown into. He definitely grew into his big frame, and I can't stop the quick looks even as I try to hide them behind my hair.

He nods giving me a long once over as well. "You aren't the gangly teen I remember. I can't believe it was really you after so long. The name change had me questioning myself. Are you married or seeing anyone?"

The change of direction brings me up short as I wonder how to answer it. I don't want him to think that I hid because of him, even if it *did* play a role in the choice at the time. If he had been there after the funeral, how differently would my life have played out?

Clearing my throat, I smile and shake my head. "No, to both. The state wanted to take me, so I used my grandmother's maiden name and ran. Didn't want to be put in one of their group homes."

If I wouldn't have been watching, I would've missed the way his shoulders stiffen as the new registers. "I should have been there Nevaeh. I'm sorry I wasn't."

All I can do is smile and nod. "It's okay, everything worked out in the end. I got my degree in teaching, and I'm happy."

He steps up and takes my hand again. "I am glad to see you happy. We have missed far too many years, let me take you to dinner Friday night."

"Oh! Uhh... I already have plans for this weekend." There goes the blood to my face again.

Something flashes in his eyes, but it's gone so quickly I'm not sure I saw it in the first place. "Then the next. I want to know everything that you've been doing all these years."

"I'd like that," I say before I can stop myself.

Brushing over the back of my hands again he nods. He lets go and holds out his hand. "Give me your phone."

It's in his hand before I can stop myself. Damn it, why did I let him do that to me? A few taps of his fingers and a beep sounds on his person.

"Call me, da?" The plastic is put gently back in my hand before he steps away.

Mute, all I can do is nod. *What the hell, Nevaeh!* I hope he is still the protector I remember. Still I can't let him get close.

He's nearly out the door when he looks back. "Lock the door Nevaeh."

My eyes roll and I nod as he steps out the door. "I will."

"I'm waiting," he grumbles from the other side, making me laugh.

"Yes, Dad!"

The wood swings in at an alarming speed, and he strides back in. Determined steps force me back to the wall seeking some distance. Arms land on the plaster on either side of me as he leans level with my eyes. Thankfully, he isn't touching me.

"Don't sass me when it comes to your safety moya liliya. You won't like what happens if you are careless. I still honor my vows. Do you understand me?"

My lungs freeze at his closeness. I haven't been this close to a man since my ex was arrested. Memories of that night steal my breath. His leering face shoving close, skin reeking of beer. Blackness creeps into the edges of my vision as I whimper, unable to move or speak. An angry hiss fills the air as Tallie darts out, arching his back in the biggest display of attitude I've ever seen out of his small body, but Volodya barely gives him more than a passing glance.

"Nevaeh?" Warm palms slide over my chilled cheeks pulling me back to the man in front of me. "You're safe, you know I'd never harm you. What happened? Who hurt you?"

My smile wobbles but I force it anyway. I haven't had one of those flashbacks in years and I'm thankful that it doesn't have me curled up on the ground like before. "I'm okay."

"You're not," he rumbles, a distasteful look crossing his face, but he stays where he is. He knows something is wrong, and thankfully he isn't pushing.

"I promise I'm fine." I grab my cat and hold him close as he noses my chin. A few calming breaths settle me in the present. "I'll lock the door."

His dark eyes search for the truth in mine. Long fingers flex in light strokes for several seconds on my arms, before I pull away uncomfortable with the touch. "You know I will always protect you. One word and I will be by your side. You mean the world to me, moya milaya malen'kaya tigrovaya liliya. You always have."

The breath clogs in my throat at his words. They aren't new, he's said them since the beginning, but they still have the ability to render me powerless in his presence. "I know you will, but I promise I'm okay."

His warm lips ghost over the top of my head like a thousand times before and disappear just as quickly. They are gone before my brain can register his closeness. Millions of memories and emotions clamor to break through the walls. I can't let them out. Not now. Not ever. Stepping slowly back he turns and heads out the door.

Knowing that he is standing there waiting for me to follow through, I set the locks in place and grab my phone. I can't let him in any more than he already is. All we can have in civility. I can feel him still waiting outside.

I open my phone to tell him to go home. Of course he saved himself as Volodya. He never went by his birth name with us. I don't think I ever heard it unless his mother was spitting mad, and that's probably why it didn't register when he picked the kids up.

Me- You can go home now.

Me- I'm locked in safe and sound so you can leave.

Volodya- Good girl. Sweet dreams moya liliya.

Me- Goodnight

Chapter 5

Vlad

She's on a fucking date. Three weeks of telling me no, of saying that she was busy. She's been putting me off each time I reach out. She snuck this one in right under my nose.

Red clouds swirl in my vision. Every time that shaggy, blonde-haired hippie lays a finger on her. He shouldn't be touching her! After fourteen years I have her in my sight again and I won't be letting her go this time. She is *mine*! *My* girl to protect. *Shit.* I need to calm down. She isn't my woman, but she is part of my family no matter the lack of connecting blood. I won't fail her again.

I want to jump out of this car and rip the bastard apart for even thinking he could sniff around her. It's got to be a pity date. There is no other explanation. What the fuck would she even see in the boy to entertain the thought of a date with him. When she flinches at his touch, for the second time, I lose it. I can't sit here and take it anymore.

Me- If that boy puts his hands on you AGAIN, I will personally remove them.

TL-??? What the hell!Are you following me?

Me- He clearly makes you uncomfortable. Why are you letting him paw at you?

TL- LEAVE!!

TL- What I do and who I see is none of your damn business!

Me- Do not push me moya liliya. Tell him to get his fucking hand off of you!

TL-Go home. I'm trying to enjoy myself.

Me- You aren't enjoying yourself. Come to me and I will take you out.

Me- Moya liliya, come out now. I can't stand watching you flinch each time he moves.

Me- Nevaeh stop this. Tell me where you want to go and I will take you.

Me- Nevaeh Annette Hawkins answer me!

Me- You are playing a game that will not end well. I do not like being disregarded.

She doesn't even look at the messages. She fucking turns the phone off and slides it in her coat. "If that is how you want to play, let me show you how the game works."

I shove the door open violently and get out. When my guards move to follow, I tell them to stay put as I make my way into the diner. More than one customer's head turns in surprise as I make my way to her table.

Gripping the back of a nearby chair, spinning it with an easy twist to sit. I'm down beside her before she knows I'm there. "Having a good time, Nevaeh?"

Both of them jump at my sudden appearance and sit back in their seats. The little minx that thinks she can ignore me blinks in stunned silence before the fire flares to life in her eyes. The sight makes me highly satisfied. She has been far too tame.

"You need to walk away," she hisses. The steel I remember finally making itself known.

Keeping the smile to myself, I lean back, not interested in giving her what she wants. Instead, I reach over to run my fingers through her hair. It's unbound, drifting like a waterfall as I run my fingers through the length. Strands of bright red highlight the brown of her hair in the most beautiful way. "Your hair looks wonderful today, Nevaeh."

She bats my hand away, and turns away with a deadly scowl as she growls, "Stop it."

Oh no, that will not do. My voice deepens in warning, "*Nevaeh.*"

"I don't know who you are, man, but I don't want you here and neither does she. Just get up and walk away while all of us can still be friends." He puffs his thin chest out as if he can make me back down.

My focus remains on the steaming woman beside me. I wonder how good her Russian is after so long. Maybe it's time to test her. "I know you don't want this man close to you. Why are you forcing this?"

Her eyes burn into mine as she leans closer with a rusty hiss of near perfect Russian. "You have no say in what you think I want."

A low rumble of humor escapes. My hand lifts to play with her hair again, but she slaps it away with a dark scowl. "This boy isn't what you need moya liliya."

"You don't know that."

"But I do, and Frankie would agree with me."

"No, you don't and leave him out of this." Her palm slaps loudly on the table causing several nearby tables to glance our way.

"You need to leave now." The boy stands up with an angry growl.

"Nevaeh, no boy playing at being a man will be what you need," I say ignoring the non-threat.

"Is he your boyfriend, Nevaeh?" He turns to her, fingers gripping the table in anger.

"No. I'm sorry, he thinks he's doing what my brother wanted and is keeping men away from me." She sends him an apologetic glance, pissing me off even more.

"Whatever, I'm out of here." Shaking his head in disgust, he doesn't spare us another glance before leaving. Fucking finally.

"I can't believe you! And *who*—in all your wise wisdom—would be right for me," Nevaeh demands, facing me head on now that the man is out of the way.

"A man Nevaeh, not some little boy who can't protect you."

She snorts, twisting to face away from me. "Right, someone like *you* I suppose?"

Her words slam into me hard. Shattering something in me, I didn't know was there. Leaving me to see things I've never noticed about her before. My heart stalls as I realize she's right. It should be *me* next to her. I loved Anya, despite our engagement being contracted and arranged by our families. But she's gone now, and the woman in front of me is shining in brilliant anger. The fondness of our youth expands into something much rawer and deeper.

All humor evaporates in an instant as the truth hits me, and I push forward, crowding her so she's flush to the seat rest. Lifting my right hand, my fingers feather over her ear and dive roughly in her hair. I watch her breath stutter and the irises blow wide as I lean into her so I can whisper in her ear, "You know the answer to that already."

That little tongue sweeps quickly over her bottom lip making something stir hungrily in my chest. Her pretty curls sway as she shakes her head as far as my hand will allow. "I wouldn't ask if I knew what you meant."

"Frankie would have run them from the city after a beating. I'm being nice by not making things bloody. Stop seeking out these pitiful creatures neither of us would allow close to you when I'm right here." Closing the distance, I let my lips linger on her soft hair. "The sooner you stop fighting the better things will be for us."

Brown eyes dart over my face, looking to see if I am telling the truth. Lips shimmering with the gloss she applied press into a thin line. They look far too delicious for her own good. Fuck I'm not thinking straight now that I can see how clearly, I want her with me. Tied to me and no other. A little sister to care for no longer but the woman I long to have at my side for the rest of our lives.

I'm so entranced by her eyes, that I don't see it coming. Sticky ice-cold tea pours from my head down onto my face and clothes. My body freezes as I take in what just happened. Did she just...

"Go home and clean some of that over inflated ego out of your big head Vladimir Sokolov!" Her empty cup thumps on the table before she jumps up, spins on her heel, and stomps her way out the door.

Blinking in stunned amazement, all I can do is watch her cute little ass march its way out of my sight. Fuck, where the hell did that thought come from? Damn this woman. I can't help but laugh at her sass. No one would dare to do what she has and live to tell the tale.

I had planned to come in here, deal with the hippie, and walk out with her as nothing more than my best friend's little sister. I wanted her in my car. Talking and laughing the way we used to *before* losing Frankie. It would be the perfect end to my night. Especially after running into more dead ends on the trafficker front. She's thrown a wrench into the mix. Need. A feeling I never realized I had for her. It leaves me feeling a bit unsteady, but also strangely light.

Lifting the paper napkin from her empty place I wipe the spill from my face. "Well played moya tigrovaya liliya, it seems you have won this round."

I toss a hundred on the table, before striding out the front door. A small price to pay to compensate the waitress who has to clean up the mess. The little minx is embracing her wings, and it makes me so damn proud. I need someone in my life, besides my immediate family, who is not afraid to call me out on my bullshit when it is needed.

My team asks if they should stop her, and I freeze in my tracks giving them my full attention. "Two of you will guard her with your lives and nothing else. *No one* is to touch her." I pause briefly, letting them feel my sincerity. "Or the death I give you will be long and painful. She is *mine*."

The last three words come out before I know what I'm saying but I don't backtrack. She isn't mine in that sense. Not yet. But now, I see beyond our past, and I'm certain that there is only one way forward. I won't let anyone stand between us ever again. Not even my father.

I take two steps toward my car, before I pause and call back to them once more. "Don't interfere unless necessary. She also speaks Russian. Watch what you say around her."

They snap straight, standing at full attention with an empathic *yes.* Two of the best quickly turn, trailing after her as she stomps her way home. My orders will be followed to the letter, or I will personally be staking bodies. I let her down years ago and I'll be damned if I do so now. Nothing else will hurt her without coming through me first.

The thought that anyone would think of touching her makes my blood boil. She's changed over the years. Become far too jumpy around other people, and there is *no* way it *isn't* tied to the bastard in jail. Rage slithers through me- could and lethal. Tonight, I will comb through every inch of her past. I need to get to the bottom of this, and find out what's happened to make her so afraid

This does not bode well for the teams that are still out in the field. Or the Bastard waiting to tell me who sent him. A quick text reinforces my orders, "Do not touch him until I get there." For once I feel the need to let my monster free and feel fresh blood over my hands.

***

The damn club is louder than ever, but that's probably a good thing. Not that anyone could hear the worm screaming. The thicker walls and sound proofing make sure of that.

Finally, the blasting noise cuts off in silence as the hidden door closes behind me. Well, not fully silent. The fool that thought he could try to bring heroin to my city— fucking laced at that— is trying to coerce my brothers into joining in on a deal with him. Both are laughing at his attempts. Making bets in Russian of how long he'll last under our hands.

"Enough of the useless bartering," I order, stepping off the stairs, not bothering to look his way. My cufflinks clatter onto the desk followed by my jacket before I turn to face him with the bag of trash in hand and a deadly scowl.

The plastic swings between two fingers as I take him in. If Makhail hadn't sent me his id information, I'd call him a liar that the fool is only twenty-two. The rumpled clothes covering his skinny frame do nothing to hide the limbs jerking. Oily blond hair, blown red rimmed eyes, head twitches, and shaking hands. He's obviously been using his own product. With the level of acid in the powder I'm impressed he's still upright.

This is exactly why we are so adamant on our streets staying clean. These type of drugs infect every inch of the person and turn them into mindless drones with only one goal. "Who gave this to you?"

"Dude it's not-"

"Dude," I growl, tossing the bag to my twin so he doesn't jump in to start beating the man. "Do you know who I am, boy?"

His throat jerks in a rough swallow. "No."

"Of course, they'd send someone who knows nothing about how we run our part of the city," Dimitri grumbles, tossing the bag in the trash to burn later. "Bet they got him hooked first and then send him in here without any information. Didn't tell him we wipe out the people bringing this shit onto our streets."

“That’s because no one in their right mind would come onto Sokolov streets loaded. That’s waving a red flag announcing their death wish,” Mikhail snorts, palming the handle of his knife.

I have to agree with Mikhail given how strongly we’ve gotten the message out over the years. “My brothers are more ruthless than me about keeping this shit off our streets and away from our children.”

For a second, doubt is clearly written on his face. Then Mikhail shifts off the desk to his full height. The sharp glint of the blade Ember gave him catching the light with a sinister glow.

Dimitri steps closer, hanging an arm over Mikhail’s shoulder in disgust as the boy pisses himself. “They sent in a pawn but maybe he isn’t useless.”

“Who sent you?” I demand.

He shakes his head vigorously, hair flying wildly, as he shivers under my glare. “I don’t know.”

“Well, what *do* you know boy?” Mikhail asks, squatting down to his level. He runs the sharp edge along his jaw before pointing it at our guest. “Who gave you the drugs?”

“No one!”

“It would be in your best interest not to lie to me again,” I repeat, cracking my knuckles and stretching before rolling my sleeves.

"I don't know," he pleads louder. "I never speak to anyone. Never see them either."

Fucking liar, I can smell the deception rolling off him. "Then tell us what you know."

His eyes dart around, desperate for a friend but he's shit out of luck. Mikhail has the blade under his chin, releasing a line of blood before the boy can cry out. The more he snivels on the floor the more pissed he's got us. We never play with drugs. While most think they have more control with the shit we've never needed it to keep our men in line.

God, his crying is getting on my last nerve. I'm not going to give him much longer to speak up. I want the truth, and I want it now. "Mikhail."

A shrill scream blasts through the space and blood trickles from the shallow cut under his ear. "Start talking."

Chapter 6

Nevaeh

The *nerve* of that man! What the hell was he thinking? Coming in here and interrupting my date, like it was his God given right. Sure, he had a point about Dwayne not being the right guy for me. But, I barely got a word in and every sentence out of his mouth was about himself. Add on the funky way he smelled and no thank you. But it was my decision to be there, not his.

I was one touch away from decking the guy myself when Volodya decided to strut in like a damn king. He acted like he owned the place! I don't need him coming in like a knight in black armor. He made his decision long ago, and left. So, I severed all ties with his family, not wanting to be dragged back in. Didn't want to set myself up to be hurt again, because he's the only one who can. And now here he is trying to run my life.

Hell, I didn't even want to go on the stupid date. But there was no way for me to gracefully back out of it. Not after Mrs. Brighton set it up for me. She has sung nothing but high praises for her nephew. No matter how many times I said I was busy she kept pushing. How am I going to explain what happened to her at school on Monday?

And what did he mean by he was the only man for me? Have I always had a crush on my brother's friend? I can't deny that, because I've always dreamed about a life with him. Even knowing it was decided that he and Anya were to marry, I foolishly always hoped things could be different. Life has a way of opening your eyes and I'm not the starry-eyed little girl I used to be.

"Stupid freaking men!" An angry tear slips down my cheek as I unlock my door. "Always have to come in and think they can tell me how to live."

***

Quiet surrounds me. I'm sitting on my bean bag, picking at my sandwich when my cell phone rings from my bed. For some reason, the call has dread sinking in the pit of my stomach before I pick it up. I answer it anyway.

"Hello?"

"Miss Nevaeh Hawkins?" A stern woman's voice echoes over the line.

Her tone assures me nothing good is about to transpire. I swallow thickly, trying to clear my throat so I can speak. "This is she."

"This is Captain Baker, at Camden County Jail in Tennessee. Miss Hawkins, the reason for my call is to inform you that Chris Boyd was paroled early yesterday morning. My records show you have a standing restraining order. Is this correct? "

"Yes," I answer. "You said... yest-" I stop and pull in a breath, grounding myself before trying again. Fear explodes in my mind at the sound of his name. "Yesterday you said?"

"Yes ma'am."

"Thank you for letting me know." The line cuts quickly after that. Numbness takes over my body as his face flashes before my eyes. "No," I cry in denial, refusing to let even a memory of that *monster* put that fear in me again.

I'm states away from him, and I've cut all ties with anyone who could even remotely lead him to me. I'm surrounded by security, and if all else fails one *word* to Volodya and he will rain hell down on the asshole. He may not be happy with me over Saturday, but he made a promise long ago and I know he will do what he needs to make that happen. If not for me he'll keep his promise to my brother.

Until I know Chris is around for sure, I won't say anything to anyone. Now more than ever, I need to stay away from Volodya. I know he's going to come for me at some point. I know he'll keep his promise to find me. The same way I know Volodya will keep his, and I can't let that happen. I'm going to have to watch every interaction all the more. The tiniest thing could be used against me if he finds me, and I won't allow anyone else to get hurt..

I'll keep watch over everything around me. I am not the same girl he took advantage of. I've grown sharper, and when I moved here I took precautions. Taking the courses that legally let me own and carry a firearm in this state. I know how to shoot and protect myself.I will not allow him to take me down this time .

With no parent duty this week, I will head to the store after work tomorrow and stock up on canned foods and noodles. For once my shelves will be completely full. I pull my locked safe from under the mattress and lay the pistol out to clean it before reloading. Once it is safe to use, I slip it under my pillow for easy reach. Crawling under the covers for the night I stare at the stickers littered over the ceiling more intently than normal.

Savy's faded orange and black stuffed form finds its way into my arms before I can think to reach for him. "I can protect us. We don't need to send out an S.O.S. to him."

Unable to get comfortable, I toss and turn for a long time. Sleep hovers in the shadows but refuses to welcome me into its hold. Too tired to fight anymore I let my mind wonder. Thankfully it's one of my happier memories and not the nightmares of my past with the monster that tried to ruin me.

Chapter 7
Vlad

For the love of all that is holy, I whisper prayers for patience to act without bloodshed as I find her on another date, for the third week in a row. She's doing this to piss me off now out of spit. My hand grips the wheel till it feels like they're welded to it. She actually seems to be having a good time. She's smiling and laughing as he talks.

When her guard called to tell me that she was meeting with another man, I left a meeting with the mayor. There was no way I could listen to him ask for more money to piss away when my woman is with another asshole. Alone! Without telling me and ignoring my calls.

Where the HELL is her sweater? He leers at her breasts for the tenth time in that far too revealing shirt. Her arms push them up in that thin green tee, as she leans down to look at whatever he puts on the table. When his hand brushes hers in the middle of him pointing at a different page she doesn't let the touch linger, pulling away quickly.

I move when she gets up to take herself to the restroom. Going in the back door, I wait to make sure that she's the only one inside. The door opens as she moves her foot into the hallway to return to the table. My hand grips her shoulder, pushing her back until I can lock the door behind us. I'm still not sure what I'm going to say, but this behavior is going to end now. One way or the other she is going to understand that I want her, and I won't let another try to step in and take what's *mine*.

"Volodya what are you doing?" Her big eyes stare up at me, too shocked to put up a fight.

I don't let her get anything else out. Her lips yield in surprise, allowing my tongue further into her sweet mouth. My hands pull her close as I feed on her, desperate to mark her in some small way. Gripping her hips, I lift her onto the sink and step between her warm tights. Each taste is better than the last. Nothing has ever felt more right and I swear I'm instantly addicted. The groan pulls itself out at the same moment she whimpers, tilting her head for more.

The need to breathe has both of us pulling back, and gasping for air. I refuse to release her, holding her firmly as she wiggles to dislodge herself. For the first time, in far *too* long, I have her right where she belongs. *My* girl. *Moya milaya malen'kaya tigrovaya liliya*.

Her soft palms press firmly against my chest, pushing for the slightest fraction of distance. "You can't do this." Her face is flush, and desire still lingers in those gorgeous eyes. I want to drown in them. She fights to deny the both of us, but I won't let her.

"Are you going to tell me you don't feel the same as I do?"

She tucks her chin and won't meet my eye, shaking her head on a whimper. "We can't. I don't belong to anyone, and I never will."

Firmly holding her chin in my fingers, I force her to still beneath my gaze. The deep sorrow in her eyes has my heart stuttering, but I need to tell her. "You are wrong, little one. Our pasts are full of hurt, but the future is bright because we have each other. I can and will do more than this because you are mine."

"You don't OWN me." Her eyes flash in rebellion as she nearly shouts the words at me. "No one does!"

Alarms are blaring through my mind. I've called her mine all of our youth, and she's never had such a reaction before. "Nevaeh, tell me what has you so upset?"

"No one owns me. *Never*. Never," she whispers fiercely. "No man will *ever* own me."

"Moya lilya," I say, tipping her chin up. "You are mine as you have always been. My dearest friend. The woman who is my light in all of the darkness around me. You are the woman I want and need next to me for the rest of our days."

"I'm no such thing," she hiccups against the tears flooding her eyes. "Not for any man, most of all... *You*. You deserve better."

"I have the best woman right here," I intone strongly, cupping her jaw. "You are. It just took both of us time to figure it out. We can take this as slow as you need. You are my brightest and dearest friend, and I don't want to live in a world without you any longer." Rapid breaths have her breasts brushing against me with each inhale she pulls in, and I force myself to stay still.

"There is no *us*," she hisses, working harder to get away. She pushes with all her strength, which barely makes me lean.

"There is," I whisper, lowering my tone as I touch our foreheads together, tucking her wiggling form close. "Forgive me for not finding you sooner, Nevaeh, but I will make up for all the years we lost."

"You can't change what happened," she sobs, shoving me away and I let her. Nevaeh backs away with trembling eyes, under my subconscious reach to comfort her as she denies me again. "You have to stay away from me."

Her tells haven't changed since she was a teen. I can see through the lie just as I always could. The longing in her gaze. Arms folding close to keep from reaching out like she used to. Biting her bottom lip to keep any other words from spilling out. Turning half away from me and grabbing the sink to hold herself back.

"You don't truly want me to stay away, moya liliya. I see it in your eyes. Why are you fighting this now?"

"You HAVE to stay away, Vladimir."

I don't miss the use of my full name, nor the tone she uses. The thin edge of unbridled fear has me closing the gap and pulling her close to soothe my hands over her spine. Someone hurt her. Has her scared. I know our separation wounded her, but this is different. This isn't because she's scared of me. More like she's afraid someone is watching, and she doesn't want to get caught.

God, what happened to her over the years? What's hunting her that's she afraid to get close to me? I've pushed enough so I won't ask why, but there will be more guards watching those around her. No more chances where she is concerned. This is going to stop *now*.

"I'm done allowing you to walk away from me. You are mine and no one will ever hurt you again," I promise softly. Leaning in, I drop another long heavy kiss to her supple lips before backing away. I brush a stray hair from her cheek while she's still occupied, dazedly blinking up at me as I continue. "No matter the years my vow will never waver."

The ends of her hair snap sharply over my nose as she whips away to look over her shoulder. Not pulling away but refusing to meet my gaze. "Please stop pushing."

That's what I thought. She thinks she's going to keep me safe by running away from me. "If you want to keep pushing me away thinking you're protecting me... Just know that whatever blood is shed, I will gladly let it stain my hands if it means keeping you safe. Many claim I'm a monster, and I have no problem proving them right when it comes to you."

Red blooms on her cheeks as stabs a finger in my guts, and stomps her foot in defiance. "You can't do that!"

Her denial rings off the walls making me slightly unhinged, but I tamper my temper down. Something has her spooked and I won't make her more afraid than she already is. "Send him away, moya tigrovaya liliya. I won't tell you again."

Her angry wordless shout has me smiling as I make my way back out to my car. The fire is as hot as ever in my little tiger lily and it makes me feel more alive than I have been in many long years. It's time to step up my game I believe.

Time to remind her how much of her pretty little self has remained cemented in my soul.

***

"What has you in such a good mood today brat," my twin asks, kicking his feet up on my desk.

"What once was lost has been found," I answer vaguely, knowing he will get it out of me quickly. Especially since I'm not giving the usual direct answer, but I want to see the look on his face when I tell him. I want the world to know to stay the hell away from her,but for now I want all of her to myself.

"Don't be mysterious, brat. It's a woman, isn't it?" He asks, making all of Mikhail's team perk up. The news that their Pakhan is seeing a woman is something that they have all been waiting to hear.

I sigh, laying the papers we are supposed to be going over back on the desk giving him my full attention. He is about to lose his shit and I'm going to fully enjoy his shock at the news. "Nevaeh is back."

Dimitri jolts from his seat with a big smile and Mikhail tilts his head trying to place who I'm talking about. From the look on my twin's face, nothing is going to change between them. The two of them were always playing pranks together. I can't give a number to the amount of times Frankie and I walked right into their hands. It only slowed when he found a girl to fawn over, but they still caused chaos each time they were together.

"Nay's back?" The fucker's face turns giddy and he's nearly bouncing in his seat. I just hope they pick someone else as their favorite target. Thankfully Nikolai is still in Russia and not here to join them. I internally grimace at the mental images of what they could do as a trio. We don't need an all-out pranks war in the house. At least he won't be coming home for another seven months.

Knowing the men in this room won't let it go any further than the few of us, I give him what he wants. "Yes, she teaches at the school. She hasn't lost her touch just so you know. She showered me with sweet tea the other day."

The room erupts in howls, even the most serious of them enjoying seeing that someone stood up to me. Our life isn't easy or kind, but she has what it takes to stay with us. They will easily give her the respect she deserves when I finally bring her home.

"I need more," he demands laughing, rubbing his hands together eager for more.

I ignore him in favor of the report in my hand. Ten new missing persons cases in our city alone and they aren't the low-class people they usually target. They're closer to the middle class and not part of those that run the streets. The traffickers are getting bolder.

Taking them doesn't make sense to me. "Why go after these people?"

"They are getting too comfortable," Mikhail hisses angrily, throwing his file.

His team stands around us in silence wanting to get out there and kill the bastards we have been hunting for years. Only Maskin is missing from the group as he has taken on the role of Ember's personal protector when Mikhail is busy with me or his missions, not that she seems to need it. The woman truly is a force of her own that I whole heartily welcome. Her and the children are keeping us centered while we fight the darkness.

Our silence is broken by Mikhail's phone ringing. "Da, Viking," he rumbles out, flicking his eyes up to us as he listens to our new brother on the other end of the line.

Excitement dances in his eyes before they narrow in anger. "You're sure? ... On our way."

"What happened," I demand, eager for a shred of good news.

"We have a new lead. Eyes on target and hostages. We are moving now." His eyes spark in excitement as the team straightens behind him eager to move.

My heart eases a fraction at the words of hope. We need a win and soon. If I can take even one thing off of my overflowing plate it will make things so much easier. If we can bring even one of the hostages home, we should be able to find a way to take a step towards making the Earth just a bit safer.

Chapter 8

Nevaeh

Damn him, he wasn't lying. I agreed to meet with Jeff again just to let the asshole know that I wasn't about to let him run my life. He's got more men following me too.

While I don't see the man as anything more than a passing friend, the second date was even more awkward than the first. At the end of the night, I told him that I wasn't interested in him in any romantic way. He laughed and told me we were square, because he knew from the start we wouldn't last. We agreed to stay friends like we've been since he started teaching last year.

When school began this morning, he wouldn't look me in the eye. He froze like a rabbit, before I got a wave from across the hall, and quickly ducked into his own room. It takes me most of the day to find out why. He was mostly successful in covering up the discoloration of his eye, but nothing can take away the swelling in his jaw.

I have a few minutes before my first class comes through the door and I plan on using them to tell off a certain Russian who can't leave me alone. I will *not* live under the rule of another man who thinks he owns me. I'm going to give that man a piece of my mind. Nasty Nevaeh hasn't surfaced in years. He is not going to like bringing her to the light again. Remembering my response to how he tasted and way he touched me is only adding fuel to the fire.

My finger hover over the call button as I close the door and look up to avoid running into any of the tables I moved last night. A single, brilliant, orange tiger lily blossom floats in a small glass bowl of water in the center of my desk. The flash of purple draws my eyes to the roots and the flashy male beta fish swimming below. My feet slip on the tile as my mind stops functioning to give them directions to keep moving.

It takes a moment for my eyes to clear. I know who left the gifts on my desk. The fact that he was able to get on to school grounds to leave it here doesn't even surprise me. He could always charm his way into anywhere that his name didn't hold enough weight for. How can he still remember? Instead of calling my fingers, tap out a message.

Me- Why?

Volodya-Why what moya liliya?

Me- The flower.

Volodya- Because you and that flower are the same. Strong, resilient, good, and beautiful to your core.

Me- Gifts won't make this better.

Me- You need to leave me alone.

Volodya- Impossible.

Volodya- You know I keep my word.

Me- A decade too late.

Volodya- Never too late. I'm sorry I can't be there today, but have a good day at school and a happy birthday moya liliya.

His words bring tears to my eyes, leaving me unable to see to respond. I wipe the tears away, barely have time to do so as kids begin coming in with the morning rush. Pulling the emotion in check, I put a smile on my face and get on with my day.

"Alright kids, we're painting mosaics today."

***

I'm so ready for this week to be over. The bitter, early winter wind cuts through the layers under my jacket to let me know it's time to invest in a heavier coat on payday. I don't make it to the bottom of the stairs when the feel of eyes on me pulls my head up.

Casually leaning against the hood of his car, Volodya looks up at me with soft hope in his blue eyes. "I will take you home."

"I'm fine, thank you." Stepping forward I keep a calm pace as I start to make my way past him. Sharp winds whip around, and I can't help but shiver as the gusts continue to grow stronger till they nearly knock me off my feet.

Heavy heated wool settles over my shoulders before big hands pull me into a warm body, and I let him as the force of the wind has me stumbling. "Please, tigrovaya liliya, it's too cold for you to take the subway today."

The air rises to an angry shriek, sending a storm of flurries around us. Burying my face in the hollow of his shoulder, I drag in a breath of needed air that the wind seems determined to rip from my lungs. He turns us back to the car, and sets me inside before climbing in behind the wheel. Heat is already blasting from the vent as we turn into traffic.

The silence has me looking over my shoulder. "Where are the kids?"

"They left early for checkups."

"Oh," I whisper, trying not to stare. He came here just for me. I ruthlessly stomp on the warm, fuzzy feeling, attempting to grow back into its tiny box. He needs to stop being so thoughtful.

Being this close isn't good for my sanity, but I can't help greedily sucking in the scent of spearmint and chocolate. Inside the soft leather interior, there is no way for me to get away from him. Has he always smelled so good? I remember him smoking back in the day. None of the smokey cigarette scent lingers. Maybe he quit.

I'm so busy watching the streets go by that I can't help but jump when his big hand closes over my clenched fingers. Without missing a beat his fingers latch onto mine with a gentle grip. "Your fingers are freezing."

"I'm fine," I say, trying to pull away. "And you know I don't like when you call me that."

The air rumbles with his chuckle as he lets me have my way. "Noted. Now, stop putting me off. Have dinner with me tonight."

The demand is so unexpected that all I can do is laugh. Years ago, I would have given him my everything if he asked. But he broke me without a care. Though he claims differently, I don't trust him like I did back then. I won't let him have the chance to do so again. I trust him with my body but not my heart.

"No."

"Nevaeh, I've been clear since I found you again. I want you in my life. By MY side." He keeps calm as he levels an eye my way.

"I told you there was no *us*, Volodya!" I don't mean to raise my voice, but he needs to understand. I'm too broken to stand by his side. I can never let him know what happened or the streets will run red with blood. "I don't want you like that."

"That's not true. I know that you love me even when you refuse to allow yourself to see it burning between us."

Damn it, he needs to stop talking! The words hit far too close to the bone. I do want him in some way but that can't happen. "You don't."

He keeps going like I haven't said a word. "Yes, I loved Anya before, but I have always loved and protected you, too. Having you in my life again has me looking to the future, just not getting through the day."

"Stop it," I plead, shivering under the weight of his coat. "I'm not good enough for any man least of all you so let it go!"

Like a viper he rips his hand from mine and twists his thick fingers in the loose bun on the back of my head to hold me still. The pull isn't hard or violent but my mind races to past touches from another hand. A hand that offered nothing but fear and cruelty. What air I have in my lungs leaves in a loud gasp when he pulls my head back to make me look at him.

"Don't touch me," I scream, trying to tear myself from him, unable to keep the fear in.

The car slows but he's still driving. "Nevaeh calm down and look at me."

His voice pulls me back from the edge. When I open my eyes, I'm staring at the ceiling above but I still refuse to look at him. Keep calm. Don't let him see, I tell myself, but I know he will. He always does. There is no way to avoid the bone deep reaction to such a touch. It's too damn much. Air saws through my lungs as I fight to get my breath back.

My words come out as a stumbling whisper. "Please let go."

His fingers tighten on reflex and immediately loosen so he can whip the wheel with precision. Cars around us blare their horns in anger, but he continues to cut people off in his determination to come to a sudden stop on the curb. The set of his jaw lets me know he won't let it go. All I can do is grip the door handle in one hand and his forearm in the other. I know he's good at driving and that he would never put me in danger, but I'm still frozen by fear to the leather seat.

Metal is still vibrating as he unbuckles me, pulls me over the consul, and into his lap. Steel strong hands grip both sides of my jaw, as he demands complete control of me. Muscled thighs move to arrange themselves into a cradle to hold me close. I try to close my eyes, but he shakes me so quickly that I have to open them again, so I don't get sick.

"*Who touched you*, Nevaeh?" He growls so low I can barely hear him. Barely controlled fury fills the car, but his touch is never harsh on me. "What fool hurt you?"

I would shake my head, but his grip won't allow even that small movement, so I keep silent. I can't tell him, if I do there will be a river of blood when he finds him. I don't want that on my hands. There has already been enough blood.

"Give me a name. I will rid the world of any who dared to touch you," he seethes, eyes blazing in demonic fury.

His promise brings tears to my eyes. Soft whimpers bubble up without my permission, but I still refuse to answer. I can't. Saying the name aloud will give it far too much power. Saying it out loud after hearing it the other week will bring back the nightmares. I just want my normal boring life.

"No."

"Tell me," he demands, snarling with wild eyes as his fingers flex over my jaw.

"It's not your evil to burn. I can handle it on my own."

"Moya liliya, I will find out one way or another. I would much prefer to hear about it from you." Those eyes bore into me refusing to let me break away.

"No." The whimpers become sobs as I sit there shaking in his hold.

"Nevaeh, *please*," His voice drops filled with hurt and restrained anger at my continued resistance. "Let me help you, moya liliya."

"I'm not your problem anymore! Take me home," I whisper lacing it with all the emotion available to me.

"Nevaeh." His eyes soften as he brushed stray hairs from my eyes. "I'm never leaving you again. Tell me how to help you now. You know how much I hate seeing you cry."

His eyes plead with me to let him in, but I can't. Too much has happened over the years, and I can't let him break me again. "Please, Volodya."

"Okay, I will take you home," he sighs, pulling me into a tight hug. His big hands are solid and strong in their hold until I calm down. Only then does he slowly return me to the seat.

As soon as the car slows, I jump out and run for the safety of my room. Bypassing the elevator, I sprint up the steps as fast as my feet can carry me. The red walls are a blur as I dash down the hall. Keys rattle in my hands in a struggle to unlock the door. A few too many tries, and I manage to twist the lock tumblers to push my way in. It slams into place, and every lock is secured before it feels safe to draw in a deep breath to calm down.

Angrily, I blot at the damn tears and turn around. I slap a horrified hand over my mouth before a sound can be made and the tears begin anew. Strewn across the tiles, are blood red rose petals torn apart from being shoved through the thin gap. A quick glance shows that no one is in my home which gives me the ability to take another breath. A note lays in the middle of the flowers. With a shaky hand I reach down and grip the edge of the thick weighted paper. The scratching on the paper is instantly recognizable.

"No," I wail, falling to a heap on the floor.

Chapter 9
Vlad

The car hasn't fully come to a stop before the door is opened, and she's bolting across the sidewalk. The remainder of the way here she didn't acknowledge my presence even with my hand begging for her to focus on me. Her fingers remained limp and horribly cold in my hold. It was like she wasn't there.

For the second time in our story, I watch her run from me. This time will be different. This time I will not leave her alone. My vibrating phone alerts me to my needed presence back at the house. I silence it without answering. Unable to avoid my job, I make sure her guards are in place before I reluctantly leave.

I haven't made it five blocks down the road when the blasted plastic starts blaring again. Gritting my teeth and thoroughly annoyed, I answer the call, knowing that hundreds of men depend on my leadership. "Da?"

"I have what you were looking for."

"I'm on my way." The phone makes its way to the seat Nevaeh left just moments ago.

In the forty minutes it takes to navigate the overpacked streets, I let the anger fuel my blood. Death is calling for blood to wash my hands. Moya milaya malen'kaya tigrovaya liliya won't give me a name so I will have to find it for myself. My money is on the man she holds a restraining order against. What did he do to make her so terrified?

Parking in the lot, I push through the back door on the way to my office. The space is empty just as it should be. No one has access but me and my brothers. Everything is coded to our retina, and logged into the system on my phone. This way, I always know who is doing what in my space.

This office is similar to the one I set up at home. Too many would call it outdated and dark. I find the wood paneling and storm cloud blue to be the only things that calms me when I must be away from my woman. The fresh lilies kept in the room remind me of my humanity. Of why I can't lose control.

The moment I'm in my seat, Maxim walks through the door. A menial file is in my hand and not a word uttered between us as I begin going through the information before me. It scatters across the wood a moment later.

"This has been scrubbed."

"Look at the last page, Pakhan," He taps one of the pages that didn't go flying and hands it back to me.

"Well, isn't this interesting?" Dumping the papers back into the folder I sit back in my chair.

"My thoughts exactly, sir."

"Benson isn't high enough to hide these damn bastards. There is someone or more likely several above him that he is covering for." My hands clench, and blood lust rushes through my body. I cannot afford to give into them yet. I need to know if he has the other information I asked for. "Have you found the bastard who touched her?"

"No." His eyes harden, darkening a fraction and I can see the same blood-lust in him that festers just under my skin. "He was released on good behavior and dropped off the grid. Only comes back long enough to check in with his parole officer. I will keep digging. He can't hide for long."

Nodding, I wave him away. The best lead we've found in years lies before me. All it will take to bring them down is one misstep and I *will* find it. The bastards have hurt my city for far too long and I'm eager to clean them out. If I can't get my hands on the bastard who hurt Nevaeh, then making these assholes bleed will have to tide me over till then.

***

By the time I make it back to the house it's past midnight, but Mikhail is pacing the floor in an attempt to calm Katya. Dark rings sag underneath his eyes, and his shoulders rise, less and less in their bouncing.

"You look terrible brat," I say softly, walking to him. "Is my plemyannitsa giving you trouble again?"

"No more than usual." His feet stop with a small smile, but his arms don't stop the slow movement. "When are we arranging a meeting? I'd like one thing handled before my daughter turns me into a zombie."

The fact that he already knows about the new evidence doesn't surprise me anymore. My little brother has ears everywhere thanks to the multiple contracts he and his team oversee. "Seven hours."

Katya's soft whimpers take a sharp turn, as she lets out a piercing howl, making her father grimace in his rush to comfort her. "Please little one, daddy and mommy need some sleep."

Moving forward, I ease her small body into my arms without giving him a chance to complain. No matter how gentle we try to be in the transfer, her tiny arms wave in protest. The feel of her fragile body in my hold always makes me feel too powerful to be near her but I steal her every chance I get. "Go rest brat, I will not be sleeping any time soon."

"Thank you, brat. Ember fed her just before you walked in so she shouldn't be hungry for a few hours." More gently than I've seen him with anyone else, he presses his lips over the soft tuft of dark hair on her head before he heads for his bed.

We make our way into my office to sit in my chair. Leaving the lights off, I hope it will allow her to settle faster. Cupping the back of her head over my heart, I begin humming lightly, not minding the continued sniffles rubbing drool over my clothes. The words escape me at first as I have not heard them in many years, but I remember the cadence as I do my own heartbeat. The song's rhythm humming softly in the night air.

Her cries gently ebb back and forth for a time, but I don't stop the lullaby. Little fingers curl into fists, clutching handfuls of my shirt as she works herself closer to sleep. One song turns into three as we hold each other, and I pat her back. Before long, her soft breaths puff into the space of my neck.

Nevaeh is out of my reach tonight, but at least I have this one to keep safe. "If not for you, our family, and the woman across town I don't know if I would have the chance to come back."

Spinning the chair, I let myself take in the expanse of the garden highlighted by the snow and stars. How many nights have I spent staring out into the darkened space as I am doing now? Allowing my parents to set my future. Learning to care for Anya. Losing her on the day of our wedding. Finding no sign of Nevaeh after she ran from Frankie's burial.

Too many years apart have done neither of us any favors in repairing what was broken between us. Besides being there for her and letting my actions do the talking, I don't know what else to do. Something went wrong in her time away and she won't talk to me about it. How can I make her trust me again? How can I show her that she is all I have ever loved and needed?

"Sweet dreams, moya lyubov'. Let's see what your Tetya Nevaeh has for us next hmm," I whisper to keep the baby sleeping.

Reaching into my desk I pull out headphones and start the next book of the series. My woman has a brilliant flair for storytelling and after a long day listening to the words she wrote helps my mind quiet. If she had a better place to write would that make her work that much richer? The room beside this is empty. Something to think over later.

Chapter 10
Nevaeh

It's just trash. When I open the door, I demand my mind to imagine that the note and roses on the floor outside my door are nothing more than something someone dropped. The locks have kept him out of my space at least since I replaced all the old ones. I need to find a new apartment soon, but I plan to get more locks anyway. Snatching the items from the floor, I crumple them up and throw them into the trash can without giving them any more thought.

He wants me back without a thought or care for what I want or who I have become. Years ago, his scare tactics would have had me running back to him like a dog with its tail between its legs but not now. What he will soon learn is that I am not the girl he remembers. Today, I am a woman who knows how to stand on her own two feet.

I don't mind the shadows Volodya assigned to me as much as I did at first. At least not as bad as it was after I dumped the tea all over his head. I'm still not sorry about it. The arrogant fool deserved it. Even with them guarding me, I will keep my eyes open on the way to work just in case. Poor guys have had nothing much to do but make sure I get to and from work.

Is it wrong that I secretly enjoy the thought of my well-being in his hands, even though I don't want him close? Most would tell me he is being exactly like my ex. With all the stalking and demanding I bend to his will with just one word. No one would believe me if I told them that this man is different. He may be a man willing to walk outside the law, but he wouldn't and will never take pleasure in my pain. Everything he ever does is to keep me safe. My Volodya is still inside this hardened version of Pakhan Vladimir. While I miss him deeply, I can't afford for him to get any closer. I'll keep him in my back pocket for when I have no choice.

During lunch, I explore the internet for any available places within my price range. Which isn't a lot honestly. Most places I wouldn't want my worst enemy to live in. The thought has me pausing. Maybe *that's* the solution to my problem. Maybe I need to be in a place that he knows I would never put myself in. Before allowing doubt to creep in, I fill out the required information for three of them and call it a day.

I'm grateful that the last of the students are gone as I make my way out of the building. I'm ready to go home and work on my newest book. The Christmas break couldn't have come at a better time. Most of the kids have been losing focus in class, which makes my job that much harder. I hate raising my voice to get their attention.

It's not like I can really blame them, when it's the weather is making everyone miserable. Even, I've been praying for a storm to come in and give us a snow day or so, just to have some peace and quiet. Between the rowdy kids, my ex, finishing my book, and the still pursuing Russian who refuses to back down, I swear can't catch my breath.

Marketing my newest upcoming release hasn't been any easier than the ones before. I never have any idea how to hype myself up out there for attention while staying under the radar. Still, I'd rather work on that than keep constantly pushing Volodya away. I'm grateful that my publisher knows enough to help me out. You would think with over a dozen releases under my belt so far that I would have a firm grasp on things by now.

Getting out of pick-up duty took some doing, but I don't want to keep taking chances. I try not to give Volodya more than one-word answers to his insistent questions each day, now that he doesn't see me when he picks up the kids. The man just can't take the hint that I don't want him.

I'm lying in bed, jotting down a new story outline, and singing to myself when my phone goes off with a text. Tallie yowls in annoyance as I dislodge him from my chest to reach for it. Arching his back, he flicks his tail, and disappears under the bed at my sudden movement.

Volodya- Open the door moya liliya.

Me-Who says I'm home?

Volodya- Don't play Nevaeh. I'm coming up, please open the door for me, so I don't have to put everything down.

Me- 2 minutes and it's getting relocked.

Sighing, I do as he asked. It doesn't surprise me that he's only a few feet from me, leaning on the wall across from my door. His arms are full of six different sized boxes. His fingers are curled around the plastic handles of three grocery bags, and I spy Russian labels through the plastic.

"How long have you been out here?" My arms cross as I sink on the door jamb with a frown.

Smirking, he straightens and steps close. He plants a firm kiss to the top of my head before I can react. "I came to make you dinner. Did you think there would be no Christmas for you this year, moya lilaya malen'kaya tigrovaya liliya? No more lonely holidays for you."

Pulling my sweater closer, I shake my head. "I already ate."

"Half a cold cut sandwich isn't a meal, Nevaeh. If I knew you wouldn't fight me, I'd drive you home to spend the holiday with the family, but you've made it clear you aren't ready for that yet, so I am respecting your choice."

Shifting the wrapped presents and bags to one arm he slips the other around my waist, pulls me into his side, and leads me back inside. Without letting go of me, he places the items on my table before spinning me to sit on my bed and turning to lock the door.

I shouldn't stare as he takes off his coat and rolls up the sleeves of his button up shirt. Truly I know better, but I can't help it. I peek at the smooth skin on the inside of his forearms, marked with Russian words. Justice and truth. Two virtues he has always stood on. Damn, I think his arms are three times the size they were when we were teens. He's obviously kept himself in shape, and I'm not sure what to make of how my stomach flutters at the sight.

"See something you like?" He grins, crossing them over his chest, so they strain the fabric over his biceps. His eyes sweep over the fuzzy pants and thin top I threw on after my shower earlier. He doesn't try to hide the heat in his gaze.

Of course, I'm not blind. If I let myself, I could sit here and watch the play of those muscles for hours on end. The way they move under the ink staining his skin. Things are getting too warm in the small space. Grabbing one of the flat pillows, I sling it towards the asshole's face. Laughter rumbles from him as he lazily bats it away, only for it to land on the floor at my feet.

"Not in the least," I snark, crossing my arms and refusing to back down. "Just a man taking over my home, that can't seem to take the hint and leave me alone."

"Only for you moya liliya. I'd do this for no one else, so sit and watch me all you want. I enjoy your eyes on me." One big hand lands on my head, messing up the half of my hair that didn't fall out of the tie I'd carelessly put in.

Growling, I slap at him, which only makes him laugh harder. Pulling the elastic off, I gather it all up and throw it into another messy bun. "Asshole, I'm not enjoying *any* of this forced attention from you!"

He keeps laughing, but turns to take the food from the bags without another word. Potatoes, milk, fresh veggies, and grains begin filling my small counters. "Sing for me while I get our feast cooked."

"Why?" My guard shoots up at the request. I haven't sung for anyone since Frankie was killed. It's something that I'd done for him since we were kids. Now it hurts too much to attempt it for others, even for him.

Something must have come through my guarded tone. Lowering to his knees between my legs, he takes my hands and kisses the top of my knuckles. Each soft brush sends shivers down my spine. "Because it is one of the most beautiful things in my world, and I have not heard it in far too long."

Licking my lips and swallowing past the lump in my throat, I shake my head in sad denial. They used to have me sing for them all the time, but I haven't been able to sing in front of others since the funeral. It's like a hand grabs my throat and squeezes till I can't breathe if I try.

Tremors wreck my voice as I stutter out the words, "I can't."

Clear, storm-colored eyes search my face as I sit trembling before him. Rising slowly, he sits next to me and pulls me into his hold. One large hand cradles the side of my head, the other curls softly across my back. Words aren't needed. I'm shaking and he holds me tightly. All that matters is the comfort of his arms as he lets me sit and cry in silence.

It takes a few moments for me to calm down but when I do, he takes the smaller box off the table and holds it out to me. I slowly reach up and take it from him. My fingers shake lightly as I lift the lid to see what's inside. Pale gold greets my touch as I pull out the small round object. My breath stops short as I open the top and a tune starts playing.

Sung in Russian, a sweet female voice sings the song from my favorite childhood movie. He found me a replica of the music box. On the inside he had engraved, 'Through the coldest years of my winter you have kept my heart warm with your summer soul.' Tears threaten to fall, and I struggle to hold them back.

"Volodya," I start to whisper but have to stop as the tears form a lump in my throat. The polished metal warms under my fingers as I look up at the man. It takes a moment, but I finally am able to get out a few words. "Thank you, I love it."

He gives me a soft look that sends a wave of butterflies through my stomach, before planting another brief kiss on the top of my head. Then he calmly turns back to the food and hums along to the music still playing from my hands.

I can't help but stare at his broad back and hold his gift close like the treasure it is. It doesn't seem possible that he would remember something so small after over a decade, but he did and made it all the more meaningful with the engraving on the inside of the lid. He's just as considerate as he has always been to me and I desperately want it not to mean a damn thing.

"What is your newest story idea, moya liliya?"

The sudden question makes me jump, and I barely catch the metal box before it slips from my fingers. I look up in confusion only to blink at his back as he keeps cutting up the vegetables on my counter. "What?"

"Tell me the details of the story that you are planning." His head jerks to the side where my notebook rests on the pillow beside me.

My cheeks go hot, and I pick it up quickly, not sure if I want to hide it or burn it. I've never shown anyone any part of an unfinished story before. Not that anyone has been close enough to me to know that I write in my spare time.

I know that he's stubborn enough to pry the information out of me, but I hope that he'll let it go tonight. "I'm just jotting down what comes to mind, but I don't know where any of its going right now."

The knife never stops moving as he turns to smile at me. "Things are about to get hectic for me in the coming weeks." He stops with a wordless groan as if the thought has him mentally cringing. "I have meetings I cannot get out of, so I won't be able to see you as often. Let me help you in some way before that. Maybe we can get the plot figured out together while the food cooks."

There's no way I'm going to cry from those simple words. *No way.* "You really want to help with my silly stories?"

"None of your stories are silly," he rumbles, stopping his hands long enough to stare me down, so his message is understood. His next words come out more as orders, "Tell me."

Chapter 11
Vlad

I hate being away from Nevaeh. Hate being hours and worse *states* away from her. Unable to see her every day, to make sure that she is safe and well with my own eyes. The reports from her guards are keeping me sane- barely. It should be me there next to her, protecting her, and making her laugh.

The past six weeks have been a new hell. Learning a more rigid form of control over myself hasn't left me in a good mood. The short calls and daily messages I send at every spare second, I can find have not been enough. I carve her presence. Need to be near her again so the monster inside me quiets. I need her voice, smell, laughter, the way her hair falls around her face, and the way she looks at me. The hidden longing mixed with the determination to keep me away. I just need her. She should be getting home from school within the next few minutes, and I want to know how her day went.

"What do you think of the proposal to join our families, Mr. Sokolov? Between the two of us, we could make a lasting change in this country."

Annoyed by the questioning of the man on the other side of the table, my scowl deepens as my eyes snap over his form. Igor Popov is perfect on paper. Tall, blond, from a good Russian family, and solid ties to others we associate with. He's everything we should want in an alliance, but there's something about the man that just rubs me the wrong way. And it's not just the fact that he wants to shackle one of his daughters to one of us, like she's cattle for sale.

I don't need to look at Mikhail beside me to know how he feels. The hostile rage and blood lust is positively radiating off him with each new word out of the man's mouth. Marrying Ember, and having two daughters of his own now, has made his hatred of contract marriages even worse. No one is going to be good enough for either of them.

Hell, there is no way I'd allow one of my sweet plemyannitsa near one of these men. We'll fight to the bitter end to keep their purity from the evil of the world. And knowing their mother she's already training them to fight the world on their own.

Anya and I's engagement was the last one our family would force on others. We love our women and we sure as hell honor them completely, not use them as bartering tools. We don't need marriages to make us stronger, nor do we need to rely on favors. I've cleaned up our family, and set us on the mostly straight path with the full backing of my parents. Not even the family in Russia oppose the changes. They understand we have to adapt to survive.

Keeping my face blank is harder than it should be, but I'm getting tired of the same thing being pushed on me. It never fails. It's always the same story of them wanting to find a way to worm themselves in and live off our power. Or to be tied to a family big enough that can protect their smaller factions.

"Whom my brothers marry is of no concern of mine and I will not let them be bullied into one just for an alliance." A single glare has his mouth snapping shut before he can get a sound out. I continue speaking. "As for myself I am not interested either. I am already spoken for."

Mikhail's bulky frame rises beside me. I stand and straighten my jacket, ready to be completely finished with them. Stuffing my hands into my pockets, we make our way to the door, wholly done with the useless talks at last. The seventh such meeting we've had to endure over the last few weeks. All of them bring up the same damn thing. Fuck. I'm ready to drop my brother off and go see my woman.

"Surely, something can be worked out between us," Igor growls, jumping to his feet to follow. "We could make each other stronger."

The room goes still as my brother casually lays a hand over the butt of his pistol. Sighing, I lay a hand over his to stop further action. I just want to get out of here, and cleaning up bodies is the last thing I want to have to deal with right now. We've been away for too long already, and my patience is about to snap.

"We have nothing more to discuss when it comes to the matter of marriage. The Solokov family isn't in need of any more strength. I suggest you *let it go*," I demand, keeping my voice as devoid of emotion as ever. "Come brat, we have places to be."

Neither of us looks back once. They won't risk the war that would follow if they tried to back stab us with a bullet. Not when my men are covering the area just waiting for the fools to try. San Francisco's hot air slams into us as we exit the building and head for the car. The driver wordlessly opens the door for us to climb in and closes us inside without incident.

"Next time leave me the hell at home," Mikhail grumbles, stretching his legs and crossing his arms. "If I have to listen to the same song and dance on marriage more time, I'll call Ember and let her deal with the idiots."

A small smile and chuckle slip free despite myself at the thought. Even with Katya at her breast, Ember would have no trouble setting the record straight. I wouldn't put it past her to take over my seat if I let her, despite running two of her own businesses *and* taking care of the kids. Even for our most dangerous men, one cross look is enough to send them running.

"Noted," I sigh, as we slow down to merge onto the packed highway. Fuck, I hate the west coast. My fingers grip my phone, but I restrain myself from pulling it out knowing Nevaeh won't be able to answer yet if I did.

"I'm serious," he snaps, pulling the phone from his pocket and grumbling about his woman still not keeping her phone on her when he needs her. "I hate being dragged along for these things. Dimitri is the one who should be here, not me."

"Relax brat, if there was something wrong Maskin would let you know. She's probably in the forge enjoying some time to herself without you hovering."

His head whips my way and tilts to take in my expression with narrowed eyes. "She told you to drag me along, didn't she?"

"It was my choice," I answer honestly. "Dimitri is taking care of other things for me."

"But she asked," he accuses, crossing his arms silently daring me to deny it.

His tone has me gripping my phone tighter, so I don't slap him upside his thick head. Now I see why she did. He's probably been driving her crazy with his unending hovering and sleepless nights with a teething baby. Staring out the window, I don't give an answer. He snorts and starts muttering under his breath again.

Lord, give me the strength not to murder my brother on the flight home. I can't take any more of his whining about missing Ember and the kids. He isn't the only one missing their other half.

***

Finally! My heart feels like it's ready to break from the strain as I make my way up the stairs to Nevaeh's apartment. Is it after eleven on a school night? Yes, but fuck it I need to see her now. Need to see that she is safe with my own eyes and maybe take her in my arms.

Her guards give simple nods as they watch me come in. Not wanting to scare her, I make sure to send her a text letting her know it's me before running up to knock on her door. Still my knock must have woken her up because it takes a bit for her to answer.

"Volodya?" she sleepily mumbles, rubbing at her eye as she peeks through the crack without undoing the chain. "What's wrong? It's really late."

"I know, but I needed to see you. Will you let me in?"

The door closes on her eye roll. Damn it, please don't let her ignore me all night. If she doesn't let me in the door, I'll fucking sit here all night just to stay close. Metal clicks as the locks disengage before the wood finally opens.

Arms curled around her stomach she steps next to the counter watching me. Brown eyes drift over me as I walk in. She sways lightly on her bare feet. A soft gasp parts her lips, and she takes one small step forward. Her fingertips slide over my jaw and cup my cheek, while taking me in with widening eyes.

The touch has me sighing and my rigid shoulders falling. "Nevaeh, I didn't mean to wake you."

Lips parting, she gives me a soft smile and brushes her fingers under my eye. "It's okay, Volodya. The bad can't hurt you here."

Fuck, I don't know how she can tell that something has me on edge. It's just something she's always been able to see, and I don't have the energy to tell her differently. She pushes my jacket off, tossing it on the chair and I let her. Tension leaks from my form with each gentle swipe of her hand.

Feeling her touch has me nearly melting wholly into her, but I hold myself back, not willing to scare her when she's touching me so freely. "Moya milaya malen'kaya tigrovaya."

Both hands grip one of mine. I let her pull me with her, and sink onto the mattress next to her. There isn't much room for both of us, though I follow her without a fight. I kick my shoes off, making sure she slides back under the cover. Then, I let her toss a bit of the blanket over my legs. She knows I'm not a fan of being fully covered. Quiet settles around us. We lay on our sides, facing each other on the thin mattress. Sharing this space, this heat, and the thin pillow has sleep pulling at us.

"This isn't how I wanted our first Valentine's to go," I whisper, gently brushing hair behind her ear.

Lashes flutter and her hand slaps off my chest with no more force than a fly. "We aren't an item, so this is just fine."

Not yet for her at least. I keep the thought to myself not wanting to start a fight, but can't stop the small tease. "Then, why did you pull me into your bed with you?"

"So arrogant," she snorts, rolling her eyes. "Just because I don't want a relationship with you doesn't mean I'm so shitty a friend that I'd let you stand in the hall hurting all night."

"Even friends deserve Valentine gifts, and you are much more to me than a mere friend." A yawn has me pausing. "I just didn't land in time to pick it up like I planned."

"Shut up," she grumbles, eyes drifting closed. Words slurring more with each one she speaks in denial. "And this is a one time thing. We're only friends."

As much as I want to stake my claim again, she's already lost the fight to stay awake. Thick lashes fanning over her cheeks, breathing deep, and still holding my fingers tightly in her hand. She can deny it all she likes but her body tells a different story. She'd never let me this close or sleep so peacefully next to me after all the jumping she does around others if she didn't fully trust me.

Whatever the bastard put her through hasn't killed what she feels for me. It will just take time, and I've learned to wait for what I want. Nevaeh will be mine in the end. Once we overcome her fears nothing will stand in our way and God help the next fool that thinks they can come between us.

Chapter 12
Nevaeh

Things continue the same way they started with the first note three months ago. Since adding the new locks and door sweep there have been no new additions to my home thanks to Chris. However, every morning a new message is outside the door with more of the same words. None of them have been threatening yet, but I know it is only a matter of time. Hell, I'm surprised none of them have turned to outright threats yet.

Vlad knows something is wrong. Even if my only responses are over the daily texts he sends. The damn man always knows when something isn't right with me. It's like he has some sixth sense when it comes to my feelings. He's been extra attentive since he came back from his meetings on Valentine's Day. Thank God I was up first and destroyed the note before he was out of the bathroom the next morning.

I wish things were still so simple. Back then any attention he sent my way had me so giddy all I could do was smile and tell him everything. One word to him and he would make all the bad disappear. Too bad things have changed so much for us.

This morning, I had to call off work because my stomach is cramping so harshly that pills and a heating pad are barely making a dent in the pain. The cramps have me sick to my stomach. I've been sick several times already, but I know a trip to the hospital isn't needed. I've just got to get through the day.

God, I wish the hot water was working at full strength right now. Lukewarm will just make me cry. Soaking in the heat would be a blessing as they move into my lower back. No position is comfortable. I'm not sure how much more I can take without just spending the day in tears.

I haven't eaten since my attempt of peanut butter toast last night which didn't stay down. Any thought of food makes my stomach heave, and I ran out of peppermint tea hours before now. Lord this chamomile sucks. Why did I buy it? I need something stronger even if I have to go get it.

Changing into some semi decent clothes with stretchy bands, I make my unsteady way to the door. Another damn note and flowers lay in wait just as every morning. Something has me reading this one.

......

Pain is fleeting but we are eternal.
Consider it punishment for allowing
another man to touch what is mine.
Be glad this is all you get for your transgression.
Our new home is almost ready.
-Love C

......

If there was food in my guts it would be on the floor. How long has he been holding out before sending me this? I knew it was only a matter of time before the threats started. I had hoped to be long gone from this place, but things have taken a turn. I was too late, and the place won't be ready for another month. For now, I'm stuck here.

It might be time to alert Volodya to the danger at hand, but the threat is clear. He's watching and I couldn't live with myself if something happened to someone else I care for. It may be time to simply disappear again. Better to live on the run than watch those I care for be hurt for getting close to me. My savings aren't big, but I could get a head start. Make Chris follow me, but if I did that Volodya would be sure to follow too.

By the time I make it to the street door, I'm ready to turn around. The pain is spiking so bad, I want to crawl back in bed and forget about finding something to help. From the corner of my eye, my shadow's vehicle shines like the answer to my prayers at this point. They've always kept their distance, so we've never even talked before. Would they even be willing or would they tell me to go back inside?

"Fuck it." Pulling myself together, I walk out with as much strength as I can manage and tap on the window.

He does a decent job of hiding his startled reaction before he quickly jumps out to stand in the cold next to me. Serious eyes scan me from head to toe before enclosing me into his own jacket when I can't hold the shiver in. "What are you doing out here Miss? Are you alright?"

"Would you take me to the store? I don't think I want to walk that far today. Well, more like I probably can't." I hold the edges close for warmth when I want to shove it away with the smell of horrible cigarette smoke on it. My warmest coat has nothing on the ones these guys have.

"Are you hurt?" His dark eyes scan over me quickly a second time. "Do you want me to call someone for you ma'am?"

"Please don't play dumb," I groan, breathing through another pain. "I know Volodya has you watching me."

“I don’t know what you’re talking about,” He stammers, tripping over himself as he tries to deflect.

“I've known you’ve been trailing me since the beginning. Will you please just drive me before I say fuck it and climb back in bed. Please, I just need a few things, or I’ll call him myself. I don’t want to deal with a pissed off Volodya and I’m sure you don’t either.”

“Of course. Get in the car. It is too cold out here for you.” Hesitant hands propel me into the seat after a few stunned blinks. Like he isn’t sure about touching me, but upset about the swaying that I can’t seem to stop. Volodya probably threatened them.

“I’ll be fine in the back.” Words are all I can fight with, and even they come out weak while he lowers me down. The moment my rear touches the heated leather I groan in appreciation. Fuck this feels so damn good.

The back of the seat suddenly starts warming as well. Then, the driver gives me a nod waiting for the man to get in. He seems a tad unsure, flexing his hands on the sleek black wheel uncomfortably. “Is better?” That deep accent is a touch thick to digest but I’ve had practice in the past.

Heat soaks in the tightly coiled muscles of my lower back and has me melting deeper in search of more relief. This is exactly what I need. I don’t know if I want to ever come out of this heaven. “Thank you.”

“Which store?” He rasps once his friend is settled behind me.

“The nearest pharmacy is fine, thank you.”

Grunting, he deftly moves us into traffic and heads down the road towards the store that will hold my salvation. A few thousand feet and I’m that much closer to getting the next thing to settle my tossing guts. Somehow the man pulls up without issue right in front of the store. Must be a magician. I’ve never been able to find such prime parking no matter where I’ve lived.

Spirits lifting, I grin in spite of the pain and nudge his shoulder. “Nice parking, magic man.”

His raising a questioning brow at me, making me laugh. My door opens as soon as my hand moves to do so myself. Several blinks later and I clear the instant glare of the sun out of my eyes. A girl could get used to this type of service.

The one who gave up his seat for me waits for me to climb out. “After you, Miss.”

For the first time since they became my tail, he follows me into the store as I make straight for the teas. I grab one of each caffeinated mint knowing one of them won’t last me long if this pain continues the way it's been.

A basket appears at my elbow, and the boxes are taken from my shaking hands. “Oh, I’m sorry. I wasn't thinking.”

He dismisses my words with a head shake, and he keeps the basket only to wave me on. After the teas I grab extra strength pain meds and cans of chicken soup that I will hopefully be able to keep down. A box of the salty crackers are next.

Turning down another isle a wave of pain has me stumbling. My shadow grabs my elbow, keeping me on my feet. Still, I'm doubled over, trying to ride out the pain. Fuck, I've always had bad periods. But the abuse from Chris has done permanent damage, only making them that much worse. I can't think of that, or I will never stop crying.

"Miss," he asks worriedly, not sure what's wrong or how to help. "Should I take you to the hospital?"

"No," I groan, and seeing him reaching for his phone quickly add. "And don't call him either. This will pass."

"Are you alright dear," a familiar voice asks gently. "Ivan what is going on? Why would you let your woman out in her condition?"

"I'm ok," I say before he can and do my best to stand tall. "Just ran out of meds and I am not his. Volodya sent him to watch me."

Her voice is closer now. "Volodya?"

"The Pakhan," Ivan speaks up, giving me a worried look.

"You mean my son?" She looks between us with shock. "Why does he have you watching her instead of him?"

Great, he hasn't told the family yet. Why wouldn't he tell them? I've never known him to lie to me before, but this is confusing when they are all so close. Is he truly serious about being with me or is he messing with my life? This is so confusing.

I snap my head up and gasp to see the woman's face. Gosh she hasn't changed much over the years. The same dark hair as her boys and the same never wavering smile. Her familiar warmth has my heart aching for the past. How I'd often wished she was my own mother.

I rush to calm her before she calls for her own guards. "Everything is fine, Mrs. Solokov."

"Do I know you dear?" She steps back to look at me fully. "You look very familiar."

"Nevaeh, Frankie's little sister." That is all I can get out as another round hits before releasing for a bit. Damn it, that *hurt*.

Both hands cover her mouth in surprise. "Oh, little one, look at you. You've become so beautiful. I'm sorry it's been so long since we've seen you that my memory is a bit fuzzy."

Blushing, I can't help but smile at her. Ivan backs away to give us room to talk but not far enough away that he can't jump in if he is needed. The man is taking my safety as if his life depends on it, which it probably does knowing his boss the way I do. A Pakhan's word is law and the results of failure are never good. It's one of the biggest reasons I haven't attempted to lose them since they started. No need for more blood on my hands.

Pulling my focus back to his mother, I give her another tired smile. "It is so good to see you. Maybe you could help me with something?"

"What do you need?" Her smile lights up the air with the same shine as ever. "You know all you need to do is ask."

We spend a few moments talking and she is more upset than I have ever seen her. As briefly as possible I tell her how he's been acting since he came to pick up the kids. How I don't want his attention. I played nice with the guys because they have no choice but to listen to him, but his mother doesn't have to worry over those things. It doesn't take much for her to promise to handle things for me and we part ways with a fond hug.

Ivan is by my side as I get back to shopping. "It was not wise to do that."

"Do what," I pause, and meet his eyes for a second before moving again.

A simple touch on my arm stops me. His eyes show the shade of true grief. "Vladimir is my Pakhan and my friend.

All he has ever wanted was you by his side. He has never stopped looking for you even when he was told not to.

"Ivan, *please*," I desperately whisper to stop his words.

"Both he and Anya wanted you back. The loss of both of you has troubled him deeply for many years. Only the hunt for the ones responsible for her death has kept him moving forward."

My breath stops as his words sink in, and I stumble. Nearly falling to my knees if not for Ivan's quick actions. Tears fill my eyes as the truth is brought to light. Anya's face flashes with her big smile in front of me and I swear I can hear her laughter. Her gentle teases, bright eyes, and steady hands as she helped me with my schoolwork.

She just didn't die. She was murdered and not too long after I disappeared. No wonder he's clinging to me so tightly. I still don't want to get close enough to get either of us hurt again. But I can understand why he wants to protect me. Why he doesn't want to let me go.

Another breath and I pull myself away. "I'm sorry Ivan, I didn't know."

"None of us wanted you to."

"Why do all of you have to play the hero all the time," I grumble rubbing my stomach as the pain flares up again. Damn it, I might need something stronger tonight.

He smiles with a small chuckle before moving me on to the next aisle. "It is who we are."

I think the only one to be embarrassed throughout the entire trip is me as I hunt for my usual feminine products. Of course, they moved the darn things to the top shelf where I can't reach even if I could tolerate standing on my toes. He never gives me the opportunity to ask for help because two boxes are in hand before I can even be frustrated by the situation.

My only struggle comes when I try to pay for my things. While I search every inch of my purse a firm hand guides me out of the pay area. Words don't have the time to leave my mouth, and the card is back in his pocket.

"Volodya won't let me pay? What else did he tell you to do?" Crossing my arms I wait for him to answer which he doesn't. Damn bratva men.

All he gives me is a small smile as he takes my bags and leads us back to the car. Maybe if I was the same girl I was back then I would let him pamper me with car rides all the time if things were different. With Chris watching that isn't an option. I won't let him hurt anyone else.

Chapter 13
Vlad

Something is wrong. Every fiber of my soul insists that I need to go straight to Nevaeh, but I'm stuck in a meeting with my brothers. The topic of discussion is not making my mood any lighter. My gut clenches, wrapping itself tighter with each passing minute that I am forced to stay still.

"Tell me you have found something new." My teeth grit, praying for answers to end the mission that has consumed me for years.

"The last proven information was Mikhail and Ember catching those Albanians in the mine. Benson is playing dumb, but he knows. Hasn't been alone since the meeting. Being too clean." Dimitri shakes his head before shooting back the last of the vodka in his glass.

"My team is watching for the opening," Mikhail says, pausing to check on the baby over the feed on his phone. "We've found seven new houses and freed several dozen women, but we have lost just as many. They are still staying ahead of us far too often."

With each new failure to bring this group to their knees it brings the loyalty of our men into question. Such thoughts turn all our stomachs sour. Most of them have been with the family all of their lives. The bonds of blood and trust run deep within all of us. Their word should never be something that we have to take as anything but the exact truth. None of us wants to doubt our family.

"They have to come out of the shadows at some point. Someone powerful must be protecting them." Mikhail spins his blade staring out the window into the frosted garden.

I don't need to look to know that Ember is walking with the kids. They are never far from his sight, not that I can blame him. He nearly lost them before he ever truly had them. It was pure luck and the grace of God that the team got the tip that led them to her in the nick of time. It was God's grace that brought Nevaeh back into my life too. Shaking the thoughts from my head I bring my focus back to the room.

Before I can say anything else, mother rushes into the room. Thunder is written all over her beautiful face. "*Vladimir Sokolov, what* the hell do you think you're doing? I taught you better than this."

Dimitri and Mikhail wisely back up and stay silent as they eye up the situation. Mother only cusses when she has truly lost her temper with us which leaves only a few valid options in my mind. "Hello mother. What has you so upset?"

"Why are you harassing that poor girl?" Her slim hands slap flat on the surface of my desk. Another mark to show how upset she is. "That child has been through enough without you showing up and putting demands on her life."

Fuck! I do not want to have to deal with this on top of everything else we have going on. The fingers of both hands press into the edge of the wood as I lift to my feet. I lean forward bracing on my hands as I lay the most withering gaze I've ever directed at her on my mother. Some things are about to be understood in this household...this *very* second.

My voice is one octave from deadly as I stare her down. "Nevaeh is *none* of your concern. We will decide how we move forward without any more interference from anyone else. I will never forgive myself for listening to you and father's orders before. I refuse to do so again."

"Vladimir..." Her eyes widen but like a true bratva wife that is all she allows to show in the face of my anger. "We only..."

"NO!" My fist slams hard enough to mark the oak beneath my fingers. "I let you rip me from her then and look what became of that choice. Nevaeh has lost herself due to the abuse of some asshole she won't tell me about and I have yet to find."

My brothers shift uncomfortably at the vague mention of her past abuse. A crime I plan to take justice for as soon as possible. Just because she hasn't been with us does not mean that she was out of the promise of my protection. Christ she won't say anything to me about him but she's more on guard now than before. Maybe it's just knowing he's walking free again but my instincts tell me it's something more.

"You both told me to give her time when she ran from the funeral only, we never found her again. I lost the future with a woman I was content to love only to lose her to demons. I have chased those pigs for the last fourteen years and mourned both while doing it. I have found my light again, and you will *not* take it from me." My rant ends loudly to echo out of the room bringing the guards to attention.

Everyone moves uneasily. In the time since we found Anya's body, I haven't raised my voice in years. First, moya liliya's disappearance after her brother's death. Then the condition of Anya's body the day before our wedding.

This life has made me a cold, calculated, and ruthless man. My raised voice is bound to put them all on edge when what they are used to is my iron control.

"I know things have not gone the way we hoped but what you are doing with Nevaeh is not right. Our world is not her's. You don't know if she would be able to handle it." Her fingers lift to reach for my arm.

My training doesn't stop me from pulling away from her touch. I can't bear it with the memories coming to the surface right now. "Nothing you can say will change anything. That woman is my light, the only thing besides the kids that are good in my world, and I intend to bind her to me for eternity as soon as she lets me. She means more to me than this damned title."

"Vladimir," Her tone is sharp at my words, but I will not take them back.

Dimitri steps forward and takes her arm gently, pulling her back into his embrace to settle her. "You know he would never do anything to put her in danger. Only they can work out what they want for themselves. You need to leave this alone. Vlad is the head of our family. His word is law."

"Vlad, she said *no*." She tries one last time letting the tears slip past her defenses. There isn't anything on this planet I wouldn't do for the woman who gave birth to me except put my heart back on ice and damn my soul to the darkness.

"Because she is scared of her past," I sigh, trying to calm down, but the monster is too worked up for that right now. "That woman is my life. She will be my wife one way or another even if that means walking away from this life." Done with the conversation, I walk out of the office and head for my car. There's only one person who can calm the storm raging through me.

My anger has cooled enough by the time I reach her door that I can lightly knock instead of pounding it down. The tapping of keys stop and I know she's looking through the peephole when it doesn't open straight away. The slide of the lock lightens my heart.

It cracks open as far as the chain will allow showing just a portion of her down turned face. "What do you want, Volodya?"

"May I come in?"

She won't look up. "Now isn't a good time."

"Please, Nevaeh. I just want to talk for a bit." Unease ripples in my mind as she continues to look down. Something isn't right just as my gut has been insisting all day.

"I'm not feeling the best." The tips of her fingers grip the edge of the door as her eyes pinch in pain.

"Let me take care of you if you're not feeling well. I can make soup like I used to." Hope leaps high in my chest even as I take in her ashen features. Her hands have a slight shake that she is trying to hide. My poor liliya always has to try to hide from me no matter how many times I tell her to let me in.

Her head shakes but I can make out a hint of a smile lifts her lips. "You always burned it."

"And you always asked for more."

"It was better than Frankie's famous grilled cheese every night." Her eye flicks up shyly to mine under the fringe of her hair. Such a simple thing I've missed in all our time apart.

"I've had practice thanks to the kids, but I can burn it for old times sake if that would make you feel better."

The door closes, and I hear the chain move but she doesn't pull it open for me. She doesn't need to. Removing the chain was all the invitation she needed to extend. When I step through, she's already sitting on that damn bean bag working on her newest book. I could never find the lumpy things comfortable.

The quiet is broken only by her rhythmic tapping puts me at ease as I search through her things to throw something together for us. Every now and then I hear the keys fall silent and watch her rub her belly. Shit it's that time for her. She always had a hard time of it. Maybe I should send one of the men to the store for some orange chocolate. A few slices of those always made her feel better.

That damn shake moves up her arms to the rest of her. It must be sheer will that allows her to work as though nothing is wrong. I can't take watching her small body tremble. Grabbing the blanket from her bed I let it drift around her not that she notices. Her entire focus is on the screen in her lap as her fingers fly over the keys.

The simple soup doesn't take long, and I have more than enough for the two of us. The bowl thumps lightly on the crowded space of her work area making her jolt but she keeps her head low while she sets her things down. There isn't any other furniture besides her bed and that is too far from her for me to be comfortable. At least she has decent carpet instead of hard concrete.

She raises a spoonful slowly and sips it. Her jaw flexes for a moment before she takes a larger bit around a sad smile. "You got better."

I wait for her to swallow several mouthfuls of the broth. I don't think she has eaten much today if the pains hurt her as they did years ago. It is difficult to see her this way and not be able to do anything about it. "I pestered my mother until she taught me. Wanted to do it right."

"I'm not hard to please." We share a quick laugh and get to eating. She's not wrong, just about anything you put in front of her disappeared rather quickly.

The silence is settling. Peaceful. Just being in her presence has the monster in me laying down to sleep in the back of my mind. This. This is why I can't let her go. I need her to bring me back to this world. I need her to keep my demons at bay. To keep me human. Someone completely my own who understands all the darkness in my past and still sees the best in me.

"Thank you." Her soft voice pulls me back.

Her eyes try to avoid my own, but I wait until her nerve returns. She has to know what is in my heart. "You know I will always take care of you."

The fire that lit her eyes earlier wasn't bright, but it seems to be gone completely now. The food doesn't seem to have done more than nourish her body. Fleece encased limbs tremble within the shadow of the blanket around her.

Frowning, I set my own bowl aside and lean closer to her. "Tigrovaya liliya ?" Her chin sinks lower to avoid me. "Nevaeh, look at me."

"I appreciate you making me supper." The climb to her feet isn't steady as she stumbles toward the bathroom.

Jumping up I reach for her, but she closes the door before I can make it. Sighing, I step back to wait for her and knock over her trash can. Cursing, I drop to clean the mess up. Crushed roses litter the floor with wadded up scraps of paper. I shouldn't look at them, but they open without any direct thought. One becomes two which leads to five. Each new discovery burns away the quiet man from just moments ago. The monster is awake and ready to spill blood.

The door opens behind me, and I hear her sharp intake when she sees what I hold in my hands. To her credit she doesn't speak or back away as I move to stand over her, but she doesn't lift her gaze to meet my eyes either. Her trembling form focuses my chest. I lift the papers and wait.

When she continues to ignore me some of the anger slithers to the surface as I shake the slips of paper in her face. "Why?"

Her shoulders tense but she doesn't back away from me. "It isn't your problem."

"Why haven't you at least contacted the police?" I know the answer already, but I want to hear her say it.

Her face tells me everything I need to know. She drops her eyes, refusing to look at me. "I only have the notes. He hasn't been near me yet."

"Invading your locked space isn't getting near you? What if he starts hiding and comes out when you get home," I yell.

Fear lingers in the back of her eyes, but she doesn't back down. She stands straighter ready to fight me on her safety. "But he hasn't, and I added more locks. I just got confirmation on a new place, but it won't be ready for another month."

Locks? She thinks more locks and moving is going to stop someone bent on taking her? Someone she was scared enough to have a restraining order out against, and she thinks hiding is going to keep her safe? "How long?"

Her skin pales further. "I have it handled."

"Nevaeh tell me," I growl, knuckles cracking from the force of my fingers as I try to stay calm.

"Volo-"

"How long have you let this bastard scare you without coming to me?"

Her eyes dart away and she grips her arms, shifting back and forth. Her mouth opens and I know she's going to lie or deflect which has me growling.

Finally, she looks up with tears spilling from her eyes. "Please let it go," she begs.

"No," I snarl, taking an aggressive step forward but stopping when she shrinks into herself. "As much as you fight the feeling, we both know that you are still *mine*. Mine to protect, no matter what is between us. I won't force for more until you are ready, but I want to know how long you've played with your safety. How long have you been hiding this from me?"

Shaking takes over as she hugs herself tighter. "Please, I don't wan-."

The way she stops herself has me furious, but I change tactics. Whatever happened she still is terrified to face it. "Why didn't you tell me he has been a problem at least? The men watching you should know to watch out for danger."

"I don't-," she cries, choking off a sob before continuing over her wringing hands. "I don't want you to have more blood on your hands because of me."

The words make me pause. Even the monster sits silent, stunned that my sweet woman has kept this to herself because she wanted to spare me. That she thought even after all this time that she has to protect me. Shaking the anger from me, I ease forward and gently take her hands in mine. They jerk at my touch, but she grips me hard. Her flesh cold and shaking like she's going to fall apart. I cup her chilled flesh to my chest, laying my head over the top of her silky brown hair.

Closing my eyes in a deep breath, I try speaking in a lighter tone. "Moya liaya malen'kaya tigrovaya you do not ever need to protect me from the threat of added blood. I would gladly bathe in it every single day if it meant keeping you safe."

"I know," she whimpers, shivering but she refuses to sink into my heat. "And that's why I didn't tell you. Why I didn't go to the cops because you would know right away. I don't want you doing that for me. Don't want the evil of my past touching you."

"Nevaeh," I sigh, fighting to stay strong and not let her words pull me off course from the information I want. "You are my family. The light in my world that allows my heart to keep beating to push the devil away. I will protect you to my last breath and love you for eternity. Nothing will ever make me walk away from you."

Her breath hitches, head shaking as more tears fall. "I can't be who you need."

"I know you don't think you are ready for that right now," I whisper, stopping long enough to lightly kiss her brow. "I know you aren't ready for that yet and I will wait as long as it takes. Just please, please tell me what I need, so I can protect you."

My words seem to finally breach her defenses as her shoulders fall in defeat. She won't look at me, but she starts whispering, "He got out nearly four months ago. The notes started shortly after."

"Never hide something like this from me again. Especially, when it comes to keeping you safe," I quietly demand, shelving the information for later.

Her shoulders hunch and she tucks her chin to her chest. Eyes darting every which way but to me. Fighting between staying quiet and arguing some more. She's always taken things on by herself, but she would at least tell me what was going on. We need that communication back. He could have busted in at any point to take her, and no one would know to look for him.

Emotions that I don't have time to name churn through me inside and out. She's been hiding the danger to herself from me for months. Shouldered the burden so well none of our men have caught on that he's close or seen him in the act yet. Rage has me releasing her long enough for my hand to tear through the sheetrock with the angry bellow of feral bloodlust. How the hell is he in my city but still being reported in person by his parole officer? How did he find her so quickly? How dare he touch my woman?

I'm about to explode so I take the only way out available to me that does end in someone's blood. I have her pinned to my body before she can do more than gasp at my violence as I take her lips. Crushing her mouth under mine and gripping her head so she can't pull away.

Chapter 14

Nevaeh

Volodya's touch has always been firm and demanding without any harshness no matter how much he may want to shake the shit out of me. His last kiss was a reminder. An order to redraw the lines between us. This kiss. This kiss is full of fury, want, need, anger, and desperation. There is nothing I can do but surrender to him. To let him take from me before he sets the world on fire.

Time stands still. The world around us goes silent. I'm not sure if he pulls me or if I push, but we wind up entangled in each other's arms without an inch of space between us. Desperate fingers dig tunnels under the band holding my hair, leaving it hanging loosely over the backs of his hands. My fingers dig into the back of his wide shoulders at first before they drop lower.

A deep growl spills into the room when my nails scratch at his back trying to get closer. One moment I'm being held up as my knees fail me and the next the plush mattress sinks under our combined weight. He lies on me to keep me in place, but not so much that I feel trapped beneath him. Just enough for me to feel his weight, presence, and protection.

I gasp for breath as he leaves my lips to attack my neck. Tiny nips, open mouthed kisses, groans as he presses closer. My body flushes with a heat I haven't felt in years. Nerves more sensitive with each new touch as he explores me like he needs to memorize all of me. A hand on my breast has me stiffening and pushing at his chest desperately trying to get him off as Chris's words try to find a crack in my armor.

Volodya stills above me at the first shove. I can feel his gaze but can't make myself look at him. The past presses in making tears come to my eyes and desperate wordless whimpers pour from me. His hands drift down to grip the span of my hips as he flips us to lay me out overtop his firm chest.

As fast and hard as we started, he brings us to a near standstill. Kisses become feather light and his hands slow to lightly map the dips in my lower back. I don't know what sound I utter when his fingers slide over the tension knots but whatever it is he leans back with questions in his eyes.

Chris's face grins down at us from above. At me as he rips me off the chair and flings me to the floor. Screaming at me for getting close to a friend. For laughing at another man's joke. I can still feel Volodya's heat and gentle hands as blows of the past rain down over my body. If I scream even a little, I'll make it worse, but I can't stop the panicked whimpers.

"Nevaeh? Tell me what is wrong." He grips me hard, making my breath catch as the panic creeps in.

My insides still as his touch registers in my mind but all I can hear is Chris's insults and him telling me how much I've disappointed him. "No," the word rushes out and I begin shaking. "No. No. No! I'll be good. I'll be good."

"Shh. You did nothing wrong." Arms lock around me without feeling like a prison, but refusing to allow me to move away from him. Holding me close, we're suddenly upright with him leaning on the wall of paintings.

"I'm sorry. I'm so sorry," I can't stop saying the words over and over again. Panic threatens to take what little control I have over my body.

"Navaeh, you're safe." He pauses at my first soft cries. "Listen to my heartbeat. I'm right here. I will never let anything happen to you."

Whimpers roll into one continuous sound and tears leak past my lowered lids. Strong beats thunder under my ear as he presses me close. The sound. The smell. The feel. That devil isn't the one holding me. Vladimir, *my Volodya* has me. I'm *safe*. Still, I can't stop the shaking no matter how hard I try. I have to speak. Say the name that has always chased all my troubles away. For years only whispers of his essence dared to be vocalized in the smallest degree. Said in the dead of night when no other soul was near. The only thing I could rely on after the way he left us.

He starts singing in an old folk song in Russian. "You know the words. Sing with me Nevaeh." He starts again and again till the first notes break through me.

"Again, moya liliya. Let me hear your voice," He whispers, running his hands over my back. One stroke after the other moves over me as the beautiful Russian words pour out and through the still air.

***

Nonstop vibrations pull me up from the deep well of sleep. A large body of extreme heat shifts under me pulling the warmth out of my reach but I latch on refusing to let go.

"Don goo," the whisper comes out more as a growl. I burrow my face back into my heater's warmth. I have no idea if the words came out correctly, but they give me what I want.

Two perfectly weighted arms cinch around me again with an amused huff. Quiet is bliss and it doesn't take me long to sink into the deepest edges of sleep. Caught in the safety surrounding me, I push closer wanting to feel a fraction of my former self only my dreams allow. Free to love the man I can never have.

"Volodya."

"I'm right here moya liliya," his voice whispers roughly next to my ear.

"Hmm." I curl tighter to the warmth than a leach to fresh blood. He should be here now. Where is he? "Miss you."

His deep voice rumbles lower while pressing soft kisses over my hair. "Ya vsegda budu zashchischat' tebya, take zhe kak ty vsegda bushesh' oberegat' moyu dushu."

"Volodya, where are you? I need you." The arms tighten but no other sound permeates the air. The fullness of sleep opens its arms to pull me into the phantom of the man I wish I could have outside of these dreams. It's so peaceful here.

"Nevaeh. We need to get up." Kisses rain over my head again after a time.

"Go away," the demand isn't as firm as I want. That would mean waking up to deliver it the right way and it is too comfortable to move.

This time it's clear he is truly here and wants me to listen. "We need to get moving, Nevaeh."

"No," I whine rolling away reaching for the pillow. My fingers barely brush the frayed pink corner, and it's ripped from my hand. I'm not even going to question why Volodya is in my bed right now. I don't care as long as he shuts the fuck up and leaves me alone. My stomach isn't trying to kill me and I'm finally comfortable. Sleep is all I want right now.

"Up." One heavy palm lightly strikes the underside of my ass.

"Fuck off, asshole!" Rolling I try to take the covers with me. The world can go to hell for all I care today.

"Such words should not come out of that mouth," he says, but the humor in his tone can't be hidden.

"Fuck off and let me sleep!"

His bulky body drops over mine, pinning me to the bed facedown as his thick fingers dig into my sides for an attack I'm in no way ready for. His touch has me shrieking vile words. Kicking out and withering under him, desperate to get away. I hate being tickled and he has me in the exact position he wants with no way for me to get away from the torture.

"Volodya stop, please!" My hips buck trying to throw him off, but he doesn't move an inch. "I surrender! I'm up. I'm up okay."

His fingers stop in time for him to lean over my shoulder and look me in the eye. "Are you going to call me names again?"

"I won't call you names," I pant, glad to be able to catch my breath.

"That mouth is going to get you in trouble, moya liliya." A kiss wets my forehead and my nose. Dark grey nearly masks the blue of his eyes. Leaning above my shocked face his eyes soften and a rare smile lights up his entire being. It makes him seem younger. Like the young man I remember hasn't disappeared altogether. He shifts so he's now lying beside me.

I can't help tossing in one last dig. "Unless you need it Mr. Pain in my ass always has to be right."

His chuckle rumbles through my space like distant thunder while he moves me closer to lay over his elbow and curl under his chin so his other hand can run over my back without interruption. I can't help but sigh at his touch.

Years before we would lie like this all the time. Each venting about things out of our control or he would teach me more of his first language. A simple time with simpler problems. A star-crossed girl wishing for things she could never have with the only man besides her brother who made her feel safe. That safety net still resonates with us even when it shouldn't.

"What makes you so damn sassy? Always have to have the last word."

"You never had a problem with it before." The familiar taunt brings some of my old words to the front of my mouth. "You always had to be so damn bossy and never letting me have fun. Always so pigheaded about sticking to the rules."

Pinching my chin in his fingers he pulls me close and kisses my nose. "You are the only one besides my brothers, the children, and my parents who are allowed to speak to me with such disrespect."

I can feel the heat of a blush creep up mid stutter. "Why?"

Framing my face, he leans in, stealing another slow kiss that has my heart hammering in my chest. "Because I love you, and you own me in every way possible."

His confession leaves me reeling. For so many years I wanted to hear those exact words and now that he's said them, they've come too late. "No...I don't own anyone."

"Nevaeh Hawkins, you have held me in the palm of your hand since the moment I met you. Now we need to get up or we will be too late."

My eyes dart to my alarm clock to see it is well past eight. Well shit, I've never slept through my alarm before. Did I set it last night? "I'm already late for school. They aren't going to be very happy with me."

"No one is going to be upset with you about being late today. I've made sure that you have a sub for the day already."

"How?" I demand as he rolls out of my bed.

His shoulders shrug mid-stretch as his back pops and loosens from sharing my small bed. "I called."

"How did you manage that? I have to give my passwords for verification."

"I told them the truth. You were not well enough to call yourself. They said it wasn't an issue when you had already called out yesterday."

"Then where do we have to be?"

"When we get there, you'll find out. Now get up and take a shower." His hand lands lightly on my head as he walks out of reach.

Jesus, he's so damn demanding. He better feel lucky I don't have the energy to spare to fight with him any longer. Snorting, the blankets get tossed back and my body drags itself from my warm hole. Goose bumps raise over my arms prompting my feet to move faster. Please let there be a good amount of hot water!

Chapter 15
Vlad

Listening to her grumbles shouldn't have me so entertained but it does. It helps curb my control when I remember the extent of her fear. It has the monster stirring, ready for blood once the truth was finally out. The only thing that kept me in check all night was her soft body curled up in my arms. It reminded me of what was important. Chris will be dealt with shortly. Now that I know he's in my city there is nowhere he will be able to hide for long.

It's good to see the fire back in her. Some might question my sanity for loving it when she turns it on me. But damn it, I do. Even on the days when she's hurting like this. The first day for her cycle has always been the worst. The second day she spends being irate at the world in general. It just so happens I know how to turn her day around.

Aside from her muttering and stomping around, she doesn't argue anymore as she moves. The shower turns off far too early than it should. A baggy thread bare black hoodie is traded for a brown one less worn and a pair of loose jeans. Wet locks brushed out to hang at the middle of her back. Hands taking the peanut butter toast I offer without an ounce of her usual sass. She has never looked more beautiful.

My coat swallows her smaller frame when she finishes eating. Well, maybe this is better.The fact that she's surrounded by my things has the possessive side of my monster rearing back with a pleased howl. My heart bundled in the folds of my coat, blinking up at me waiting for what comes next. Wordlessly trusting me to keep her safe. It's a look that has my chest swelling with all kinds of emotions.

I eye the new locks, but lead us out the door making a mental note to upgrade them for her since I know she won't see reason. Crinkling paper and crushed petals under my feet bring me up short. Making sure the hall is empty, I scoop up what I know is another note. It wasn't able to be shoved under her door, so he left it there in the hall for anyone to see.

Fucker should have tried the door so we could have put an end to his ass already, because I never locked the deadbolt last night. I'd only done up the one, too agitated with what was happening to worry about more. Hell, it wasn't like we were in danger if he did try. I have my gun and fists. The monster in me growls in approval of the idea of his blood spilling over my hands

Shaking fingers curl over mine, jerking my focus down. Our eyes lock. Her wide brown eyes are lit with worry and untold fear, silently pleading with me to stop. She doesn't want me to read the note, and she doesn't want to know what is inside either. Of course, she'd just ignore what was inside and act like everything was fine.

"Volodya, *please*," She grips my hand harder, pressing close enough for me to feel the shivers running through her.

"He is a threat to you, moya liliya. Do you forget my promise so easily? I will let no one hurt you ever again." I keep the anger out of my face, wrap an arm around her back, and bury my nose deep into her neck. I breathe her in, fighting to regain some semblance of control. "I need to know how to protect you."

"I know you will always protect me," She whispers firmly, eyes never leaving the paper in my hands. "But-"

"Then we need to know what he has to say." I say, cutting her off as I lift the paper between us, waiting for her to decide. "Running from it won't make it go away."

"I'm *scared*," she whispers, so lowly I can barely hear her.

Her confession lands like a punch to my kidneys. Her form shakes under my hold, but she won't allow herself to fall into me completely. “It’s okay to be scared but I’m right here beside you. Tell me what you need.”

Her feet shift for a moment before she whispers, “Please… just hold me.”

Pulling her back to my chest, I bring the slip of paper in front of us so we can both read at the same time. Her arms keep me close, hugging mine over her middle. One deep breath and she steels herself for what is to come. “Ready.”

“I have you, moya liliya,” I say, kissing her hair and tightening my arm to calm her. “He can’t hurt you.”

“I know.” Reaching up she pulls the page open with shaking fingers.

No one is allowed to make my girl cry. Don't worry I will take care of him for you. Soon no one will keep us apart baby.
-C

“He’s truly lost it,” she whimpers, turning to fold herself into my chest. Her hands clutch at my back as the shaking becomes more pronounced.

“He will never have the chance to touch you again,” I promise her firmly, crushing her to me to keep the beast inside. This man’s time is limited for the continued harassment.I will not tolerate his continued interference in our lives. More importantly he will answer for the way he has treated her.

“This is why I wanted you to stay away! I can’t lose you to him too, Volodya,” she whispers the last words into the folds of my shirt. “I just *can’t*!”

“I am *not* going anywhere, Nevaeh.”

Fuck! I don’t know what to say on top of that. There’s nothing I can say hasn’t been said before. There is no way I’m walking away from her, and she knows that full well. I’m not worried about myself when it comes to him, but she won’t hear those words without another fight. It also means that Dimitri will have a target on his back because of me. He travels far more freely than I do, overseeing the vast array of businesses we own. The moment I tell him, he’ll act a fool just to deal with the bastard himself. I can’t tell her this, but it will give us the edge we need to draw the fucker out.

"Can we please go, Volodya?"

Pressing my lips to her hair again, I pull back and take her hand. We make our way out of the building to my car. I open the door for her and fire off a stern text to her guards to up the security. I don't know how he's gotten so close right under their noses, but it will not happen again. He's just made it to the top of my kill list, and I plan to do it personally.

"Oh, these I could get used to," she sighs, moaning in delight. She sinks further into the seat, letting the heat help her relax. The sound makes my body tighten and my mouth go dry, but I don't let it show. Now is not the time to feed that hunger. If I didn't have to keep my eyes on the road, I'd sit here and watch her all day. Head tilted back, small smile, loose brown waves, and fingers wrapped in my coat as she snuggles into it. Fuck I want her, but she isn't ready yet.

"That can be arranged with just a word if you'd stop being so stubborn," I tease, already planning to drive her from now on. Between the cold and Chris's threat, letting her walk is no longer an option.

Those notes offer a small window of the trauma that the soon to be dead man put her through. I can't see any physical signs, but the emotional wounds are glaringly obvious. The flinching, avoiding touch, whispered voice, and unable to meet someone's eyes. Those are all I need to know. I will find him and send him to Hell, so she doesn't have to fear him any longer.

The belt clicks in place before she glances up at me. "Where are you taking me?"

"You will see," I chuckle, sending a wink her way glad to be back to our teasing.

Fake annoyance spills from her lips in a long groan as she flops back to look out the window. I can't resist the pull and reach for her. Though she jerks at my touch, she allows me to take her hand and hold it with mine over the shifter. The drive falls to a comfortable silence as she relaxes next to me. The small squeeze she gives me lets me know that she doesn't mind me taking advantage of her being unable to get away in the small space of the car.

The surprise is something that is going to make her feel better. Maybe save myself a headache in the long run. I park around the corner, so I don't ruin the surprise before I'm ready. Then, I slide out of the car, help her out, and pull her close to block the biting wind. "Close your eyes for me."

"If you walk me into a paintball room, Volodya," She warns, twisting to grin evilly up at me. "I'm aiming for the most damaging shots without question."

"That is not something I *ever* wish to relive." I grimace, tucking her in closer. "Once was more than enough to learn my lesson."

I mask my face so she can't see the phantom pain, rippling through places that have never emotionally healed from that incident. One bad decision on our part for her fourteenth birthday was enough for me. Even her smile at the end of it wasn't quite enough to replace the pain. Close, but slightly lacking. Though, it was hard to be mad in the face of her happiness as she and Anya celebrated their victory with ice-cream.

Shaking her head, Nevaeh closes her eyes and lets herself be led. I nod to the man as I bring her inside and turn down the hall to the room I reserved for us this morning. Once we're in the middle of the area, I take my coat from her shoulders and step back.

"Open," I say, with a smile.

Musical laughter spills from her as she shakes in amusement. Eyes burn brightly with pure joy for the first time since we found each other again. "A rage room?"

"Better these to absorb your anger than my poor unfortunate anatomy." I smile down at her, enjoying the way she lights up from something so simple. "Enjoy yourself."

When she grabs a bat, I take another step back not wanting to be too close as she starts spinning it with daft flicks of her wrist while looking for a place to start. The tilt of her head lands like a punch to the gut with how closely the move reminds me of her brother. The unfairness of his loss is still something I haven't fully gotten over. And then it's all her as she leaps forward.

If I was fearful for my life I would have stepped out of the door within minutes of her first swing. Glass, plastic, metal, and rubber fly over the area as she rains destruction. A few shards of debris barely miss my head. When the wood splinters in her hands, she grabs an iron bar and continues like nothing happened.

The notes must have been weighing heavily on her than she wants to admit. I stay back by the door and watch her work up a sweat. She goes and goes, until she finally drops her weapon and flops to the floor. I can understand her desire to protect me. She has always watched my back, but as soon as this started, she should have at least gone to the cops. Even if she didn't want to call me, someone with authority needed to know. Sure, my contact would have alerted me to the fact. Probably why she kept me in the dark, but she'd have had protection. She shouldn't have taken this all on herself.

The first sob draws my attention sharply, and I quickly kneel beside her, drawing her into my arms. She latches onto me and presses close. Tears wet the fabric between us as she releases her emotions safely in my hold. Her pain has my heart so full of agony all I can do is wrap her up tighter.

"It's going to be alright, moya liliya. Let me take care of you. Stay with me so I can protect you from this bastard."

"He *won't* stop," She sniffs, holding me closer.Her face buries itself in the crock of my neck.

"I will not give him a choice."

"He won't. I tired. I put him in jail, and he still wants me. Still insists he's going to marry me." She quakes against me as she tells me small pieces of the truth.

Gritting my teeth I say as calmly as I can, "He will *never* have you."

"He won't stop, Volodya," She sobs harder, pushing back to tearfully lock eyes. "He will do whatever he has to, including killing me if I don't marry him. He almost did before."

Framing her face, I kiss her hard enough to make her stop rambling before I can't control myself. This one is as much for her as it is for me. Her truth is too much for me to take. The fucker put his hands on her, tried to kill her, and made her into someone who fears trying to live the life that was always hers.

"Move in with me," I plead. It's too dangerous to let her keep living alone as she has been.

She goes to speak in denial, but I stop her with a finger. "I'm not asking for marriage, moya tigrovaya liliya. Not yet. I plan to marry you but only when you allow me too. I need you safe and the best place I know is with me. At least until he is dealt with."

We stare at one another as her face wavers in indecision. I let her take her time. Most men would force the issue and take the choice from her but that isn't how we treat each other. She will make her choice and one way or another I would put myself between her and any who think they can try her.

Her eyes grow dim as she sadly shakes her head at me. "I'm not wife material for anyone, Volodya. Least of all for you."

The monster raises its head to howl into the darkness of my soul. His rage will not do. With effort I force him back to watchfulness so that I can be here for her as she needs me to be. "You are exactly the type of wife I need by my side, but you are not ready for that talk yet. Stay with me where I can keep you safe."

Her teeth bite into her lip for a moment before she nods. "Okay. Only until he is dealt with. This doesn't mean anything more for us. "

Well, it's a start. We can work on the rest with each new day. "I'll take that for now."

"And I won't stop working so you can lock me away inside the house," she demands, jabbing me squarely in the chest with one stiff finger. "I love my job, and I won't give it up. Won't let him *or* you take my work from me."

Laughter chokes me so hard all I can do is nod along with her words. I knew she wouldn't let me bundle her up and spirit her away even if it was for her own good. "The school is safe, moya liliya. I will never ask you to give up what you love."

Lines press over her features as she lifts a brow and frowns. Tone sassy and full of doubt as she rolls her eyes and questions me. "You aren't going to try talking me out of working and relying wholly on you?"

And there goes my heart again. For a few moments all I can do is sit here and smile. This is the woman I remember. The one I want to bring back to life. My sanity may be in doubt in front of others, but I love the fire in her. She grounds me. Keeps me on the right path and never doubts what I can do.

"No, Nevaeh. You would never be happy living like that which would in turn make me miserable. I'd never make such a demand even when we move past all of this and say our vows. Working with kids was always your dream and I'd never take that from you."

“I won’t give up Tallie either,” she grumbles, leveling a glare at my growing smirk. “I don’t care how much he makes Dimitri sneeze.”

“I wouldn’t dream of it. Hell, I think we may stop and adopt a few more just to keep him company.”

A sharp thrill of laughter bubbles out of her at my offer. The sound building until she has to swipe at her eyes to clear her tears. “I wanted more,” she giggles, slowly calming down to get the rest of her sentence out. “But Tallie hates other cats so that won’t end well.”

Chapter 16
Nevaeh

As soon as I break down and give into his request, he wastes no time in bundling me into his coat and loading us into the car. I can feel him glancing at me hoping to gain my focus but all I can do is stare out the windshield. The only warmth in me is the hand he keeps in his. We stop only long enough for him to take my keys and run up to grab Tallie for me before we're moving again. Everything in me is numb as we make our way through the city and into the fringes.

Volodya grips my hand firmly as he stops the car outside a massive stone mansion before letting go. Panic threatens to take my careful control without the presence of his touch, but I fight it back. I may be leaning on his strength now but once Chris is dealt with, I have to stand on my own once more. Tallie's restless kneading on my legs helps.

The house towering over me is far more than I could ever imagine. It's a great deal more than the house he grew up in. This must be the new house that was being built before he left... *Thanks to the fire.* He helps me out of the seat watching me closely, like he's worried I'm going to crack. He remains close, arm wrapped around my shoulders, and giving fleeting touches before he moves aside to let me enter the home first. Whiskers twitch under my chin as I grip my cat tighter.

Ignoring the glances from his men, we climb the stairs and down to the last room on the right. A small smile on his lips he opens it to let me in. "You will stay here in my room."

The room is huge. Spacious and clean, like stepping into a magazine. The dark grey walls and cherry floors are offset by the light blue of the bedding. There's a small sitting area on the right, facing the fireplace on the inner wall. Everything in its place, looking completely undisturbed since they were put in place.

"I can't." My breath catches in my throat, but he calms me before I can let my mind run down a wild path. Being back in the circle of the bratva is fine. But to be in his personal space feels like too much.

"You can and you will. I don't even sleep here. Too many things that need to be done keep me elsewhere. *Please...* give me this. We will get your things tomorrow." He's lying. We both know it.

Tallie, not impressed with my hesitation, jumps from my hold and disappears under the bed. "I have work tomorrow. How am I going to get there?"

My logical question seems to make him relax a bit as he takes my hand. "You are free to come and go as you please, but you won't be alone. Your guards will stay close to keep you safe. My men will be there to collect your things after you get off."

Teeth dig into my lip as I chew over what he says. While I don't like the thought of strange men in my space, I *was* going to be leaving soon enough. I had found a new place and was just waiting for the current tenant to leave. I have no plans of being in an area where Chris would know where to find me. For now, there is no way he's getting close to me here. I guess the time frame has just been moved up.

"Okay."

The lightest of touches slides across my check before he backs away. "I will be in my office if you need me. Lunch will be up shortly, and we have a few hours before the children come home so you can rest. Take a bath if you like." His hand sweeps out to the door to the left.

I have to give it to him. It sounds heavenly after using a tiny stand-up shower the past five years. But… That may be a bit hard. "I don't have any other clothes."

He spins on his heel and opens the closet. In less than a minute he's striding back to me and handing me a shirt. "Wear this. It is more than long enough to cover you... Or I can call and ask Ember for some of her things." He quickly adds, paling a bit when I don't take it right away.

"No," I gasp, refusing to let him bother her. Breathe, I scold myself as I take the material from his hands. A hot blush takes over and climbs up my skin, but I play it as cool as I can. "This is fine, thank you."

He tries to hide it, but the heat flashing in his eyes over my choice is obvious. Typical possessive male wanting me in his things. "You come get me if you need anything, da?"

I give him a small smile but don't verbally promise him anything. His fingers brush over my cheek before he turns, wide shoulders making their way back the way we came, until they slip from view down the stairs.

***

I stayed in the huge claw-foot tub far longer than I should have. I don't even know how much time has passed as I dry my hair, and slip his shirt over my head. The shortest edge of the material reaches to my mid-thigh and billows widely around my form. Knowing he won't care, I help myself to a belt from his closet and cinch my waist tighter.

Pulling in an uneasy breath I turn and stare into the open space of his private area. Someone left lunch on the bed, which is cold, but I eat all of it anyway. No way will I waste food. The cold soup and Russian black tea still taste like heaven.

I'm not sure what will happen now, but I will take it as it comes. I don't have a choice anymore. Fighting him is going to be far harder than before with us sharing the same space. I'm not blind, or unmoved by the desire and pull we have. He's all in and while I never stopped loving him, putting myself in a position to be hurt is *terrifying*. Things are just so confusing. With Chris circling, I fear I'll be watching Volodya bleed out for standing in front of me.

I can't deny that just being near him makes me feel safer, but a target is now on him. Should I give up control and let myself sink into the safety he offers? *No*. I still can't seem to let go of the ugly lessons my past has taught me. Wholly relying on him isn't possible, but he isn't going to give me a choice. If I tried to keep fighting him, I wouldn't put it past him to move in with me. So, while I don't like it... This is easier.

My head is all over the place. These stirring feelings I've been trying to ignore won't go away. It's only gotten worse now that he's barged back into my life. I should be worn out from the extent of today's emotions, but I know I will find no rest in his bed. My thoughts aren't ready to let me settle down, and it's late enough that I'd just be up at 2 am trying to be quiet while the rest of the house sleeps.

Leaving the bedroom, I make my way through the hallway and down the stairs. Children's laughter has me pausing. I decide to follow the sound into a large glass sun-room. Hunter and Josey lay on the warm tile floor playing a card game, under the watchful eye of a blonde-haired woman gently rocking in a low hammock. It takes me a moment to recognize Ember as her honeyed locks brush the floor with each swing.

A baby's angry cry pieces the air, and she is quick to shush the little one as the rocking continues. It only takes a few minutes before the child calms itself. Her faint murmuring soothes the baby back to sleep.

"Don't just stand there, come sit with us." Her low call has the kids looking up.

Hunter's eyes widen when he sees me. Josey has herself attached to my waist before I can do more than smile. "You came to visit us, Miss Hawkins! Have you seen our baby sister yet?"

"Josey," her mother's quiet but stern voice brings her excited words to a quick halt. "Settle down before you wake Katya up again."

"It's alright, Josey, we need to be quieter for your sister. Go play with your brother for now. I will play with you later," I whisper in a hushed voice and send her a wink. I hold my pinky out and she locks hers around mine with a big grin.

She's quick to return to the game with her brother who gives me a nod and smile. I'm soon forgotten as they pick up where they left off. I don't mind being ignored as I make my way to sit on the wooden rocking chair next to their mother. She offers me a sleepy smile but doesn't move to disturb the baby curled up on her chest. The poor woman looks as if she could fall asleep any time now. I hear the first months are the hardest and the proof is laying before me. A happy but exhausted mama.

"Hello Mrs. Sokolov," I keep my voice low as I take in the mother and child. The little one's features are a perfect replica of both her parents. Though, her hair matches her uncles' dark strands.

"None of that," she jokes in mock anger. A smile lets me know that she isn't upset with my address. "Ember is more than well enough for friends. If you know how to handle these boys, you and I will have lots to talk about."

"Nevaeh! Darling, what are you doing here? Is everything alright," Maria gasps, cutting off my reply as she catches sight of me as she steps into the room.

"Hello." I smile sadly. I try to keep everything in. Try to keep the conflicting emotions off my face, but by the look on her face I haven't managed that.

She wastes no time in reaching my side and pulling me into her arms. "Oh darling, everything is going to be alright."

The familiarity of her hold brings tears to the front, and I hide my head in the shelter she provides. The sobs come out silently, but my body shakes. How I have missed the comfort of her embrace. Of having someone other than myself to rely on who wants nothing in return but my presence.

***

So much paint. Red sprays of my most vibrant paint are literally everywhere. On every single surface and small crevice of our large activity station. There are several spots dripping from the ceiling. Puddles are making their way closer to the rug of my desk area.

The janitors are not going to be happy with me today. Not that they are ever overly thrilled with the mess the kids and I make in this room on a daily basis. Truly they should know better. This is an art room for goodness sake and art is messy on a good day.

The only redeeming grace is that none of my students were here when I dropped the crate. Stepping on that stray pencil was not how I wanted to end up on my ass. I am covered from head to toe. Most of my hair is spared thanks to the handkerchief wrapped around my head. I keep spare clothes in the closet just for days like this because I can be incredibly clumsy.

Damn my spastic brain. Lose focus for just a second and shit hits the fan. The next class of kids will be here in a short ten minutes. It will be close, but I should be able to have most of it cleaned up by that time. If I get to change before may still be in question.

Jumping into gear, I grab cloth towels and get to work. The ceilings are first and surprisingly easy to wipe down with very few smears left behind. My tables are not so lucky as the liquid finds its way into every tiny scratch that is etched into the surface top.

The last towel finds the washer as the door opens. Well, no time to change clothes so on with the day as I am, I guess. "Good afternoon, everyone! Did you all have a good lunch break?"

They all laugh and giggle with loud yells of yes. Each is quick to find their seat so we can begin class. All the supplies are back on the table and free of paint to start the next stage of our latest project. They easily fall into work without any prompting from me.

I can't imagine not working with these younger school kids. They are easy to love and follow instructions without the attitude of the higher levels. My first years of teaching with older kids did not go as well as I'd hoped. Most of my college years did not go as I had thought they would. Still, I try not to think about those memories. I've found my place and I'm not leaving it.

"Miss Hawkins, I need red please." One of the girls turns as I walk past.

"I'm sorry. I am out of red today sweetie. I think if you use some orange and purple, those pretty leaves will look amazing." Leaning over I show her a few different mixes that seem to please her. So easy to redirect. Show them something shiny and new and they go right back to their happy little selves.

The darn paint is still in my face as I hand the kids off to their guardian's cars at the end of the day. One by one they slip into their seats, and I watch them drive off. None of the adults question my chaotic appearance, bless them. Things like this are far too common that they no longer bat an eye when they see me.

Lord, I hope that Volodya isn't the one picking me up today. It only takes me a few moments to gather my things and make my way back outside. Damn, the air is freezing today. I can't be totally irate that he forced his coat on me again this morning when he dropped me off. It is the warmest thing I have ever worn.

A black sports car sits at the bottom of the walk, but I have no idea who it is, so I walk on the opposite side looking for my shadows. Where the hell are they? Volodya has made sure that if he could not pull himself away from his work Ivan and Kostas were to be right here to meet me.

The black car honks at me before the door opens and Volodya steps out. No, it isn't Volodya, but he is a near mirror image of my protector. This man smiles too much, and his air is open with friendship. His face is smoother and less stress filled. I grip the strap of my bag close as he starts towards me.

"Dimitri?"

"Hello Nay, it has been far too long." His grin spreads as my eyes widen.

"What are you doing here?" I ask.

"What? No hug for your long-lost friend, little Nay-Nay." He laughs, rushes in and pulls me into a bone crushing hold as he sweeps me into the air.

Laughing is easy with my bubbly friend. They may be twins but even in their youth Volodya was only carefree with his family, Frankie, and me. Dimitri and I used to prank the boys every chance we got. The scoldings we sat through! All while trying not to burst out laughing as their father ranted at us. Though, the lines in his eyes told us he was laughing too.

"Where have you been? Two weeks and no sign of you," I demand as soon as he sets me down. I playfully punch his arm unconsciously, as I step back to take him in. A fissure of fear sears through me for a moment, but he never stops smiling.

"You know what a task master my brother is. I only just got back and told him I would collect you. Especially, since he couldn't excuse himself from his meeting." His grin is infectious, and I can't help answering it with my own.

"Trust me I know. Let's get back so he doesn't see this mess," I grimace, waving at the red that is still staining my hair.

"What mess? You are as beautiful as you have ever been." His arm settles casually around my neck as he jokingly pushes me around.

Rolling my eyes, I punch him again but let him lead me to the heat of the car. The leather is just the right tempter for my cold backside. "God! These heated seats are heaven."

"Anything for you NayNay."

"Shove off asshole," I tease, sticking my tongue out.

Gasping, he falls into the door with a hand to his heart. Ever the *dramatic* pain in the ass he has always been. “You wound me sastra.”

“Oh, please you know I haven’t done anything yet.”

“Ah the team is finally back together again,” he says, his hands rubbing together in childish glee. He grips the wheel to take us home with a bigger grin.

“Uh oh. Do you plan to get me in trouble,” I joke though I know the answer already. When the two of us got together someone always came out on the bottom of some crazy pranks.

“Always and forever dear Nay.” He sends me a wink.

The familiar words and his presence have me settling further into the seat eager for more. “So, who are you going after first?”

He just flashes me a grin. “All in good time Nay.”

Chapter 17

Vlad

"Are those beads?" Mikhail leans over the back of my chair with a raised brow.

My brow ticks at his question though I don't glance at him as I shift through the orange glass orbs with a critical eye. "Good to know you don't need glasses yet brat."

The furious scowl he aims at me doesn't escape my notice. I finish and dump them back in the multi compacted set of colored beads to go with the ones I just bought. He wants a different reaction, but I ignore him and twist to my adorable plemyannitsa. The humming seven-year-old is contentedly sitting upside down on the thick cushions of my office couch. Her favorite spot to be when I leave the door open. Both of her hands are floating around each other in one of her many imaginary games.

Bigger issues come before dealing with my younger brother's teasing. "Josey, come here little one."

She's bouncing out of her seat and ducking under my arm to climb into my lap before the last word is finished. Her arms curl around my neck, hazel eyes glittering up at me now that she's perfectly comfortable. She doesn't have to say anything. I have her full attention and she's waiting for me to tell her what I want.

Mikhail groans the moment I slide the closed container in her hands. "Why must you get her more when she has an entire drawer full?"

"Because I can," I snort, enjoying the pain on his face. Our parents line her closet, Dimitri feeds her, and I give her whatever toy or craft she lays eyes on. Mikhail would spoil her just as much if doing so didn't have her mother after him. It's just how things work.

"At least she can't yell at me for it this time," he mutters under his breath with a huff.

Turning my attention to the little one in my arms, I lay the box into her hands earning another big smile from her. "Would you make some pretty bracelets for Tetya Nevaeh to cheer her up?"

"OK," she giggles, bouncing in my hold.

"Slow down Milaya," Mikhail sighs. One hand playing with her hair, earning her giggles and his smile returns. "Make as many as you want, just make sure these aren't left for anyone to step on this time, please."

"Yes sir," she promises brightly and jumps off my lap to return to her spot.

His eyes flick to mine as he lowers his voice and switches languages. "You had trackers put in those didn't you?"

"Of course I did," I snort, opening my laptop to get payroll done, not feeling the least bit wrong for doing so. "She's stubborn but she won't take off anything the kids make for her."

While I don't mind the silence, the sudden jolt has me turning to take him in. His mouth works without words and then a smile that spells nothing, but trouble takes over. "Brat you may be on to something there."

He pulls his phone from his pocket and heads for the door before I can inquire about what crazy new idea he's just thought up. "Be good for your Dyadya for a bit Milaya."

Josey doesn't look up from the line up of beads she wants to use. "Ok Kail!"

Glancing to make sure Josey is still content, I get back to the work in front of me. Payroll is the one that needs the most focus. I start with the hardest jobs first and work my way to the easier things. Dinner is in two hours, and I want this done so we can eat together.

"Josey, go get washed up for dinner," Ember says, pulling my eyes from the screen to see her leaning on my door.

It can't be that late already. Or maybe it can I see checking my watch. Time has flown by. Good thing the payroll is done along with some winning bids to keep the crews moving. The emails can wait till tomorrow. Closing everything down, I stand only to stop short under the narrowed glare from the woman still standing in the open door. She doesn't look happy, but I haven't done anything to upset her lately besides the beads.

If I didn't mind being late, I'd simply wait her out, but I want to spend as much time with the family as possible. "What's the matter?"

Hazel eyes flicker to a deeper green. "Stop giving your brother more ideas."

"I do-"

A wordless scream has us both out of the office in time to see a figure stumble and fall down the lower half of the stairs. Whoever it is covers their head and howls. Sobbing, they climb to their feet without dropping their arms and they finally spin to face us. Dimitri's panicked gaze locks with mine and suddenly turns angry.

"I'm going to end her!" He yells, stomping.

"End who?" Ember asks, blinking up at me from my side.

All I can do is shrug, clueless to what he's crying about. "What is the problem brat?"

"She's gone too far," he shrieks, drawing men from their rooms.

"Who?" I demand, feeling a headache coming on with all his shouting.

"*Nevaeh*!"

God, please tell me they haven't started their childish games already. "What did she do?"

Groaning, he slumps forward and looks away. Shoulders rising around his ears like he's trying to hide from us. The men at my back grumble about his outburst and now his reluctance to speak.

"Dimitri," I growl, crossing my arms.

A low whine spills from his throat and his hands slowly let go to hang at his sides. I automatically zero in on his eyes but come up short as something out of place grabs my attention. What the hell happened to his hair? The locks still hang longer than mine but instead of the matching dark tone my eyes are met with hot pink. The color is so bright it's nearly a neon sign.

Ember sees it at the same time and starts laughing so hard she starts wheezing. Clutching her stomach and bending over to not fall, barely able to stutter, "That color is *perfect* for you!"

"Shut up, Ember," he yells, gripping the discolored locks again. "This isn't funny. I can't go out like this."

"No," she chokes. "It's hilarious!"

"I don't know," Mikhail says, popping up on my other side holding the baby and eyeing our brother with obvious delight. "I've heard it's all the rage with some women in the clubs."

"Enough," I growl, shutting down the bickering before it goes any further. "Did you think she wouldn't get back at you for the salt in her coffee?"

"That's different. It was harmless," he whines, shaking his hair at me. "How am I supposed to go out like this?"

"Not my problem," I shrug, finally able to enjoy the payback he earned. Did he think she was just going to let him prank her without doling out her own justice? "But you have several meetings you can't miss this week."

"I can't go like this!" Again, he yanks on his hair.

"You can." Shaking my head, I spot the sly grin on Nevaeh's face as she watches from the dining room. I can't stop the small smirk when our eyes meet. Dimitri's sputtering has my focus snapping back in time to silence him with one hard look. "This isn't up for discussion. You can and will do your duties or you'll deal with me."

"Easy woman, or you'll make me drop our daughter," Mikhail laughs, lifting Katya higher as Ember digs in his pants. "It's on the other side."

Cackling, the blonde reaches for his other hip and pulls out his phone. She points it at our brother with an evil smile as shutter sounds fill the air. "This is perfect!"

"Stop it sastra," Dimitri cries, covering his head again. "Brat handle your woman!"

"What do you want me to do- drop my daughter and piss off her mother? No, thank you, I'm enjoying the show," He laughs, kissing the little head on his chest as she stares at her crying uncle with wide eyes.

Chapter 18
Nevaeh

The house is far quieter than I've *ever* experienced in my time here. Volodya and Mikhail are away on another meeting, and their parents have the kids. Dimitri has been out of the house for a few days with one of the crews. Ember and Katya are around here with their shadow somewhere. I'm just not sure where since I've checked the entire house three times and still come up empty. Only one last place they could be, though, I've never dared enter her area before.

The early spring air still bites as I step out into the gardens. Chilly but no reason to go back in for a coat when the stone building is a quick five hundred feet ahead. The flicker of firelight wavers, dancing in small waves through the window and the strong rhythmic hammering of steel on steel lets me know I've finally found the woman I've been after. Hugging myself against the wind, I hurry down the path eager to get in the warmth of Ember's space.

The heavy door swings in with little effort and the wall of heat slams into me like a hot hug. It rips an appreciative moan from me as I close it and lean back to soak it in. My eyes close automatically, and I enjoy every last bit of it. Damn, I really should have put on a sweater at least. That wind makes it much colder than the forecasted forty degrees.

Opening my eyes, I suddenly feel like I've been transported through time. The entire inside is large, exposed stones that reminds me of a medieval blacksmith shop with some modern upgrades. A deep fireplace stacked with wood but unlit, rows of forging tools, a large open flamed forge, several anvils, and machines I can't name. On the outside wall, there's a long wooden table filled with rolls of leather and smaller tools, projects, and books.

The hammering stops, and I pull my head towards the sudden silence in time to watch Ember shove the metal back into the coals. Two swift twists of her wrist have it where she wants it before she pulls it back out and dips it into a bucket. She's wearing a heavy leather apron, streaked with black. It's cinched over her front to protect her body and clothes from the hot metal and sparks while she works. Her hair is thrown up in a messy bun to keep it out of her face.

Her head tips my way with a teasing grin and a wink, as she places the blackened metal to the side, tugging the thick gloves off. "Was wondering how long it'd take you to find me out here."

"I didn't mean to interrupt your work," I mutter, sheepishly, suddenly feeling guilty for intruding into her space without being invited.

"Now, I'll hear none of that," she scolds, tossing the gloves down and walking to the back corner to pick up the gurgling baby. "You're always more than welcome to hide with Katya and I out here. Get some space from the men and have some girl time if you want."

"I..." Darn, I don't know what to say to that.

Anya was the last woman who was that close to me that we spilled all of our secrets. All of our hopes and dreams. What we wanted and what scared us and what kept us going. Even though she knew I loved Volodya and she was set to marry him, it didn't cause a rift between us. She was my best friend until the accident. Losing her steady presence and wise words was one of my deepest regrets while on the run.

"It's fine, Nevaeh. The boys always say I'm really forward but I don't see the point of saying what you don't mean," she laughs, shoving the baby into my arms. "Here, hold her for me a moment so I can get her swing set up."

The damn woman doesn't give me a chance to say no. Katya is thrust into my arms and I can't do anything but draw her closer to my chest. Her mother is already walking into the back room ignoring my sputtering for her to come back. I'm stuck, staring down at the tiny person in my arms unsure of what to do. I love kids, but I've never been trusted with one this small and fragile.

For the most part she doesn't fuss about the random handoff to a new person. Storm colored eyes with flecks of green blink up at me as she blows bubbles. Her simple trust and curiosity has me smiling as she takes a fistful of my loose hair, squirming happily with a little gurgle. My heart doesn't stand a chance in the face of her cuteness.

"What's got you so excited?" I whisper, leaning in to give her little nose a kiss. "You just trust whoever your mommy gives you to, huh?"

Ember walks back in cackling to set the baby swing next to her worktable. "Oh no, not everyone. She adores Vlad for some reason and gives Dimitri gruff every time he tries to pick her up. He hands her over in tears wondering why his niece hates him."

The image of a sobbing Dimitri cracks the rest of my unease. He was always the life of the party making every-one fall for his smile and charm. Easing tensions on the edge of boiling over and turning a near brawl into a friendly party. To have this sweet little bundle of joy reject him every single time would definitely wound his large ego.

"A girl after my own heart," I chuckle, rubbing noses with her. "Poor D has never been turned down before. He must be so confused and heartbroken."

Snickering, she tickles under Katya's chin earning a stilted giggle. "He is. That she likes Vlad over him has him clueless and digging to figure out ways to get her love."

Something buried deep in my heart cracks as I gaze down at her. It takes a few moments to get my emotions under control before I can talk again. "I can fully understand. Who wouldn't want to snuggle this little angel all the time."

"Yeah, they all fight over her. Did you wanna sit? I was gonna try to finish this order before going in and I could use the company." A stool groans across the floor as she pulls one out next to her own with a firm pat of expected compliance before I can answer.

"Well since you asked so nicely," I chuckle, easing down next to her so I don't bump the baby still in my arms.

She ducks her head but not fast enough to cover the grin stretching her lips. "I'm always nice. Now that I have you where I want... You tell me what's wrong between the two of you. I'd kick both of you in the ass to help you figure things out and get over whatever the hell is holding you back. And don't tell me there isn't anything there. Anyone with eyes can see the way you look at each other, now out with it so we can help you over it."

If I didn't fear hurting the baby in my arms, I'd be on the floor. "How do yo-?"

A brief glance is slanted my way as she threads two large needles with thin strings of leather. "It's painted all over your face girl. You are head over heels for him, and he'd burn the world for you. So, what's holding you back?"

There's no way she should know that's what I came out here to hopefully clear up. Do I want to put myself on the line to be hurt again? Do I want to allow him closer and hope that Chris can't touch us? That something won't happen to one of us and completely shatter the other? So many questions and feelings are cluttering my mind about the issue that I don't know how to think or feel. That's why I came looking for her. If anyone understands the dangers of coming in from outside their world and still making it work, she is the only one who could relate to my fears.

Ember doesn't push again. Her fingers move in steady stitches as she works on binding the pieces of leather before her. It's like she figures she has all the time in the world to wait me out. The lines of her face relaxed and focused on her work. All the while I sit, holding her daughter... Trying to keep myself from losing it and talk myself into getting the questions out.

Dang it, I need some answers!

Closing my eyes, I finally get a single word forced out. "How?"

"Bit too broad there, Nevaeh," she chuckles, not looking up as she continues working. "How did we meet? How do I put up with all the men? How have I not stabbed my husband worse than when he tried to take my dinner? Can you narrow it down for me just a bit?"

"You stabbed Mikhail?" I stutter, staring at her wide eyed full of disbelief. "Why?"

Her smile is all innocent as she turns my way but there is no way I'm falling for that. "He tried to take food from me when I was pregnant. I did warn him, and he thought I was bluffing. Hasn't made that mistake again so at least he learned."

Once my brain reboots from the shock, I start laughing and she easily joins in. Nothing in her short summary sounds healthy for a man to do to the woman carrying his child. It's a show I wish I could have been around to witness. His face had to have been priceless in the face of the event.

With the ice broken between us, the words I want to ask come out- like they weren't being held back in the first place. "How did you know it was right? That putting yourself out there wasn't going to end badly this time around and trust that he wasn't going to disappear?"

My words seem to sober her though the smile never leaves, just grows softer as she sets her project down and brushes hair from my eyes. Her movements and looks bordering between mother and friend. "Love doesn't have a right or wrong time really. When it happens, you either let it go or have the courage to step up and ride out whatever comes with them by your side."

The next words are more of a struggle, but I say them anyway. "What if they've already hurt you? That you needed him, but he was nowhere to be found. So you ran, only to find a worse evil?"

Hands pause mid reach for her work. "Does he know that he hurt you?"

"No," I whisper. Glad I haven't given up the baby continuing to play with my hair. "Well, he knows I'm upset that he left and didn't come back for me."

"Did he do it intentionally?"

Guilt hits hard as I shake my head because I haven't been able to tell him anything about what happened besides my stalking ex. He doesn't know how deep his leaving hurt me. Or any of the horrible things I allowed to happen when I ran. How I wish I'd had the guts to stay and wait for them after the accident. Or that on the bad nights, I'd dream that he found me and took me home. That over the years my memories of him were the only good things in my life.

Firm fingers pinch my chin and lift my eyes, jolting me out of the past to meet her understanding gaze. "Could he have done anything differently?"

"No," I whimper, fighting to keep the tears in. "He was doing what he had to at the time. What his family expected of him. It was done before I ever met him and there was no way for him to get out of it without starting a war."

"That doesn't make the pain any less hurtful to manage." She nods with a knowing smile. "Letting Mikhail in wasn't fast or easy, no matter what others say about how quickly we got married. Even now, we still have days where I have to walk away to get myself back on track."

In the weeks I've been here, I've never seen them have a cross word between them. When one walks into the room the other lights up like a Christmas tree. They never seem to stop reaching for each other. "But you're happy now."

"Yes, but we aren't perfect. No couple is," she chuckles, pulling my hair from Katya's mouth. "I can't tell you that what they do doesn't scare me because it does. There are days I know he's dealing with a lot of bad stuff he can't talk out with me. And I have to remind myself it isn't because he doesn't trust me but because he doesn't want the ugly to touch me. That he's protecting me and our family. Those are the days I give him more love and grace. This isn't an easy life and I won't lie to you by saying otherwise."

"What if I'm not strong enough?" I ask, just as the baby begins fussing.

Practiced hands lift the upset child from my arms and deposit her in the swing. A quick flick of her finger sets the motor running. The swing gently sways the tiny body back and forth. Katya's upset grunts, turn from whimpers to soft sighs as sleep takes her.

"I don't think it's a question of being strong," she whispers, a fond smile in place as her gaze twists to land on me. "The bigger question you need to ask yourself is can you live with the guilt of hurting both of you if you walk away."

"What should I do then?" I ask, begging her to give me an answer.

"No one can answer that but you. But before you take all the decisions on by yourself, talk to him. You can have all the fears and differences in the world, but you have to talk or there's no point in being with anyone. Relationships that are worth it are never easy."

I know she's right, but saying the words and putting them in action are two *vastly* different things. Trusting him with my body is easy. It's the dark truths of what happened that I'm scared is going to change the way he sees me.

I'm not the sweet innocent teen he remembers. The naive girl that believed the light would always win died years ago. A distrusting second guesser who fears getting close to anyone else now stands in her place. A broken and twisted shell teetering on the edge of control not meant to lead by his side with the confidence he needs.

I don't realize my fingers are clenched until she takes them and smooths them open while delivering more advice. "Stop letting all of your doubt bleed into what you think he needs. Trust him to take your fears head on, and live for the moments most people overlook. The ones where he sends a thinking of you text, gives a simple touch, whispered conversations in the middle of the night, and the secret smile he shows no one but you. When he remembers something so small no one would notice but that brightens your day because he wants to see you smile. Hold onto those the hardest because those are the ones that matter the most."

As I sit next to her ready to deny my feelings yet again, I pause. Her words carry the heavy weight of experience that only the pain of loss can provide. Her words aren't lip service, she's speaking from hard won truths.

My silence must be too pronounced because her gaze tilts my way with a warm knowing smile. She doesn't need to do anything more before she turns her focus to the leather in her hands. And as I watch her, I realize how much I've been lying to myself. How deeply my actions are hurting not just myself but the others as well.

Chapter 19
Vlad

Blood. My hands want to be drenched in an unending supply of it as I murder the slimy bastard I've had to play nice with for the past seven hours. He's given me no straight answer, sitting there, lying through his teeth and smiling at me like I'm some fool he can play. I can fucking taste it in the air.

He is dirtier than *any* of our people. I just have to find the proof to protect us before I take him to see his maker. Getting a meeting was far simpler than I expected, and he screwed up just as I knew he would. He probably didn't even realize he let slip. Just enough to let us know that we will be able to deal with our little problem sooner than anticipated. I still want his blood to wash my hands.

I swear if I listen to much more of this prattle I'll start a blood bath. Finally, he tires of hearing himself speak and I can head home. It's nearly seven and by the time I finish the drive it will be well after ten. Fuck, I wanted to be home much earlier to spend some time with Nevaeh and the children.

I need my woman. If only to listen to her breath and watch her sleep. Only she can ground me so that I don't go on a killing spree. My resilient little one, moya tigrovaya liliya, my woman that holds me firmly out of the darkness.

I told her that I was not using the room so that she would feel comfortable in my space. Through the years, I can't recall the last time I spent more than a few hours at a time in there to get enough sleep to function. The promise of the space held too many memories for me to find any peace.

With Nevaeh there, I can't seem to stay away at night. Keeping her safe is not just a want or need. It is the very fabric of my being. So, here I will sit for the tenth night in a row to watch over my woman. So that I know she is forever taken care of.

My footsteps are muffled as I move to the chair I use to rest beside her sleeping form each night. Her dark hair curls over my pillow and lays over her cheeks in damp waves. She must have tried to stay up, but lost the fight and passed out. My angel lays sleeping in peace, safe in my space as she always was meant to.

Her soft skin makes my fingers tingle as I brush back several locks so I can gaze at her lovely face. Murmuring at the touch she smiles and rolls to face me. Her eyes flutter open to take me in though I know she is not really awake. The smile grows but her dark lashes sink closed after a single breath.

"Volodya," her whisper is filled with a softness she does not voice in her waking days as she turns closer to me.

The sound has my lips turning up in a smile. She sighs again and relaxes. "I am here, moya tigroyaya liliya. I will keep you safe. For now, and for always I will protect you as you protect my soul."

I allow myself to doze for a few hours before dawn's first light pulls me awake so that I can leave before she wakes to find me. If she sees me here, I will never hear the end of it. Our trust has grown slowly, but we are not where I want us to be yet. We aren't where I can lay beside her and hold her through the night.

"Morning, Volodya," a husky feminine voice whispers in the darkness.

Jerking up straight, I stare at the perfect sight in awe. Sitting before me, her hair still a mess, and eyes delivering a stern frown. I can't take my gaze from her rumpled clothing. *My* rumpled shirt more accurately. Darkened curls tumble in wild abandon over her shoulders. They're just begging my fingers to dig in deep. And her *eyes*. She meets my eyes with a warm gaze that I've been dreaming about for far too long. There is no space for shame, even if I *should* feel some for keeping the truth from her. For gazing on all of her beauty without restraint. She is far too lovely.

“Moya liliya, I...”

Her hand snaps up, stopping my words with a firm look to tell me to stop talking before I put my foot in my mouth. “No more lying, it doesn’t suit you. You have a perfectly good bed here. Use it, please.”

“I don’t sleep here, little one. I never could. I am only keeping my word.” I want to wrap her up in my arms, but I hold myself where I am. Damn, she really does look like an angel. It is probably a sin to want to ravish something so pure as her, but I’ll gladly burn in hell to keep her.

“The mattress is King-size,” she grumbles, rolling her eyes. “There’s enough space for both of us here.” Her head motions to the large expanse of the special ordered mattress at her back.

“If I lay next to you at night, I will not let you go. You said you were not ready for that. I am doing my best to honor your choices.” My insides tighten to an uncomfortable level. She shouldn’t say things like that to me. If it wasn’t for my training, my body would betray me. I’d lay her back, under me on that bed. She’d be so ripe for my taking.

"Volodya," Her eyes mist with her dejected whisper. "You don't want me."

My body flies to hover over top of hers, forcing her back. I trap her so that she can't escape from me. Moving my arms, I cage her in to stare down at her perfect form. I have to speak honestly. I am not sure how she doesn't know it yet, but she will understand it clearly today. "You are *all* I have ever wanted."

"You loved Anya."

"Loved? No, Moya liliya, I got along with her. Was content to have her by my side, but you are the only one I have ever, could ever truly love."

Her chest brushes a hairbreadth from mine as her breathing becomes choppy and her hand presses to my pecs as if to push me away. "Not true. I saw."

"It's true. You have always held my heart. I love you, Nevaeh."

Tears gather but she doesn't allow them to fall. "No, you don't."

"You should know better than to doubt my words," I growl, demanding her attention stay on me.

"I'm not right for you. Shouldn't want to be more than friends. I'm too bro-"

She fights me, as my mouth claims hers, demanding her silence in the face of that denial. I am glad for the storm inside her, but she will learn that her fight is *with* me not against me. Her fists beat like angry butterflies over my back. Growling, I restrain them and double my assault on her honeyed mouth. Her slim feet kick uselessly between my legs as I take control of her. I draw her in deeply, and suddenly, she's clinging to me. Clutching my shoulders like I'm a lifeline she's afraid to let go of.

Needing air has me pulling back, but I don't stop consuming the treat beneath me. The flavor of her skin is richer than my favorite chocolate. Small beads of sweat gather under her ear, and I lean down to lick them away. Each new touch makes her squirm, but she doesn't push me away.

"Volodya," her husky whimper fans over my hair as she shivers.

I pull back at the fear in her tone and cradle her head for another lighter kiss. "I love you, Nevaeh. Nothing on this earth, or beyond, will ever change that. Even if you are never ready to marry me, I will never leave you. I am yours now and forever even if this is as far as we ever go. Just tell me how to help you, *please*."

My body keeps her from rolling away, but she turns her head to avoid my eyes. Tears leave tracks over her features as she gives in to the hurt. "You *left* us. We *needed* you and you were in Russia. Frankie *died* and you never came back!

I didn't know what to do! I couldn't call you, and running didn't make it better."

Pain lances through my heart. Finally, she reveals the deepest reason she's fighting us so hard. She has never been one to show her pain to the world, but I can see how much our past still affects her. The guilt of not being able to prevent my best friend's death that night still haunts me. That I wasn't there when they needed me.

She doesn't know it, but I *did* come back. As soon as I got the call, I boarded the first flight back, but it was too late. He was gone, and so was she. We never found any trace of her, no matter how many times we tried. My relationship with my parents has never been the same. There's a dark stain in our lives that I have no way of wiping totally clean.

Tears threaten my own eyes for the first time in years. As much as I need to let them fall, I have to be strong for her. "I can never express how sorry I am that I did not make it back in time, but you are wrong. I would never not come back to you. I never stopped searching."

Small sobs break free as she shakes her head. "It's too much."

"I know," I whisper, closing my eyes against the pain and laying my head over her heart. "I'm sorry."

"You left us!" She cries again. This time louder as her fists knock weakly off my back.

"I did, but I had no choice. I *had* to go." My gaze rises to the heavens as I pray for the strength to hold myself together long enough to calm her and get to the privacy of my office.

Gripping the collar of my shirt, she pulls me down until her face is flush against my chest and tears wet the cotton separating us. Her small frame shakes in my arms as I pull her in, burying my face in her hair while her cries get louder. I can't keep the pain from my face as hers becomes more pronounced. "I needed you, Volodya. I needed you and he wouldn't let me go."

"I know, tigrovaya liliya. I can't change the past, but I am here *now*," I whisper brokenly into her neck as I try to calm her.

Of all the dumb things I have ever let happen, being across the ocean from her when she needed me has to be at the top of the list. I should have fought harder for her.

"If what you need to be comfortable is my walking away from this life, I will do so this instant. Just say the words and it will be done."

She jolts back in shock, mouth working wordlessly as she tries to come up with something to my confession. "Volodya you can't."

"I would."

"But this is your whole world."

"No, not my whole world." I can't help smiling when it comes to her. "Without one ounce of regret. If it was with you, I'd never look back."

"You can't," she shouts, slapping her hands over my mouth hard enough to sting.

Gently, I pull her away so that I can see her eyes. Patting the stray hairs back I take her lips with mine. I don't ask anything. Don't take anything either. This kiss is merely a vow to do my best by her no matter what comes. Whatever she needs I will do and accept what comes so she doesn't have to.

"I will do whatever my heart tells me when it comes to you. Even if that means leaving everything but you behind."

Her fingers claw at my shirt again. This time she isn't fighting to get away, she's fighting to get closer. Her arms are cinched around my neck more tightly than I have ever felt her hold me before. The way we should have held each other in comfort of Frankie's death. It is as if she demands that I take the words back.

Rolling, I bring us to our sides so that I don't crush her under my weight, and throw a leg over her knees to curl more solidly around her. Fuck, the things waiting for my attention outside this room. Nothing is more important today than being here for her. I should have prioritized her a long time ago.

We both lose track of time as we comfort each other. Her tears have slowed, and she lays limply in my hold with the occasional sniff mixed into the quiet. Soft puffs of air warm my skin at a slow pace and I smile as I look down to find her fast asleep.

Brushing damp hair from her eyes, I settle in to enjoy the time I have to be close to her. Mumbling at the disturbance, she snuggles deeper into the crook of my shoulder. As relaxed as she is, her fingers don't lose their hold. Fuck the meetings today. This is where I need to be, where I always *want* to be. I relax into a light sleep once again. More at peace than I have been since a child.

"Vlad," Mikhail pokes his head in the door and whispers lowly to get my attention.

I only just manage to keep from flying out of the bed ready to gut whoever dares intrude on my sleeping woman. My brother's grin tells me he would be reacting the same way. Fuck, I know I wouldn't be able to hide away for the day without being interrupted. "*What*?"

"We need you downstairs. We found some-" His eyes take in Nevaeh's tear dried face and he gives me a guilty shrug before backing out and shutting the door.

Sighing, I nod and slowly pull away from my sleeping woman. It takes a moment to untangle her fingers from my clothes, but eventually I ease myself to the edge of the bed. As my weight lifts off the mattress her fingers shoot out and latch onto me.

"Where are you going?" Her tone is rough from crying as she tries to sit up. Those pretty eyes flutter rapidly as she tries to wake herself up. That will not do.

"Shh," I say, leaning over to help her lay back down. I kiss her pulse, lips, nose, and stop at her forehead. "Sleep, moya liliya and come down when you are ready."

"Where are you going," she yawns, reaching for me again.

"My brothers need me downstairs. I won't leave the house without seeing you first. Rest." It doesn't take much to get her to lay down as I pull the bedding over her. She is nearly back to dreamland before I get done tucking her in.

I remove myself and head out of her tempting atmosphere. If I spend one more second in sight of her tantalizing form, I will lose it. The office is the only space left for me to find more than a hope and prayer of giving her more time. It may be a good thing my brother came for me.

Chapter 20
Nevaeh

The bed is empty and cold when I wake up again. I vaguely remember Mikhail coming into the room before Volodya got up, kissed me and left. I know it has been some time since then. The sun is shining brightly through the windows.

My phone lays on the stand beside the lamp where I tossed it last night. At least I remembered to plug it in after spending most of the night halfheartedly scrolling through listings for new apartments. It feels like more of a chore each day. My heart doesn't really want to leave the stubborn man downstairs.

Unlocking the screen all I can do is blink. "Shit, I can't believe that it's after ten already."

"Knock, knock, sleepyhead," Ember bounces into the room, blue jeans hugging her hips as she jumps onto the bed next to me. She rolls over sending her hair flying over the pillows at my hip.

"How do you always have so much energy," I laugh, flopping back to let her pull me into a hug.

"Because I'm child free for a few hours and the boys are locked in your man's office. That means that I get to have fun without my husband up my ass. Get up, you're coming with me," she demands, bouncing back up and smacking my leg to get me moving.

"Does that involve getting dressed?"

"Hey, if you wanna run down the halls butt ass naked I don't have a problem with it. At least, until my kids get home. Hell, I'll even help you deal with Vlad if that's what you decide to do. But, it *is* safer where we're heading if you cover up." She gives me a cheeky grin and flops into the chair that Volodya has been sleeping in.

"Give me five minutes," I grumble and head into the closet to get changed. I don't bother to get anything fancy, I grab a clean set of clothes. Simple pants and a light sweater that I drag on before walking back out. "Okay I'm ready."

Standing, she grabs my hand and pulls us out the door. The few guards we pass don't give us more than a passing glance as she pulls us down the hall. "Where are we going?"

"You'll see." She flashes me a grin and turns down a darkened set of stairs I've never been brave enough to descend till now. Lights snap on automatically the farther we go until we reach a hidden door. The long hallway lays open before us. Lockers and locked safes line the wall to the right. The highly polished metal stands out starkly against the white walls.

Walking over, she taps in the code to open the large steel door of one of the safes. I have never seen so many handguns in my life. While I know how to use a gun, I can't be comfortable with the sheer number of them on display. I can only assume that the rest of the safes are stuffed full of weapons as well.

Pulling out a long-barreled revolver along with a box of shells, she turns to me. "Which are you comfortable with?"

"How do you know I can shoot?" I ask, licking my lips as I shift from foot to foot.

"I'm a military brat. Your body gives you away." Smiling, she swings around and gives me a complete mama look. Her brow arch further when I don't speak right away. She isn't going to take any of my evasive answers.

The smooth concrete seems like the most interesting thing in the space, but I know that she'll just wait me out, so I tell her. "Sig."

"Not bad," she hums, turning back to grab one for me. "Let's see what you can do."

Without a choice, I take the black metal in hand and follow her to the stalls set up to separate the shooters. We take our places and begin loading the rounds into the clips. They make their way in, one on top of the other, and I remember why I picked up a gun in the first place.

I never want to be so defenseless again. Knowing that I haven't pulled the trigger in a long time, I tune in to what Ember is saying as she does her own work. She doesn't have to look at her hands while she works. The experience in her movements has me absorbing every word. The cylinder of her barrel clicks shut, and I slide the clip home on my own.

"Ready?"

"Yes," I lock eyes with her and nod. I'm ready to do what is necessary to protect myself and the ones around me.

"Let's make it more interesting, shall we?'

"What do you have in mind?" I ask curiously, looking at her to share a smile.

"Five rounds a piece. Loser makes supper tonight."

"You're on," I say with a grin.

No way am I going to let her show me up. I can't cook the way the others in this house can, so maybe I should let her win on that front alone. Would serve him right for making me go through the emotional roll coaster he has been making me ride. But the thought of the kids enduring the tasteless things I can whip up makes me feel bad enough to give it all I've got.

The first shot is wide but still hits the right shoulder of the papered silhouette. Adjusting my grip, I shift to widen my feet and fire the second. Paper rips through the middle of the forehead.

"Lucky shot," Ember groans and sticks her tongue out at me. Her fingers work in tandem as she cocks the hammer and takes her own shots. Both find their mark right to the heart.

Three more rounds thunder down range with each twitch of my finger. They find their marks, and I turn with a raised eyebrow. "Were they?"

Laughing, she empties her load into her own target. The chamber rolls open, and she lets the spent shells fall to the floor. Reloading, she flicks her wrist to close it again. "Knew there was more to you than Vlad could have predicted. Try widening your stance another inch. Good, now let's finish this."

I may have more bullets thanks to a larger clip, but the damn woman still out shoots me. After my spectacular failing, we spend another hour going over the guns and she has me use a few others to get me used to them. She also tests me with a blade which does not end well for me.

She must love her family, because she stays in the kitchen with me and helps me cook for the kids and the boys' parents. Well, that and cooking with a wrapped hand isn't easy. Not with how big a pot is needed to make spaghetti for so many mouths.

"Are they going to come out for dinner?" I look around the room as all of us sit at the table.

Their father Gregor waves his right hand lazily. "No child, they are busy. You have been running off to work so early that we have not had a chance to catch up. Tell us what has been going on in your life."

Maria helps him fill his plate as his left arm is still mostly useless from the stroke he suffered the year after Frankie's death. "Dear, let her eat first."

"I don't mind," I jump in with a small laugh as they bicker back and forth for a time.

"Eat first, all of you," Maria commands in a firm voice. "Plenty of time for talk later."

All of us quiet down and do what she says. The only noises are the kids chatting about their day out with their grandparents. Ember smiles through it all, but I laugh as her eye twitches when Josey describes her newest dress. Other than the occasional skirt, the woman is never in anything but jeans that I've seen.

The kids finish and collect the empty dishware, so they can be cleaned, before Maria allows us to start talking with cups of coffee in our hands. I keep things simple and leave all mention of my ex out of the conversation. If Vlad wants them to know about that he'll tell them, but I won't say anything with the kids still here.

Gregor catches my eye with a knowing look, but he doesn't voice his thoughts. The stroke may have limited his movements, but that mind is still as sharp as ever. I'm sure he'll corner me soon enough to get the whole story.

Chapter 21
Vlad

Dropping into my chair I focus on the grounds outside. What was I thinking attacking her so forcefully? Did I fuck up the trust we were reforging between us with those thoughtless actions? Would it matter if I did? The papers are already drawn and locked in my desk waiting for her to take the last step that will tie us together forever. It wouldn't matter to me if they stayed there another ten or twenty years as long as she is always by my side.

"What did you do brat?" My twin's voice grumbles as he and Mikhail slowly make their way in. Both have their arms crossed in disapproval.

The snow-covered ground holds more appeal than the coming conversation. They will know that I did something without me ever saying a word. Our methods of training would have made it easy for them to pick up on what a body is saying long before they were voiced it. Only, they don't need to go that far. I'm sure they can see the hints of unease marking my face though I try to keep my features blank.

"Vlad." Mikhail's hand lands on my shoulder, heavy with worry but I still don't move. "Are you alright?"

That has me turning to face them. "I'm fine."

His gaze drills into me looking for a lie. When he doesn't find it, his mind jumps. "Is Nevaeh alright?"

"She's fine. We finally talked is all," I sigh, trying to shake things off. "What did you find Dimitri?"

My twin's grin turns giddy. "Our dearest friend was released a few months ago like you said. He is good... But I still found him. The men took him down before he knew they were there. He's been paying off the parole officer to claim he's following the rules."

Now I can smile. "Good. Is he where I asked?"

"Of course, he is. I wouldn't let him get lost so easily," He chuckles, while playing with the dice in his pocket. He doesn't need all the details to want blood payment for Nevaeh. "We party tonight."

The monster raises its head eager for the kill within our reach. "Yes, we will have the most enlightening time with him."

"Then let's get working so that our fun will be uninterrupted." Relief washes into my heart that the man who thought he could hurt my woman is sitting in one of our cells waiting for me to end his miserable life. For once, I will take great pleasure in sending another human being to meet our maker. Soon, I will end him and allow Nevaeh to breathe knowing he's no longer able to reach her.

The next few hours drag on as we go over everything that we know about the group that is still eluding our hands. No matter how many times we go over it something new pings through my brain to add another piece to the puzzle. We are getting closer. I can feel it. They can only run for so long. Had they stayed off my streets they might have lived a few more years but they got greedy. Played where they had no business being and for that they will die.

"There is still something here we are missing." Dimitri grumbles, yanking the button of his coat off in his agitation. Mother is not going to be happy to resow it for the tenth time.

I don't get a chance to say anything before my phone starts ringing. Everyone goes quiet as I pick it up and answer the call. "Da?"

"*Gone*," The voice wheezes on the other end. Levi, one of the ones guarding Chris. "Killed Alec, stabbed me-... he's gone."

"Stay awake until we get there," I demand, rushing from the room. I can hear the blood invading the air space, it will be a miracle if he is still alive when we arrive. My brothers are close on my heels as they call their teams. We don't have much time to reach him, but I have to make sure that my woman is safe first.

Luckily, she is about to go back up the stairs as we storm through the hall. "Nevaeh."

Jumping she spins, eyes wide at my tone as I close the distance between us. Gripping her arm, we sweep into the empty formal dining room so we can have a moment. "Volodya, what's wrong?"

"Do not leave the house until I return," I grit out before taking her in a deep kiss.

She lets me have my way for a minute. A moment of peace before gripping my jaw and searching my face, like she's looking for things that I don't want her to know. She must not like what she finds as her eyes turn glossy and her fingers bite into me harder. "You found him."

"We did. I need to deal with this," I sigh, letting her have that much of the truth. "Stay here for me please till we get back."

Guilt clouds her face, and her fingers grip the ends of my beard to keep me from turning away from her demand. "There's more. What happened?"

A rare full smile touches my features, and I lean in to kiss her softly. She still knows me too well, but this is not a problem I am going to put on her shoulders. Her pretty pouts will not bring forth my confession. "Nothing that you need to be worried about, moya liliya. Just stay here for me, please."

"*Vladimir Sokolov, no lies.* Tell me now," She demands, fingers threatening to pull the hair from my jaw. "Don't tell me this isn't serious when you have that look in your eyes."

I know she won't back down when she uses my full name. I swear she forgets it until I have tested her last nerve, but this isn't something I want her to know. Not when she'll try to take all the blame for something she didn't do. My men underestimated the bastard. It's a mistake we won't be making again.

"Vlad, I just heard! Are they ..." Mother rushes into the room, stopping short at seeing us. Tension vibrates through her body as she eyes our position, hands ringing together in agitation.

"What is it," I ask, keeping my scowling woman in my arms.

Her eyes flick to Nevaeh uncertain if she should say what's on her mind in front of someone who isn't permanently tied to the family. They widen as I wrap my arm tighter and nod, sending all the message she needs. Bless my angel for wrapping her arms around me in return instead of pulling away. Maybe this morning wasn't such a fuck up on my part.

"Is this what you want, Nevaeh? Do you know what you are getting into?" Mother loves the woman beside me, always has, but she has never been allowed to see anything of our business. No outsiders have. "You were so adamant about saying no to the two of you becoming more."

"What are you talking about," she asks, giving mother a confused look, unsure of what she is being asked.

"No one is free to say anything about the family business around you if you are not a member. Not even if it involves you. I've made my intentions clear. The choice is yours." I explain as carefully as possible, not wanting to scare her. She may know a few things that most do not know about us, but there is still nothing that could truly harm us if she was to talk.

"Volodya, are you sure?" A pause follows as her eyes look up in question. I made my mind up and she knows what I want. I give her a nod letting her know that this step is hers.

Laying her head onto my shoulder, her breath rushes out in a whole-body shiver. I understand the difficulties running wild in her brain. She has fought me the entire time that I have been chasing her. That she feels she isn't worthy of standing with me. A thought that is utter bullshit, but I can only push so much. This *has* to be her choice.

Once she makes her choice there will be no going back. You are part of the family, or you are not. No in between exists in our allegiances. She knows saying yes will mean that she is bound to me for all time. I will never let her go, not even in death.

Another deep breath pulls her back straight before she looks up again. Our eyes lock as she reaches up and runs light fingers under my eye. "You promise?"

Puzzled, I cock my head waiting for the rest of her words. "Say what you need Nevaeh, and it will be so."

"You will not leave the family."

"Only if it is your wish." My heart pounds far too fast as our earlier conversation runs through my brain. "I will do what I must to protect you."

"It is."

I keep myself in place as I take one of her hands from my face. Slim fingers cradled perfectly within the confines of my own. "Say the words, moya tigrovaya liliya," I softly demand.

"This is what I want, Vladimir Sokolov. I agree to be yours. Broken bits of me and all. I'm tired of fighting this. Don't leave the family if you think I can't handle things because they need you too." She stands firm before me as she says the words so close to the ones I've longed to hear.

Stepping in front of her I grip her arms, gently fighting to keep the joy from overflowing just yet. I have to be sure before I can allow it to swallow me whole. Reaching into my breast pocket, I pull out the ring I have carried for her as soon as she gives in. Her eyes go big, and she licks her lips but does not back away.

The strength she feels she doesn't have shining through. I lean closer to make sure she understands how far my vow will go. "There is no going back. We will be forever. You will be mine as it always should have been."

Another deep breath and her hand wraps around mine holding the tiny piece of metal. "I know. I shouldn't want everything with you, but I can't keep fighting it. I want to be yours, Vladimir Sokolov. There are things that I may not be able to give you, but I'm willing to stand by you through what comes if you're willing to put up with me."

Chis will die a long painful death for breaking my woman down. For now, I will keep working to close her scars and show her that she is the most amazing woman just as she is now. "All I need is you as you are. To stand by my side, believe in me, and call me out when I am wrong. Can you do that?"

Though her lips tremble she doesn't back away. Her eyes shine as she fights for courage. She still doubts her worth, but I will make her shine even brighter than before. All she has to do is say the word and I'll make it happen. "I will always stand by you. For as long as you want. Your monster has never scared me, Volodya."

My heart stutters at her declaration of what I must be to keep everyone safe. Damn, she truly was made to stand at my side. "Say the words moya milaya malen'kaya tigrovaya," I lower my lips to whisper against hers. "Tell me."

This time her eyes are firm in her decision, and she meets my gaze without trouble. The old Nevaeh stands before me now, beautiful in all her glory. "Yes, I will marry you."

The band slides over her knuckles as soon as her words are out. I have no more time to spare on words, so I do the next best thing. Wrapping her up tightly, I kiss her with all the joy that surges in my blood. Duty has me pulling back far too soon but I can't help touching her face. "Wait in the house for me, da? It may be late. Do not wait up for me."

"Da Volodya," she answers as she knows I want to hear.

"Do none of my children know how to propose the right way," Mother wails from our side. I know that she would prefer me on my knee at this moment, but that act would put thoughts in my head that I have no time for right now.

Mikhail pokes his head in with a scowl. “I did just fine with my woman, thank you very much dearest Mother.”

“Oh, out with you, young man!” Her annoyance turns to him as he runs away.

Chapter 22
Nevaeh

Jesus, I signed myself over into Volodya's hands. He had slipped the gold band over my finger, given me a slow press of lips, and gotten my promise to stay within the house before walking out the door. Every word was spoken with the full knowledge of what I was doing but I'm still stunned by how quickly I gave in. And yet ... letting go and saying yes? All I can feel is peace.

I would have stood staring after him all day if his mother hadn't slipped her hand into mine. "Come doch'. The house is on lockdown until they deal with what has happened."

"What did happen?" I ask, hoping she will tell me. Just them finding Chris shouldn't have all the men rushing out the door in such a way. Not unless he found out some of the bad things I've been hiding.

"Nothing for you to worry about dearest doch'." She smiles, giving my hand a pat.

My brows raise at her calling me daughter, but I allow her to lead me. She takes me out into the huge sunroom, where the kids are splashing in and out of the pool. All while their mother watches holding the baby. Hunter and Josey yell hello but do not stop playing.

Ember waves me over with a smile as I hesitate just inside the door. A faint glint of sadness in her eyes has me sinking down next to her and throwing an arm around her shoulders. Our men may be gone but we're still here and we have to be strong for each other. For now, it's enough.

"He finally got you to say yes, huh?" She laughs, giving me a wink.

"He can be very persuasive when he wants to be." I blush, making her laugh hard enough to make her nursing daughter upset.

A few pats and she settles quickly. "Yes, Mikhail is the same way," she sighs dreamily, and waves a hand to fan herself before lifting the baby to burp. "That's how we got this one so quickly."

I can't help the sputter of giggles as Maria shakes her head. "I don't need to know what my boys do in the privacy of their room girls."

Ember drops the now full baby in my arms so fast I nearly drop her. Wide hazel eyes blink up at me in stunned wonder before blowing a milky bubble and yawning. My heart hammers in my chest at the feel of her unexpected weight on me. This is only the second time I've held a baby and I'm no more sure about it than before.

I love having her but with everything that's going on I feel too shaky to keep her safe. "Please take her back, Ember."

She refuses with a bright smile on her pretty blonde face. "You're doing just fine. She already loves her aunt."

"I feel like I'm going to drop her," I whisper, curling her closer, scared of watching her little body land on the tile floor at my feet.

"That's a good fear but you won't just like you didn't the last time." Her hazel eyes sparkle in humor. "I think you're far too good for that grump, but... I've never seen him smile so much. I'm going to need all the wildly embarrassing stories you have."

"Are you trying to cause trouble now?" I ask with a conspiratorial grin, as I finally tear my eyes from the gurgling baby. "Volodya only asked that we not leave the house. I haven't had any fun for a while with everything going on."

Her shoulders lift in a non-answer. "Well, Mikhail should know better than to tell me to sit still and Dimitri has been far too happy lately. I think he needs another pink hair day."

"Oh, I knew there was a reason I liked you," I laugh as we lean together and start trading secrets for the next few hours before bed.

***

"This is taking too long," I whisper to the dark ceiling, unable to close my eyes knowing that Volodya is not back yet. "You should be home already."

Unease rolls through me and not even Tallie's company on my chest can make it go away. No word from the men has me wanting to go out and find them. I won't. The guards are already on edge and there's no way they'd let me out. Whatever happened wasn't good and they aren't risking our safety for anything.

The lack of news is more irritating to my soul than a room full of screaming babies. I can't take it anymore. If I can't sleep, I need to move. No lights shine though the darkness, but that doesn't stop me as I make my way around the halls. Everything is quiet and peaceful. Not even Katya is restless tonight for me to have an excuse to walk around holding her.

Passing Volodya's office, I know better than to enter that door but the one next to it draws me like a moth to a flame. I don't even need to add any strength to my fingers and the wood opens without effort. Lights are needed to see anything of what's in this room in the darkness. The switch clicks under my finger as tears cloud my eyes.

"Oh Volodya." His name leaves my lips in wonder as I take in the half-finished room.

Tears sting my eyes as I take in the work he's done. Stepping in, my fingers run over the bright cherry wood of the one wall of bare book shelves. Another lays ready to be put together on the floor in front of large French doors that lead out into the gardens. On the big wooden desk that matches the shelves sits a copy of each of my books.

"You never could let me give you anything nice without finding it ahead of time could you," Volodya says quietly behind me, making me jump.

Laying my hand over my books I ask, "What is all this?"

I turn when he doesn't answer to see him leaning against the doorframe, arms crossed, and a small smile on his lips. Fresh clothes stretch over his tired form. A small breath of relief breaks out seeing that he is unharmed. "Volodya?"

"A gift for you."

"I don't understand," I sigh, shaking my head and turning to look out the window. If I keep looking at him, I am really going to start crying.

"You have been sitting up in bed or on the couch in my room to write since you came. I wanted you to have your own space to work," he says quietly.

"These are new books."

"Yes. I enjoyed them."

Is that embarrassment or pride mixed in with his words? Maybe both? I don't know if I want to laugh or cry at how thoughtful he is being. Why does he have to be so sweet under all his arrogance? When he wants something, he does nothing halfway. It's always all or nothing with him.

Arms wrap around me from behind, and he lays a light kiss to the back of my head before looking out the window with me in silence. His strong arms hug me with such promise and understanding. He is a comfort I didn't want to fully rely on, but I have no choice. When the options were presented to me, I didn't fight. Not anymore, I've *always* been his. Always wanted and needed to be near him. Now that I've said yes it feels like a weight has been lifted from my shoulders.

The glint of the band on my finger reminds me of the position I placed myself in. For better or worse, I have bound myself to the man who left me years ago. I just pray that he will prove himself a better man now. I don't know if I have what it takes to pick up the pieces if he leaves me again. And Ember is right, he'll never know if I keep all my fears to myself.

"Volodya."

"Da?" he asks, with a quiet breath pressing a kiss to my skin and another to the back of my ear. "Tell me what's wrong, moya liliya."

Shivers race over me, and he pulls me further back into him. He curls around me, rubbing over my cool arms to chase the shivers away. His heat soaks into me and I use his strength to work up the nerve to voice what I fear most. It's still tough but I need to get it out.

"I don't know if I can survive, if you hurt me like you did the last time," I whisper, wishing I could be stronger.

He stiffens around me. So still that if his breath wasn't still falling in my ear, I would fear he had turned into a statue at my words. "I will never be parted from you again," he promises, holding me closer. "I have fought too hard to win you back to ever let you go."

As much as our past hurts, I believe what he tells me. Neither of us has told the other the full truth of what happened during that time. I never asked and maybe I need to take this step to help both of us move forward. "What happened?"

"I thought I had more time, but my future was already planned for me. The marriage was contracted when I was ten. It didn't bother me at first, I knew what was expected of me. Then I met you and your brother when I wrecked my bike. I told myself I only loved you as a sister because I knew I couldn't get out of the marriage," his voice has a slight hitch to it as he pulls me closer.

"You had lost your guard and were freaking out that he would call your dad," I remember, smiling up at him.

"Best rebellion of my life until now. I told myself I had to do what my father ordered but nothing in that came out the way he promised. I'm so sorry for everything. I should have put my foot down and agreed with Anya to stop the wedding."

"No," I say, quickly shaking my head knowing not having Anya in my life back then would have been much worse. "We can't change the past."

He releases me, only to turn me to face him, gripping my hips and watching me with sad, sober eyes. "I love you, Nevaeh, and I will spend the rest of my life making up for all of my failures when it comes to you."

His hands shake slightly, but the moment they connect with my jaw they become stronger than ever. He holds me firmly so I can't get away. His words and possessive touch make my mind surge, but I fight through it. He isn't Chris, and I can't continue to compare the two.

This is my future, so I lean in to take it on my own terms. Hesitant at first, our lips just peck before he softens and leans into me to take everything I give. Craving his taste, I push up and take full control, causing him to grunt in surprise as he rocks back on his heels. He pulls back first but we don't let go. I bury myself deep into his broad chest, locking my arms around him as he hugs me tight. For first time in a long while everything in our world is right.

Snow is swirling fiercely in the howling wind bringing in the next big storm as I stare out into the night. We have to be on the same page to move forward but I don't know if I can open the largest wound. It has only now begun to close but I fear that there is still something festering inside that needs to be cleansed. We may have started small, but we've taken the first steps.

"Will you tell me what happened to you, Nevaeh?" His fingers lighten to drift down my sides to my hips. There is no push or pull, he just holds me and lets me decide if I can tell him what is holding me back.

"I.. I don't know if I can. It still hurts so bad. The words choke me when I want to set them free," I say shakily, squeezing my eyes closed.

His arms pull me close, but he doesn't push for more. "As soon as you are ready, I will be right here. I will always be here."

"How do you know?" I choke out.

Reaching down he cups my hand bringing it up in front of me so that the rock sparkles. "Because, I will tie us together for all time. I will be your rock, comfort, strength, and shield. Whatever you need, I will always be right here."

"Even if I don't listen and make you pull your hair out?" I can't help but tease.

"Even then, Nevaeh. Forever," he laughs, kissing my hair. "Our wedding is in a week."

Shock jolts my body, but I can't go anywhere as his arms have turned to iron, and he refuses to let me go. We did agree but I have to ask, "Why so soon?"

"Because I need you. Because you should have always been mine. Because we can," he whispers, holding me still in his arms saying each sentence with a kiss to my jaw. "And I don't want to be away from you one day longer."

Something has happened. I know that he has said he wanted me and I believe him. Even though I have fought him, I never doubted his words no matter how much I'm afraid of being hurt again. But, why so quickly? He said that Chris was caught and then they all left and made me promise not to leave the house.

That could only mean that ... Oh. Oh God, he got away, and they can't find him. He wants me tied to him so that no one can contest his words about me. So that no one can legally force him to let me go. This is his way of making sure I am always cared for.

"I see," I say, shivering despite his heat.

My words have his head lifting. "Moya liliya?"

"He got away, and you haven't found him yet."

He avoids giving me a direct answer, but I know by the set of his spine going rigid. I let him shoulder the issue by himself for now as he diverts the topic. "Mother and Ember, want to take you out tomorrow and buy you the dress you deserve."

I let him shift the topic. "How will you get everything done so soon?"

Humor seeps over me from his warm laugh, "I remember you talking about your dream wedding. Everything will be exactly how you want it. I promise. I may be rushing things, but I will make it perfect for you."

"There is no way you remember what I said back then," I shake my head in denial with a light laugh.

"Corset backed, off white lace, mermaid style, no puffy ball gown, and a red velvet ribbon for your hair. A bouquet of white and orange lilies mixed with peach tinted roses for color. Flower girls with bright orange dresses and the ringbearer in a black suit with no jacket."

"Ok... you listened." I stop him from saying anymore with a sigh as I step back from him to look over the gardens.

"I always listen to you, Nevaeh. *Always*," he rumbles, turning me around to see the soft smile on his face. "Just like I'll take you shopping to fill this room the way you want."

I silence him with a kiss. Our lips lightly touch for just a moment before he lets me lean against him. The heavy thud of his heart sounds under my ear in an easy unbroken rhyme that has me falling into him more. He doesn't have to say anything to make things right and then he has to go and open his mouth. How did I hold out for so long?

My emotions feel like I threw them in a mixer and now that he's holding me it all leaves me in a rush. All the bad is gone and peace settles deep into my bones. "I would love an outdoor wedding, but what if it's raining?"

"Then we cover the pool and hold it in the sun room."

Damn man, always has the answer to everything, but I can't be mad at his thinking. "Can we go to bed now?"

"Of course," he says, reaching down and swinging me into the air. "Let's get some rest."

"I can walk you know," I scold with a scowl that holds no heat.

"I know," he chuckles, kissing my nose midstride out the door. "You finally agreed to marry me. Let a man enjoy his victory for a night.'

Chapter 23

Vlad

Benson is cracking, sweat beads his receding hairline, and he can't sit still in his seat. "I'm sorry I can't help more, Mr. Sokolov. My people have investigated every avenue and there has been no new information."

The man still thinks he can work his way out of my line of fire by playing dumb. All it took was one shabby deposit to his account to alert us to his shady dealings, and the amount of dirt that Maxim has already managed to dig up is more than enough to raise eyebrows. Along with that new beach mansion in the Bahamas he's bought in his son's name.

The fake leather protests as I lean forward and say, "You do remember the clauses in the contract you signed with us, do you not? If I find out on my own, you will not like how our business arrangement ends."

"We will look again. I swear we will find the ones responsible." He rushes to reassure me, face losing a shade of its sprayed-on tan. "It will just take some time."

I can't be in the same space as this trash for a moment longer. Slowly, I make my way to the door and stop short. "You have one week to give me what I want."

Leaving before he can give me an answer, I make my way down the hallway without giving any of the staff the courtesy of my time. My guards fall in beside me. Silence reigns as we make our way to the cars outside. The air is finally starting to warm, and the late April forecast looks beautiful for the wedding. A clear day with everything in order that will be perfect for moya liliya to finally be fully claimed for the whole world to see. No one will ever be able to take her from me again.

"He'll run before the time I gave him. Follow him but stay out of sight. Send our best," I order dropping into the car. He will get me what I want whether he knows it or not.

"Where did you let the women go today without us? I thought that we were on lockdown." Maxim reclines back in the seat in front of us.

"Nevaeh deserves the best. The wedding is already rushed, I will not allow her to walk down the aisle without the dress she wants," I try to keep the growl in as I answer him even though his questioning continues to piss me off. Partly because letting them out is a risk but she's already missed so much I'll be damned if I take dress shopping from her. "They aren't alone as you well know."

"Why do the girls get to have all the fun," he whines, flopping back and kicking his feet onto my seats.

Jacks and I ignore him, used to our friend's dramatics. It isn't difficult to figure out why he is in such a bad mood. Damn it, we're all mad about what happened. "There will be someone for you to kill soon enough my friend."

"I want the slimy bastard back there." He grins, letting the mask slip with us to reveal the made man he is.

"You will have him as soon as he tells us everything of use. He knew the law, what his contract with us states, and he broke his oath for money. Once I have what I want he's all yours," I say, before stepping out of the car as it stops.

Stepping into the house is akin to stepping into a war zone. Glitter litters every surface, pillows are ripped with feathers still floating in the air, and my brother fights off the kids trying to take him down as their laughter fills the space. Yellow splatters on my shoulder, across my back and chest from the ceiling above. Sticky gel that won't separate from my form even with my fingers pulling the strand more than a foot from myself.

"What the hell have you done to my house," I roar, outraged at the utter mess of my front room.

All three freeze at the same time. "Welcome home brat." Mikhail gives me a guilty grin. Slowly, he climbs to his feet and sets the kids in front of him.

The damn coward thinks that I won't get around them to beat his ass for what destruction they have caused. When none of them answer I bite out angrier, "*What* have you done?"

Josey's pretty little eyes grow large, having never heard such a harsh tone from me before. The look has me leashing myself quickly. "Where is your Dyadya," I soften my tone to a growl as I ask.

"Behind the couch," she quickly snitches, pointing to the only piece of furniture still standing.

"You little traitor," My twin jumps up yelling in mock horror though he won't meet my eye.

"Enough," I hiss.

"Brat," Mikhail starts but stops at my glare.

"The four of you will not leave this room until you have every nasty flake of plastic and… goop cleaned off my floors, ceiling, and furniture. Shut up Dimitri, you won't be getting out of this. Get cleaning."

Ignoring their whining, my overcoat lands on his head to keep the mess where it belongs. A distraction is sorely needed, so I make my way past my office and into the room that I am working on for Nevaeh. Of course, it would be done faster having one of our crews doing the work, but this is my gift for her. It must come from my hands, or it will not mean what it is meant to. This is me giving her what she needs to make her dreams become reality.

I take my suite coat off and throw it on the desktop before rolling up my sleeves. The next ten feet of shelves need to be screwed together and then I can move on to the next twenty feet of empty wall on the other side for her art supplies. It won't be long till the rest of the room is finished to her liking after I take her shopping.

Putting all this together and sleeping in a chair for so long hasn't been the best on my back. Real oak might be heavier but there is no way I'm putting shitty material in her office. Whatever it takes to do this the right way. I have no problem putting in the hard work to make it happen. Picking up the needed items, I grab the next board, getting lost in the project again.

By noon all the shelves line up both desired walls and the desk is moved closer to the garden doors so that it has the best lighting. A replica of my chair is tucked into the leg space so that she will be comfortable during the long hours she pulls when inspiration strikes. A few bean bag chairs she is so fond of sit tucked to the wall. I just need to get the curtains up to close off our connected offices for privacy. I want to be able to see her as both of us work at any odd hour.

Out of the corner of my eye I watch my father's form shuffling into the space. He pauses to take in what I have done so far. He smiles with a nod of pride before moving closer.

Jumping off the ladder, I pull the chair out to help him sit as his strength wavers. "Otets, sit before you fall, please."

"Thank you, syn," he chuckles, patting my cheek like he did when I was still a young boy.

Kneeling, I lower myself before the only man who will ever get me on my knees besides God. A quick look for his usual shadow comes up short for her figure. "Mother and the girls are not back yet?"

"They stopped for lunch and are on their way back. I wanted to talk to you before your mother was here to make herself sick with worrying over everything between the two of you."

Weariness zips through my blood at his words. He could only want to talk about how fast the two of us are moving forward. He can't tell me not to marry her, but he can give me the laundry list of horrible things that could happen due to bringing her into our world. How much more dangerous life will become for her by my side, but she already knows what to expect. She's always known.

Might as well get it out now. "Say what is on your mind before they get back."

"You understand the danger you are opening her to so I will not ask if you want to go through with this. I will ask if she knows what she is getting into."

"She knows. I let you direct my life and leave her behind before. In doing so she suffered a fate she should never have even glimpsed. I will not do so again. Not for anything." I can't help the bitter twinge that laces my words.

No matter what he says he won't change my mind about keeping my woman. Yes, there will be dangers, but I will not leave her side. Not now, not ever again. I know she is strong enough to make it beside me. If she can witness the monster in me and still stand next to me, then she can take on our world like the queen she is.

"You bullied her into being here. It may have been to keep her safe, yes, but you did not leave her with another choice. Would you force her into this life as well?"

"She had no one else and refused to go to the cops because he conditioned her to fear asking for help. Should I have left her to keep running on her own only to be dragged back into his hold?"

"Of course not, but have you not done much the same thing?" His raised hand has me snapping my mouth closed so he can finish. "I know you won't hurt her but many others will, simply to get to you. They will know she is your weakness."

Anger burns bright, and I let him see it as I stare into his eyes. Does my father think so little of me that he think I would do something so low. That I don't know the dangers of our world? "I told her I wasn't leaving her again no matter what her choice. I would give the title of Pakhan to my brother if she didn't want to be in our world. Yes, she made this decision on her own."

Shock is not an emotion that crosses his face often, but it is in plain view without the ability to cover it up behind his mask. "You would give up our family?"

"If it meant that I would wake up beside the woman I love every morning, yes. I would do it this very second." My mask is back in place, but he was always able to read the truth in his children. He knows that my words are not something to be taken lightly. I would give up my life here if needed.

It takes him several seconds to lift his left hand, but I don't move to help him. Whether he is going to strike me, berate me, or understand me is all up to him. When his stiff fingers curl around my shoulder he leans forward and begins laughing.

"Good man," he says, pride shining openly in his tired eyes.

"No more fight from either of you." It is no question, but it isn't an order either. Father and I have spoken as equals since I took on the mantle of the family head. Power hunger was never in his future nor mine. The transition of power was smooth, and his advice only given when asked for.

"Vladimir, if you could not give up the world for the woman you claim to love it is no love at all. I am glad that you have found yours."

"But you think I bullied her into choosing me with no other options," I accuse as good naturedly as possible though his comment still smarts.

"No syn, I just want what is best for her. We should have made sure that she was looked after all those years ago. We will do better this time. She should have always been with us. Forgive an old man his mistakes." His weak hand pats my shoulder in solidarity as he smiles his apology.

His words send ripples of shock and pride through me as I take his hand in mine. For a man who has always said what he meant and never said that he was wrong, the significance of him asking for my forgiveness is something

I never thought would happen in my lifetime. The reason is not lost on me. Our family is stronger as one connected front. But it is not me who needs to hear his words.

"I do not need to forgive you for anything. I know you were only doing what was needed for the family. While I could have been content with Anya by my side, Nevaeh is the only one who has held the keys to my heart."

"I know, I saw it even then. I am sorry for my part in your unhappiness all these years." Tears fall unchecked from eyes that I have never seen shed a single one that wasn't from happiness.

The sight of his grief has me pulling him into my arms, holding him as he did me in my youth. I meant what I said, but he needs to feel like he can atone for ripping us apart. Tears clog my throat as I battle to get the words out, "I forgive you Otets, now show Nevaeh how much she means to all of us."

Chapter 24
Nevaeh

There are far too many dresses laid before me to choose from. As soon as we got to the shop, we were taken to a large room with dresses falling within what I have always wanted. They asked a few clarifying questions and drinks were in our hands within minutes. The whole thing has my head spinning and we have only gotten started.

"The best way I've found to go through so much is to say yes or no from the start. Do not keep it if your immediate thought is not a yes," Maria says, patting my hand with a smile.

Her wisdom leaves me with twenty gowns for the three of us to slowly whittle down. It takes us hours, but I do find one that makes my breath catch. It isn't a full mermaid, the skirt flares out six inches off my hips with a beautiful lace overlay and small crystal accents. The moment I feel the silky fabric glide over my skin I know that this is the one. I don't need a mirror to tell me anything different about my decision. It fits me perfectly, like it was made for me. All I have to do is step out and let the women see my choice.

"Damn girl. Screw our men, it's us against the world," Ember whistles, sweeping her eyes up and down the dress. I'm sure she would get up and take a walk around if she wasn't feeding Katya.

"Hush doch' we don't need the boys starting a fight," Maria waves at Ember. "Let her have a moment to take herself in."

Ignoring her, Ember blows me a kiss. "Vlad won't know what hit him when you walk out."

The honesty in her eyes makes me smile. I've never had a real girlfriend besides Anya that would stand by my side no matter what, but I think that Vlad's persistence has brought one right to my lap. Not just a friend, but a sister ready and willing to take on the world for me.

Rising to her feet with her hands clutched in front of her, Maria turns her shining eyes on me. "Tell me Nevaeh, how does this dress make you feel?"

Pulling in a breath to steady myself, I turn to the mirror. The image only confirms what I already know. This is it. A tear slips from my eye, and I fight to catch my breath. How many times had I dreamed of my wedding as a child and now, it is going to happen in less than a week. Walking down the aisle to a man who would give up everything for me.

And Volodya is the one that will be waiting for me at the end of that walk. The one who has dragged me back to his side kicking and screaming. Holding on to me no matter the amount of fighting I threw his way because I was scared. A man with monsters of his own he's willing to unleash in all their fury at one word from me.

Both women stand by me, each taking a hand to give a reassuring squeeze. "What do you say, Nevaeh," Ember nudges me with her shoulder so that the baby's soft head touches me as she giggles and waves her hand at me.

"This is my dress," I whisper excitedly. I can't help it. The person staring back at me is who I always dreamed I would be when I walked down the aisle. There are no scars bogging her happiness with a past full of misery. No, her glow holds nothing but joy.

"You look beautiful, doch'. I am so happy to have you finally join our family." Maria hugs me close.

By the time I get changed back to my clothes the dress is wrapped and paid for already. I knew that there would be no way that they would allow me to drop a single penny on anything while they were within breathing distance. I'm not even allowed to know how much the dress was. None of them had a hint of a price tag.

Under the watchful eye of our guards, we decide to have a quick bite to eat at the nearby cafe before going home. The tuna melt's crispy buttery flavor tastes creamier on my tongue and my heart lighter in my chest with each bite. Our meal is just as full of smiles as before.

***

I never thought I would think of the place as such, but with my promise to bind myself body and soul to the head of the house I suppose that it is just that. It will be my house until the end unless he decides to move us. The sight of the stone structure coming into view used to lodge a stone in my heart, but now it just seems to be calling me. Inviting me inside the thick stone walls to the promised safety of its space. Is it because I've let him have me? That I have pushed the hurt away and said yes to the man I have always loved? That I finally stopped fighting my heart?

I haven't forgotten the pain of his leaving. The wound still weeps lightly but it is closing. Each day in his hands, hearing his words, and feeling the truth of his feelings, the hurt becomes just a little bit less. I can see how hard he is trying to make things right between us. The firm resolve when the other's question him. I know it won't be long before he has won me over completely.

The sight of Mikhail and Dimitri bickering while they scrub the floor of the family room puts a smile on my face as I make my way upstairs to work on my project. Tallie greets me from the cat tree by the window, too lazy to get up as I pick up my computer and settle against the padded headboard. It's more stable to write on the table but the bed is more comfortable.

I know Volodya needs to hear what happened to me, but putting the words to voice has me choking up each time I simply think about it. So, I recreated myself on the next blank page waiting for me to give him what he needs. I think that I need it too. Both of us have suffered more than enough and I am beginning to understand that the only ones who can heal us is, the other. I'm sure that I know more of his story than he does of my own. With Chris still on the run, I need to let him know what sick kind of man he is dealing with.

The need to get the pain out in a way that Volodya could understand started days ago, and I've gotten through nearly half of it. Words filled with raw pain. I dive into the words. Getting lost in my tale with no notice of the passing time. My heart bleeds into the pages faster than I have ever written before.

As I get to the attack Chris inflicted that landed him in jail the old terror tries to take over, and I can't hold back the tears. Volodya's jacket lays on the chair and I quickly grab it. The weight and smell of his presence allows me to keep the monster at bay long enough for me to continue. Holding it close, I let the tears fall as I get back to writing. They wet the keys under my fingers, as they blur while I get everything out.

"Nevaeh, are you alright?"

The bed dips and strong arms are around me before I know anyone is in the room. It isn't *him*. It isn't the one who keeps me safe. The feeling of safety is gone, and the memory I just typed is playing in my head. Uncontrollable fear rips a primal scream from my throat so fiercely that it hurts to breathe.

All I can remember is that Volodya is in the home office talking with his brothers. If I can get away long enough for him to notice he will come, so I do the only thing I can think of doing. Flinging myself back I hear the crunch of bone, and the arms loosen just enough for me to jerk off the bed and take off running. Get to the office, I chant to myself. If I can make it there, I know that he keeps a pistol in the top drawer of the desk.

Something trips me as I bolt out the door, and I scrabble on my hands and feet to keep moving. If I stop, I know that it will end in my death. Office, Volodya, and the gun. Just keep moving and find Volodya. Nothing else matters.

Men's shouts echo from below and I scream for them. Chris always worked alone. Find the men and he would fade back to the shadows like the coward he is. Just make it to the stairs. That's all I have to do, and the others will keep him from me. Volodya will paint the floor with his blood, and I will happily cheer him on as he does.

Halfway down the steps, I lose my footing and start tumbling headlong to the ground floor. By the time I land on the marble I have no air left in my lungs to cry out as another pair of arms scoop me up and handed over to the slim arms of someone else. These are not the arms of the one who vowed to stand for me. They aren't safe. I fight again with renewed vigor. I need to be in the arms of my protective monster.

"Volodya!" Screaming for him hurts but I don't stop.

"He's coming, Nevaeh. He's coming but you have to calm down... Maskin, get him now," A female voice grunts as she stops talking to hold me in place.

The voice tugs at the edges of my brain but no face makes its way to the front of my mind. I don't have much left in me, but I can't give up. I need to get out of here. Get somewhere safe until he comes.

Chapter 25
Vlad

"You were right, he is already making plans to leave in three days," Maxim laughs, dropping into the chair next to me amid the ringing of gunshots.

"Widen your feet and steady your arm," I shout at the youngest member to be heard over the noise. The boy adjusts himself without looking back, loading the next clip to continue training.

"That one shows promise in computers. I'll be watching him closely in the coming months to see how much he knows," Maxim nods at the one I just addressed.

I grunt at his words, having noticed the same thing about the boy. Several show promise but the final choice I will leave up to my friend. "Use him as you see fit."

"Don't promise me a good time if you're going to take it from me in the end."

I just keep my head out of my hands, not sure why I allow him to tease me in such a manner. Just as I open my mouth to tell him to jump off the nearest cliff, Maskin rushes into the room. He doesn't need to say anything. The stern pinched look on his face is enough and I'm already past him.

My feet thunder heavily on the stairs as I sprint up them and out of the basement range desperately running for Nevaeh. Up here, I can hear her screams. My name repeated continuously as I break into the crowd of men surrounding her and Ember on the floor. My sister-in-law is barely keeping her in hand while keeping the men back.

The bite of the hard marble in my knees doesn't faze me as I drop beside them and pull her struggling body into my hold. Her fist grazes the edge of my jaw, just missing a full connection as I turn into her. An elbow lands in my ribs as she screams again. I grunt, taking the hit and grip her harder. Locking her limbs between our bodies I wait for her to stop screaming.

"Nevaeh, calm down. Moya lilaya malen'kaya tigrovaya liliya, I am here. You're safe, I'm here."

Legs kick in her continued attempts to get free till it seems like an hour has passed for her calm enough to recognize the tone of my voice. No matter how she thrashes and cries I hold her firmly in place. As the volume of her cries weaken, I hum her favorite melody.

"Volodya," she whispers, shuddering under me now fighting to stay awake.

"Rest moya liliya, I am here." Changing my stance to a more comfortable sitting, I finally look up to see only a few men and Ember remain. A nod to Max and Maskin is all I need to have them getting the rest of the men cleared out.

"What the hell happened here," I demand looking at Ember.

Calm hazel eyes raise to my stormy ones. "I don't know what made her scream, but this was a major panic attack. None of us could seem to get her to respond. She bloodied your brother."

"What?" I demand in shock.

"I'm fine brat. She is within her right to the small break she gave my nose. I was walking past the room and found her sobbing. Wanting to know what upset her, I touched her without thinking. I did not expect her reaction, I'm sorry." Dimitri makes his way to me. Worry lines his bloody face as he takes in her limp state within my arms.

"Sobbing," I growl, turning my eyes to the woman still beside me.

"Don't give me that look, she was nothing but smiles and happiness when we got home." She matches my gaze unafraid of my dark mood. "We've been home for over an hour and she went upstairs.

Mikhail is suddenly there pulling his wife into his arms and giving me his own dirty look. He doesn't mess with anyone going after his woman and neither do I. The fact that Nevaeh is lying helpless against me is the only thing that is keeping me from spilling blood. I know this isn't her fault but not having answers when Nevaeh is trembling in my arms is driving my monster crazy.

"We were in the sunroom with the children when she started crying. Ember went to calm her thinking if I tried it would upset her more. I have called the doctor for you, why don't you take her to bed," Mikhail offers, trying to defuse the situation.

Nevaeh moans jerking in my arms weakly as if trying to get out of my hold again. Even the voices of others are upsetting her currently, so I do as he suggests. Carefully, I cradle her closer as I gain my feet and head to our room. She whimpers, fingers continuing to search for me the whole way. Broken sobs of my name spill from her lips, doing a fine job of tearing my heart to shreds.

Ember steps in after me, and pulls the bedding down for me before leaving just as quickly. Another violent cry passes her lips when I deposit her in the sheets, and she refuses to let me move even an inch from her. Struggling closer to bury herself against me. I don't even give it a thought as I sink into the space next to her.

Her eyes may be closed, and her body given to sleep but the moment I'm settled she glues herself closer to my side. Driving herself further into my hold as I smooth my hands down her back. A few soft cries slip past as her sleep deepens but a wave of murmurs and her melody ease her safely back to a place of peace. The Russian version has never failed in making her relax.

"Brat, the doctor is here," Dimitri's softened voice seeps through the door a moment before he opens it to let the man in.

"Move aside so I can see to her Pakhan," the balding man says, laying a hand on my shoulder.

Removing myself from her warmth is not easy but her health comes before my own wants. I go to sit in my chair but stop my feet when I nearly crush her laptop. She never leaves it anywhere but the nightstand or her school bag. She values it too much to leave it carelessly underfoot.

I pick it up filled with unease becoming a lead stone in my gut. Ember's hand has me moving so she can sit beside the bed and hold Nevaeh's hand while the doctor works. I don't want to move further from her, but I head out the door to look for my brother. We need answers. The family stands waiting for me just outside.

I head straight for my twin ignoring my mother's worried frown and draw the device up between us. "Was she on this?"

He doesn't need to do more than glance at it to answer. "Yes."

Our eyes drop to the closed screen. What was she doing that made her cry? Did that bastard stop with notes and find her email? Should I open it to see what is going on or should I wait for her to give me permission?

The door to my room opens pulling me from the dilemma in my hands. Doctor Jessups lays a hand on my arm and gives a reassuring pat before slowly speaking. "She'll be fine. Upset but refusing anything but tea. Just let her rest for the day. She's asking for you but don't do anything to put any other stress on her. If she wants to talk, listen and nothing else."

"Has she told you anything," I can't help but ask, hoping for a clue as to what triggered her today.

"No, Pakhan. She would like your brother to go in so she can apologize for hurting him though."

Relief and humor war at the surface under the unease of the unknown. My brother and I know what it is she's doing. If she isn't ready to say what is going through that pretty mind of hers, she'll focus on the wellbeing of others.

"Go see to your apology," I say, motioning my brother to the room.

Gripping my arm, he all but drags me in behind him. He at least makes sure the door is closed before ripping on me hard enough that I nearly trip over myself. God, I hate when he does this, but the sight of Nevaeh's shy sleepy smile from under the cocoon of blankets as we move closer has me willing to put up with his antics. Her face pales at the blood tracks still on his chin.

"What is this apology nonsense the doctor spoke of just now? Does my little sastra think of me less than a child," Dimitri demands in mock anger. "You've given me worse before this and laughed."

The fool isn't paying attention as he sends a grin my way and is met with a mouth full of pillow that she sends flying. It may be filled with soft feathers, but the thud is loud and snaps his head hard enough he falls back into my chest. The undignified shriek that leaves his mouth makes up for his disrespectful handling.

Playing into my woman's hand, I step back and push him aside. I listen to him fall as I take in the beauty rising to sit up in my bed. Blankets pool around her hips, face still pale, but the glimmer of fire burning in her eyes tells me that the worst is over.

Her eyes drop to the machine still in my hand and she closes her eyes. Gently, I set it safely on the nightstand. Only once it has left my fingers, do I move to sit on the mattress next to her. It's a struggle to keep my hands to myself but I manage it.

"I have not pried, moya liliya. When you are ready, da?"

Her shoulders lower in a deep exhale, but my words bring her gaze back to mine. The brush of her fingers makes my nerves jump but I let her do as she pleases. That soft skin inches its way onto my open palm till fingers slide over my wrist and take hold of me.

Words whisper in the air between us, "Thank you. It is mostly finished." Her gaze flicks off mine for a heartbeat before coming back up. Trembling fingers twist in the heavy fabric of the bedspread. "It's for you."

Tilting her chin with a finger, I study the shame invading her posture. In all our years together this trouble to hold her ground in my presence sets my teeth on edge. She wasn't like this when I first found her again and she was scared to let me close. Scared but forward in her defiance. Holding my gaze is a struggle for her but whatever she finds in me firms her resolve.

Once she takes a breath I ask, "For me?"

"You need to know. The words get stuck in my throat the moment I try to say them but to write them." She pauses, shuddering as she pulls in a deep breath. "What's done will have you spitting mad." She nods at the device I just set down. "The worst of it at least."

Her tale lies just to my right waiting for my suddenly uneager eyes. The truth I've been demanding to hear from her since she returned to me waits within reach. Now, I'm not so sure I'm ready to hear it. Not sure I have the strength to sit here and learn it all without scaring her with my reaction. I haven't even touched it, and my monster is ready for the fight.

"I think I will step out and get back to my duties," Dimitri grunts, shifting with an awkward cough.

Nevaeh's voice raises before my own. "Stay."

"Nay, what is in there is not for my eyes or ears." He attempts to back away a second time. "If you want to share it after he knows I'll be here."

"Dimitri shut up! What's in the pages isn't good. Please, I think both of us will need you to keep him from going on a blood hunt tonight," her tone softens at the end, unwilling to meet my eye.

The effort to keep myself from reading the horrors stored on her computer has never been so hard to find in me. She says I will go on a blood hunt. Those specific words did not leave her mouth by chance. What terrors does the darkened screen hold in its depths to make me go on a killing spree? Can I calmly sit here and know that she lived through it all?

"Volodya," Nevaeh whispers, pulling my focus immediately back to her. The item that she thinks will cause me to lose my mind is gripped lightly in her hands. "You don't have to read it now if you don't feel up to it."

With just the three of us in the privacy of our room, I let myself be vulnerable and take it. Dimitri nods in understanding and sits in the chair. His unspoken support means as much to me as the woman willing to look past my darkness and continue to stand firmly with me in life.

"Would you let me hold you, moya liliya," I ask softly to keep my body in check.

"Please." Plush lips wobble with a light sobbing laugh as relief washes through her face. "I think I need that too."

We move at the same time. I take her place, and she crawls into my lap, legs draping over one of mine, ear over my heart, and arms gripping my sides. A shudder races before my fingers as I stroke her chilled skin. The hold she has on me lets me know that she fears the words as much as my reaction.

It seems like the world holds its breath as I open the computer and begin reading. The facts of her brother's death and the struggles she faced without the strength of my family by her side. Her quick thinking to rename herself and make her way south. Years of living under the radar. Working at a shitty diner to get herself through college. While it hurts to read about her first few years hiding out in the small town it doesn't do anything but fill me with grief. She should never have felt the need to run.

Her eyes never drift to the words, but she must know that I'm at the start of the tale I'm not going to enjoy. Glancing to the top of her locks tucked into my clavicle, nose pressed flush causing my shirt to fold over her cheeks has me uneasy. She's hiding. Not from my reaction but from the sentences yet to come.

It doesn't take long for the absolute horror to slam into my guts like a sledgehammer to my unprotected kidneys. What began as a harmless friendship was quick to turn into a relationship that she found she could not easily find a way out of.

Within three months, he was set to dead on marrying her. Had her believing that she was his everything, and while it was me she wanted she believed that would never happen, so she let him take over. Small things turned into more. A slap for her talking to another man, a customer at the diner. She was so desperate for acceptance that she allowed him to continue the harassment and only realized how wrong things had become when it was too late.

Each new incident brings the darkness to life until the terrible monster I've kept caged writhes under my skin, demanding its release. It wants this man's blood. I want this fucking man's blood. Verbal abuse, physical strikes turning into cracked ribs and broken wrists. Beatings he'd beg her forgiveness for only to do so again. Hospital visits filled with lies.

The last few pages sit unread in my shaking hands. I owe it to moya lyubov' to finish it. The woman sitting in the cradle of my thighs, branching herself for my reaction to read the last of what is before me. Only, I don't know if I can.

"The last is the worst," she whispers to my heart.

I take a moment to hug her closer. The contact steeling my nerve to be strong for the both of us. The contents of her tale have been the stuff of my many nightmares. For a brief second, I doubt my ability to get through what I'm about to learn.

The bed shifts and my twin's arms encircle the two of us to lend his support. His close-cropped hair rests on my shoulder, and he locks an arm firmly over Nevaeh's heart holding all of us together. Three parts of our gang bonded again to face all the troubles of our world. The jokester no more when such things need handled. His faithful support is the boost I need to find my courage.

His eyes meet mine with a sharp nod. "Finish it brat, we need to know the rest if we are to catch the bastard and give him the justice he deserves for hurting our girl."

"He has much to answer for already, brat," I choke out, nearly strangled from the bile rising in my throat.

He laughs, patting Nevaeh's head. "Then there is enough for the both of us to have our fun, da?"

......

We left before dawn with a packed bag, a tank of fuel, and nothing else. He'd pulled me from sleep, put me in the car, and refused to answer a single question. His silence hangs like a storm cloud as the miles pass by.

Ribs aching worse with each rut, all I can do is sit with the hope that things will be different. The tall trees and dirt road are not giving me the comfort that they usually would. Our speed slows and an old ramshackle house covered in vines stands as if waiting for us.

The car hasn't stopped before he twists to give me a hard look. "Get out."

I do as he says slowly, knowing if I don't move at all his anger will turn for the worse. My legs feel wooden as I follow him up the damp steps and into the interior which is cleaner than the outside would suggest.

Dropping the bag by the door, he takes my arm in a far gentler hold than I've felt in over a month. I fight back the startled reaction my body has to his touch because if he sees it, he'll tell me what a disappointment I am yet again.

"Chris, what's going on?" I ask, trying not to fall as he leads me out the back and into the woods.

Ten paces off the rear of the house he spins me in front of him to frame my face in his hands. His eyes are soft as they were when we first met as we slowly back further into the forest.

"You need some time to think, baby. Here you'll have plenty of that without any outside interference to distract you."

"I don't understand,' I try again, confused by his tone.

Something is wrong, but I don't know what. Instincts rise up fast but not fast enough as he pushes me back. I step with the movement to keep my feet, but there is no ground to meet the sole of my shoe. My back lands with a harsh thud taking the breath from my lungs. The sight of Chris wavers above me but the wooden door in his hands is perfectly clear. A devilish grin lights his features in an evil glow.

Chris lowers on his heels, laughing as he takes me in. "I'll be back to bring you supper. Do as I said and consider what I told you to."

The wood leaves his hand and slams into the top of the box now holding me in its darkness. Only once the first trickles of dirt rain lightly over me does my voice work again. My screams go unanswered.

....

Dimitri and I stiffen at the same time. I can't move. Can't speak as her words tumble on repeat through my mind. *Jesus Christ.*

Chapter 26

Nevaeh

As the hard case falls from his hands and tumbles off the side of the bed, I brace myself to endure whatever reaction he will hand to me now that he has my most horrible of truths.

Panic rears its ugly head as he remains still beneath me. Does he not want me now that he knows the worst of things done to me? Can he now understand why I don't believe I'm good enough for his beautiful soul any longer? Will he finally let me go?

His throat gurgles on several unsuccessful starts and he clears it quickly. Breath whistles through his teeth as he finds his voice. "How long?"

Tears well up because I know exactly what he's asking. Somehow the memory stays in the past as my brain demands allowing me to get the words out. "Two weeks. He opened the lid once a day to give me a bottle of water and a sandwich. I beat my hands raw and one night the lock wasn't closed properly. I ran, didn't stop till I fell on the black top of a highway. A state trooper found me. The state of my body and testimony had him behind bars and denied bail within a day."

Volodya's rigid hold of control astounds me all the time. Now is no exception as his finger coasts over the lines of my body. Fury burns hotly just under the hard flesh that surrounds me, but he keeps it all tightly coiled with his iron will.

The hurt and pain he feels he sets aside to put me first. His selfishness has sobs bubbling out unchecked and all he does is hold me closer. His unwavering need to protect me kicking in. Both twins close in on me to block out the world. To shield me and destroy anything that would dare to do me harm.

"When that scum is back in my hands, he will repay every hurt he has put upon you moya tigrovaya liliya. I swear down to the smallest words of injury he slapped you with," his voice breaks with his vow but the vengeful undertone holds a wealth of promise.

"You don't think any less of me for what I allowed to happen?" I can't help but hold my breath dreading his possible answer. He can't think of me as the same pure young girl after being told all the bad things I allowed Chris's miserable hands to take.

Solid muscle stiffens behind me, and Dimitri jerks in shock at the words while Volodya goes eerily still. Identical eyes glare down at me with burning rage as I'm pushed an arm's length away.

"If you ever utter that nonsense, from your pretty lips again I will slap your bare ass so hard that you won't sit for a week. You were taken advantage of, plain and simple. None of what he did was your fault." Volodya growls, face set in a grim mask, but I see the guilt lurking in his eyes.

He is taking all the bad that has befallen me on as his own. Blaming himself for not coming to me and keeping me safe. It's not his fault. I left instead of waiting. All the blame is squarely on my soul but how do I make him understand? I was a fool to let all those things pass without seeing the red flags for what they were.

Mustering my courage, I take his rough chin between my palms and brush my lips lightly over his. "If it isn't my fault, it does not belong to you either."

"The blame lies squarely with the man who did the deeds." Dimitri cuts in to end the unspoken debate. "And he will soon answer for each offense."

"As long as you don't get caught and come back to me, I don't care what you decide to do with him." I take the out to let them know that the revenge they want to hand out doesn't bother me. "You promised to stay this time."

The monster doesn't leave but his anger softens as he curls around me. Soft kisses skim lightly over my skin as he drags in a heavy breath. "Nothing in this world can keep me away from you ever again."

"His every misdeed will be accounted for Nay," Dimitri says with a growl and a huge squeeze as he climbs off the bed. "He used you when you couldn't fight back. Unluckily for him, he has no idea the family you belong to. I have plans to make for his ultimate displeasure."

Raising my hand as high as I'm able, I grip his fingers to stop him before he goes. "Thank you."

His feet stop before he reaches the end of my hold, and he faces me again. All of his usual joking mannerisms are wiped off his features to be transformed into the most tender look he has ever given me. "You're my family Nay, always have been. I'm sorry I wasn't there when you needed me. There isn't anything I wouldn't do for you."

Guilt fills me at his words. They came back for me, and I wasn't there. Like a coward I changed my name and took off before child services could get their hands on me. How close were they before I fled and sentenced all of us to years of misery?

"Get out of your head, moya liliya," Volodya growls, nudging into the hollow of my neck. The hold forcing me to wiggle closer, nearly out of his lap so our fronts are touching.

Tingles advance into shivers at his continued touches. It takes considerable effort to relax into his hold. Not because it repulses me or makes me uneasy but because it makes me long for more. Longing that has me wanting touches that I know my brain and body are not ready for.

“Thank you both. I know I haven’t acted very grateful.”

“Hush little sister, all is well between us. Not the first time you’ve had me bleeding and it won’t be the last,” Dimitri laughs, walking out the door.

"You are loved Nevaeh, you always have been," Volodya whispers in my ear, tucking a stay hair out of my face.

“Promise me something?”

“Anything within my power that you desire I vow to do. The only exception being I will never let you go.”

“No, not that,” I say, shaking my head. “I want to watch.”

Shock jolts him straight and his head lifts in question. “Watch what, moya liliya?”

Clutching his arms closer I pull in a steadying breath and get it out. “I need to watch him die. Watch the life fade from his eyes so that I know he’s never coming after us again.”

The denial is on his tongue. In the pressure of his fingers gripping me. But he can't say those words. His vow is still fresh in the air and he's trying to think of a way to talk me out of my request. "You promised, Volodya."

"You don't want to see what we will do to him before the end," he promises and swallows the rest of the words.

"I'm not a stranger to blood." Tears threaten again and I don't have the strength to stop them. "You vowed! I have to do this. I have to see his end! Please, give me this Volodya!"

Cursing under his breath, he tucks himself around me. "Alright... I don't like the thought of you being there, but I'll allow it. You won't leave my side when the time comes."

"Thank you." Blind eyed from the onset of tears, I reach up and take the back of his head holding him in place. The move may surprise him, but he ducks in closer allowing me to do as I wish. His steady breathing a welcome balm in the face of what I have been able to share with him.

"And you still want to marry me after... well all that you know now," I can't help but ask. I still fear his rejection though the weight of it is not as heavy as it has been.

Lifting his head he pinches my chin with a true smile. "Always and forever, moya milaya malen'kaya tigrovaya liliya. You hold my very soul in your hands. I answer to no one but you and the almighty."

"You don't intend to make this easy for me do you, Vladimir Solokov?"

The rumble starts first. Vibrating up from his belly and shaking him so badly that it makes me quake in his arms as well. Those big hands grip my hips, lifting me and forcing my legs to either side of his own wide set. Careful shifts of muscled thighs bring us to our sides before he rolls to hover over me.

Lowering his sizable bulk to his elbows, he traces my eye with no more pressure than a feather. "I plan to spoil you rotten my stunning wife. As much and for as long as we both live, Nevaeh Annette Solokov."

A name is nothing more than a name until you give it the power to set your life on a new course. Even with the dreams of a hopeless teen romantic, I never hoped to truly hold the title now standing before me. Butterflies erupt in my belly and tears cloud my vision, but I blink them away.

"God, you don't have to use the full name Vladimir Aleksandr Sokolov."

"I'll use it as much as I want Mrs. Sokolov."

"I never thought to truly be called such." Unsure but needing to touch the warmth of his skin, I flatten my hand over his heart. I swear the beat skips for half a second as he puts his palm over mine.

"It was always meant to be yours, moya lyubov'. I'm just sorry it has taken me so long to do right by our love, moya liliya."

I pull in a sharp breath at his use of the word but the sting of it is not as harsh the more he says it. It's not conditional like Chirs. It's an endearment given freely and without ties. I find that I want to hear more of it from his throat. "Say it again, Volodya."

"Say what Nevaeh?"

"Say the words again."

He shifts back to read my eyes. "What words do you need from me, moya lyubov'?"

Laughing, I let them wash over me. They don't hurt so bad and a small kernel of warmth sprouts in my heart. "Again, Volodya. Say it again!"

Chapter 27
Vlad

She couldn't hide the reaction to my words of love if she tried. Now that I know why she feared the words with such violent aversion it does not sting my heart so badly. He used them as a way to punish her and often only said them as he abused her. The fucker is going to have an extra painful death.

Getting her past out in the open seems to have lanced the festering wound and is cleaning the infection at a rapid pace. Each utterance seems to be less painful than the last. She made me repeat the words too many times to count until she lay resting peacefully in my arms. I am fine with waiting for her to be comfortable to say them back to me as long as I can tell her my own every day.

My men give me second glances as I make my way to the office to meet with my brothers. I can't blame them, as not more than a handful of them have ever seen me smile in the slightest. Least of all, the large grin that takes up my mouth as it does now. Can't seem to help it now that everything is moving the way it should.

"What did you get her to do for you to have you grinning like a fool brat," Mikhail chuckles. Katya wiggles, cooing from the shelter of his arms as he sways her side to side.

Plucking the little angel from his arms, she cuddles into me quickly. Not one peep of anger leaves her as the coos increase the way they always do for me. Kissing her growing fluff, I smile at her father. "She's finally talking and healing. Laughing by the end of our talk."

My answer seems to intrigue him. His head tilts and raises a brow for me to say more. There are times when he outmatches my twin in reading me, but he won't hound me to get what he wants. The little bastard is a genius in waiting me out. If I don't break down quick enough, he'll use the girls to get me softened up before moving in for the last blow.

Can't blame him for it this time though. I'll steal the little beauty in my arm at every chance presented to me. And though they weren't close when they were younger, he'll defend Nevaeh just as fiercely as Dimitri and I simply because we love her. He deserves a small bit of the truth.

"That sorry excuse of an ex was worse to her than any of us could have imagined."

His humor evaporates in an instant. Thunder clouds his stormy blue eyes, and a hard line thins his lips. "And yet you stand here smiling like a fool."

I can't fault his tone of disbelief when he knows the horrors of what can happen to women in his line of work. He has had to help pick up the pieces for women who have gone through things just as bad as Nevaeh. Those things still don't overwhelm the happiness burning in my heart. "Don't look at me like that brat."

"A reason I shouldn't?"

"She let me tell her that I love her. Demanded it actually, until she fell asleep in my arms. The words would have sent her into a panic just last week and tonight it put her to sleep."

"Your girl is stronger than any of you give her credit for Vlad," Ember says, sliding under Mikhail's arm to stand in the doorway. "She just needed some help to see her own power."

"Of that, I never doubted. She has seen things of our world I haven't told our parents about. I know she will have no trouble standing by my side." I admit, lowering my voice to a whisper just in case mother is lurking around. No need for her to know of the blood on my woman's hands.

The two share knowing smiles as he drags his wife closer. "Come brother, you can't leave such an enticing morsel at those bare bones. You gotta give me more than that."

The memory of her hands dripping blood as she ripped the knife from a man's chest when he tried to kill me has me smiling. After another fight with my father about my leaving without my guards. I found a way to get drunk off my ass. Somehow, I made it safely to the Cooper's home. Frankie was at work, but she opened the door before I could turn off the bike. Her thin shoulders bracing me with each step and neither of us saw the bastard coming.

"Vlad?" Mikhail's hand grips my arm pulling me out of the past.

Katya coos up to me, and the future I dream of is so close to being in reach of my hand it is hard to have the patience to wait for the day she is eternally bound to me. Nevaeh is all I have ever wanted in my life after losing Anya. My life, light, hope. The one who pulls me free of the shadows that wish to drag me down. The one guilty pleasure that I refuse to give up again and the possibility of something more.

"Don't go getting any ideas while you hold my little one brat. You have your own woman to share such thoughts with," Mikhail says, quickly scooping his daughter from my arms.

The back of Ember's hand bounces off his arm as she scoffs at him. She tries to hide her amusement in irritation, but the love is plain to see in her features. The companionship and love they share is what I want in my own life.

"You would hit me with our daughter in my arms, moya plamya," he gasps, holding the baby between them as if she can shield him from her mother's blows.

"Don't give advice you can't follow yourself Kail. You would have made sure that I was pregnant before we left the hospital if you hadn't already accomplished the job in Harrisburg," she chastises, but gives him a kiss to soothe his ruffled feathers.

The quick eyes of my brother must see the longing because he pulls his family deeper into his arms. "Give her time, brat. She is sharing her pain after such a short time with you. She may not know how to say it all right now, but she trusts you."

My eyes seek the door hiding her sleeping form from my view. The urge to return to the bare space beside her grips me hard, but I cannot follow it just yet. There are things to be done. A man to find so that I can bleed the life from his wretched body for touching what is mine. And a crooked politician that thinks he can get away with undermining our contract.

"I need your team watching over her until I can deal with the bastard who wronged her without disrupting her schedule," I order, making my way to my desk. I trust my men to do the job, but Mikhail's team needs to be kept busy until they get called out again. Better to have the best.

"You plan to let her continue working," he asks, brows shooting up in surprise that I am not putting her on a strict lock-down.

"Whether I tried to convince her to quit for her safety or my peace of mind she would never allow it. She is just as head strong and stubborn as the one in your arms brat." I allow a chuckle to slip out as I shake my head.

"With men like you, we have to be. It's the only way to get you to listen or get anything we want done, handled in a timely manner." Her head snaps sharply my way before turning back to her husband sending the untied blonde hair back over her shoulder to clear her eyes. "Just like our still unfinished talk of houses."

His eyes shift, darting to me before returning to his wife. "Why must we rush?"

The green flashes brighter in her narrowed eyes. One finger jabbing into his chest. "Because we agreed this was temporary until things got settled and it's been a year already. I don't like being in the city and you know that. Stop stalling and man up!"

The open office suddenly feels very small, making my skin itch. Even Katya's gurgle mixes with a whine as her father bristles at the challenging words. "Are you calling me a coward, woman?"

She just smiles and crosses her arms. "I don't know. Is that what I'm saying, Mikhail Sokolov?"

"Brat, take your plemyannitsa. I need to have a talk with my wife."

He all but thrusts the baby into my arms and has Ember over his shoulder before she can get out of reach. Two steps from their door she shouts teases, and he slaps her ass firmly. Her head dips into his side, and his knees start to buckle but he keeps to his feet. Neither spare me a passing glance as he kicks the door shut behind him.

I can only guess that she bit him because he may be spewing vile punishment promises but she is laughing like the cat that's had the last of the cream. You can't punish the willing when it comes to those two. I foresee many long nights now that I'll be in the room closest to them. Maybe I should look into sound proofing.

"You look good with a baby in your arms, Volodya," my woman says, catching me off guard.

Nevaeh's sad tone draws me to her standing in the doorway. Another of my shirts hangs off one shoulder as she leans on the frame. I'm sure she's trying to hide her sadness from me, but I don't need her to speak to tell me that something is troubling her. Some deep hurt lies on her that she hasn't shared with me yet.

The few short steps to reach her take too long for my liking but I keep my feet slow so as to not scare her. "What is wrong moya, tigrovaya liliya? You should be sleeping."

Her fingers stretch forward to hover over our niece's head before lightly making contact. The hesitation gives me pause. I know that she always wanted children of her own. Dreamed of having a house full of them. She's touching her like she's afraid to break her. Nervous to move closer or take her from me which is stranger because I know Ember's given her the baby before.

Her voice a bare whisper as she asks, "Do you still want children?"

"Only if I share them with you," I smile, hoping to make it light and teasing.

For several moments she stares down at the content little girl in my arm. The shimmer of tears on her has the monster in me stirring. Shifting the baby to one arm I take my woman into the other. Soft shivers run over her, and I rub down her arm to chase them away. "Nevaeh, tell me what is troubling you."

"What if I can't give you an heir?"

It's hard to hear her whispered question but it has my brain screaming at the implications her words suggest. Was there more to the abuse she endured that she hasn't shared with me? "What are you saying, moya liliya?"

"Can you still want me if I can't give you any kids," she sobs, shaking more in my hold.

Brown eyes filled with misery rise to lock with mine as the truth falls into place. More has happened than what she has written down. I need to know the extent of his crimes so that I can repay all the misdeeds he has to pay for the both of us. "Nevaeh, I will always want you. Tell me."

"Volodya, please I-," she pleads, straining to get the word out.

My twin pauses at the top of the stairs. Eyes flicking between the three of us before he walks down and takes the baby from my hold without an ounce of the usual fuss. A hand on my arm with a tight smile. "Take your time, we will handle whatever comes up just fine without you."

A decade of being the responsible one has an argument on the tip of my tongue, but I bite it back. Letting others take over is something I've never done before but I allow it so that we can get the rest of the truth out. I know she doesn't want to relive the nightmare, but the wounds have been festering for too long. She needs to get them all out.

Keeping her tucked into my side, I take us back up the stairs and into our room. Sitting her on the bed, I kneel at her feet and take her hands in mine. I will need her touch to remain strong for the words to come. "The truth, Nevaeh. No one but me needs to hear what he has done. I need to know so that the both of us can make our life together."

Tears spill like a waterfall from her eyes as she tries to deny my words. I let her have the time to gather herself to speak. Cradling her fingers in mine, my thumbs soothe in circles over the back of her hands. This will not be easy for her to say nor for me to hear, but it needs to be done.

"He beat me," she starts. Stopping to drag in more air. "So many times where no one could see."

Her words are a puzzle, but it isn't a stretch to connect the dots. The most precious thing she wanted for her whole life has been stripped from her by the hands of the foulest creature on the face of this good earth.

She must take my stillness as rejection because she tries to jump from the bed, but slips in the tangle of ruffles at our feet. I wrap her up and pull her into me, so she doesn't hurt herself. Heart breaking for her as the tears come faster.

"Please Vlad," she sobs, pushing weakly against me. She keeps her head down refusing to look at me. "I'm sorry, I'm failing you."

"No," I growl, pinching her chin to force her head up. It's a struggle to keep the monster from voicing his icy rage so I don't scare her. "I am Volodya to you and no other. For better or worse you are mine and I will never let you go! This changes nothing between us, and you can't fail me when you've done nothing wrong."

The fight leaves her in an instant leaving her hanging limply in my hold as she sniffs. "But the doctors said th at...He hurt me so bad I might not be able to give you an heir."

"Then my brothers will take on that duty. All I need is *you*. Whole and well to stand by me no matter what we will face. We have lost too much of our time over the years." I hold her gaze so she can see how serious I am.

That she thought I would throw her away because of events beyond her control has me wanting to lash out. The monster wants blood for all the wrongs in her life but more than death he wants to horde her away from the world. To keep her all to himself so no one can ever get close enough to hurt her again. I can't bring death right now, so I clutch her to me and let my tears wet her hair because watching her hurt is tearing me apart.

"I swear, he will pay for taking your dreams from you." My vow is cold in the face of her past. A past that I can't change but a future that I will make sure is filled with nothing but light and laughter.

"I'm sorry," she sobs, muffling herself in my ribs, fingers gripping my shirt and twisting it to the point of pain. "I'm sorry."

"You did nothing wrong," I promise, pulling the monster back under the surface. "I love you as you are, not for what you can give me."

"I should have said before. Should have told you so you knew before you got your hope up."

Fuck! There have been too many heavy topics tonight. Too many secrets coming to light that she feels responsible for when none of it is her fault. I hate that she dragged the vow out of me before I knew what that would entail. He probably won't be recognizable at the end, and she wants to see him die. To watch me become the monster the evil of the world forces me to be as I hand out her revenge.

"Stop pushing yourself, moya liliya. When you are ready to tell me things I am here to listen and not before. No matter what you are all I need, the rest is just extras."

Shivers run through her, body sagging tiredly into mine on a deep sigh. "I know you have work but-"

"Nothing is more important than you tonight. It will be there tomorrow," I whisper, already lifting her and moving us deeper into the center of the mattress.

Sliding us under the rumpled covers, loosening my hold only to let her twist and curl into my side. Head in the dip of my shoulder, fingers twisting in my shirt, feet gripping my leg. It doesn't take long for her breathing to even out as sleep takes her though it takes me a bit longer to find any relief from the truths running rampant in my mind. Plans for all the crimes I need to avenge.

Chapter 28
Nevaeh

The day of my wedding arrives slower than I expected. With all my past now in the open between the two of us, I have nothing left to hide. The memories still leave me grasping for something to hold onto, but no matter where I am, Volodya always seems to be near to chase them away.

He has been relentless in making sure that I know how much he wants me. Where he let me sleep undisturbed before he now wakes me with words and kisses before leaving the warmth of our blankets. Going over both our schedules so if either of us needs the other throughout the day we know where to go. Texting throughout the day, kisses each time we pass, small touches, and smiles all in view of the men. Cutting meetings short to make sure he's at the table with all of us for dinner.

The little things I give are all he asks for. I'm not sure why he doesn't demand more from me. Maybe he can tell that I doubt myself being ready for that with him. That I'm scared to take that step just yet. Maybe he wants to do everything right by us and wait for us to be bound before God. He's always been very traditional in those views of his faith. His level of patience and restraint is astounding, but also strangely thrilling in contrast.

I look into the mirror, taking in the woman staring back at me, wearing the dress of my dreams. The reality of what's happening today is more beautiful than I ever could have imagined, making it hurt to breathe. I barely believe I'm the same woman. In the light it looks as if I'm glowing, about to burst from happiness. I pinch myself to ground my mind, but can't stop smiling. My childhood dreams are coming true because I couldn't build high enough walls to keep the man out of my heart. Vladimir Sokolov will be my husband in less than an hour, and I plan to stand tall at his side. I'm not running any longer.

Tonight, I will put every single one of my demons behind me. My husband will have all of me because it is what we both want. What we both need in the years to come if we are to have the life we deserve. And more than anything I don't want to leave his side again.

Ember slings an arm over my lacey shoulder as our eyes meet in the mirror. Mikhail always says her hair reminds him of honey, but it reminds me of warm creamy caramel.

A stark contrast to my own dark locks. Her green and blue hazel eyes glow with an inner fire that chases all the darkness around those near her away.

She is the perfect woman in my mind, but I keep the thoughts trapped inside. The woman would have no shame in telling the men to kick rocks while trouncing me until I believed her when she tells me I'm beautiful. She doesn't allow anyone to talk down about themselves or others.

My thoughts must not be as masked as I hope because she grins wickedly at our image. "You're stunning. I'm happy to have a sister who isn't afraid to put these men in their proper places."

I can't help but laugh, because I don't think that the three of them are all together that bad. Sure, Dimitri and I pull a few pranks here and there but it's never anything permanent. The bright pink I dumped in his shampoo doesn't even show anymore. Mikhail doesn't join, only because he's working or playing with the kids. But he never snitches on us either, and only keeps Ember and the kids from joining in too much.

I can't say anything about Nikki. Since his prank at Ember's wedding his father was quick to send the fourth who I barely remember back to the motherland for a stern dose of reality. I remember him being a wild boy as a child even at five. But it seems that he has taken things far further than his brother and I ever have. Our pranks were wild, sure, but never destructive to anyone. I wonder when he will be allowed to come home.

A knock on the door draws both of our attention to Dimitri who closes the wood behind him as he walks in. A bright grin stretches his lips as he takes in the both of us. "There the woman of the hour is. You look stunning, sastra."

"Thank you, brat." I blush, leaning into Ember's arm and pushing a sprayed curl behind my ear.

His finger tilts my chin up with a smile. "Don't doubt yourself so much, Nay. You've always been beautiful. Now before the tears start, put this on. Vlad was adamant that you were to wear it."

His hand holds a small blue velvet box. When I am too slow to take it, Ember plucks it from him for me. The hinge is soundless as she opens the lid for me and neither of us can keep our silence. Three bright tiger lilies with emerald leaves woven in a tight knot around a heart shaped aquamarine stone. Small red rubies fill the seams as if to hold it all together. My favorite flowers and birthstone holding his own stone shaped like a heart. Not big, the whole jewel set is less than two inches hanging from a sturdy gold chain. A pledge for all to see that I am his alone.

What little air I have left in my lungs squeezes out as my emotions choke me. "When did he have this done?"

"It was meant for your seventeenth birthday," he chuckles, to cover up the past and winks. "The heart is a new addition."

"And I disappeared. I couldn't stay still and wait for the two of you to come for me like I should have," I moan, trying to keep the tears out of my voice.

Two sets of arms take hold of me. Ember says nothing, but lets her body do the talking for her. Dimitri whispers words of comfort. They crush me between them and don't let go. I can't help but take in as much comfort as they are willing to give. Years of having only myself to rely on and now a large willing family stands ready to come beside me for any and all reasons.

"Always Nay," Dimitri whispers with steely authority. "We will always come for you, sastra."

"Enough of this or you'll have to get Maria back here to fix this mask of makeup she painted on my face." I try to laugh as I dab at the start of them.

"Well, there certainly is no time for me to do so much work again when you need to walk down at this moment." My mother-in-law sweeps into the room with a swirl of peach-colored skirts looking as elegant as she has always managed to with so little effort. Her smile is soft as she takes the three of us in, tears shimmer in her own eyes.

Breaking away from them I reach out and catch the one tear that escapes her. "If that's the case none of us has the time to stand around. Don't want to keep Volodya waiting till he thinks something is wrong and comes to find us, do we?"

"Hmm-" Dimitri starts but the three of us slap a hand over his mouth.

"Prank times over brat," I scold lightly, with a smile. "It's time for us to go."

Maria shakes her head with a scoff and delivers the glare that still has the boys jumping to act better. "You've done enough wedding pranks. Now, let your brother and Nevaeh have peace for the rest of their day."

"Yes mama," he mutters sheepishly.

The four of us head out the door and meet Gregor on the ground floor. Standing to the fullest height his aging form will allow, dressed in a full black tux with an orange lily in the breast pocket. Dimitri hands me over to his father with a quick kiss, and I grab Gregor's elbow to keep him up straight. We stand back to let the others into the large sunroom ahead of us where they have the hard panel covers on the pool for safety and extra room.

My hand won't stop shaking, so I grip him tighter. It's hard enough for him to give me a reassuring pat. He doesn't allow me to move more than a step, which has me turning to face him. Deep lines of pain darken his eyes, making worry clench my guts. "Are you alright? Does something hurt?"

"I am sorry my girl for the troubles that you have had to face. I never should have left you the way I did, but I did not expect you to run away so quickly. Maria and I were too late to keep them away from you." I have never seen his eyes look so sad and hurting. "You should have been with us."

I grip his hands, forcing him to stop talking. It takes me a moment to gather myself and find the right words. "I am the only one who can bear the blame. If I had the trust I should have, I would have waited for one of you to come for me. I will live with the outcome and learn from all of my choices."

"But not alone anymore child. You are finally home, and we will not leave you. Let us make our family whole my doch', da?"

No words are needed, but I still pull him into my shoulder. Hugging him to hide the threat of tears as another crack starts healing. He bends his large form very little to meet me so our heads are lying against each other. His quiet acceptance has peace settling over me like a familiar blanket. Patting my arm, he leans back with a smile and chuckle that sounds like thunder.

Spinning, I stand by his side, my smile is free and easy as our long-ago roles sink back into place like long lost friends. “Lead me to my husband, Otets.”

The French doors open for us, and I can only continue to feel at peace as we walk towards the man waiting for me. Volodya stands by the outside door with the priest. His stern face breaks into a wide smile at the sight of me, open for all in the room to see. His beard is freshly trimmed, tux pressed crisp, standing with the baring of his office in the small sea of his peers.

Countless potted lilies create a sea of orange leading to those waiting for me at the front. Ember looks like a dream in her strapless floor length gown in the same shade as the flowers Volodya brought in to be planted after today. Her hands grip Josey so she doesn’t sprint down the walkway to me. Hunter stands at Mikhail’s side with the restraint of a grown man, chest puffed out trying to look like the other men. Mikhail holds Katya in her own little orange gown, full of glitter like her sister.

I should be uncomfortable with the number of dangerous men in the room, but I’m not. I feel completely safe, because I know that my family will never let anything happen to me. I'm sure that most of them are pledged to us as it is. With all he has done to up the amount of security around me, now that he knows the truth. The men watch over me far more closely, hands close to weapons each time we go out. The school watched closely at all hours, especially when I need to stay late.

Gregor places my hand in Volodya's and the world around the two of us fades. Hard callouses from years of gun play sooth my jumping nerves of excitement. His eyes brighten when they land on the jewels around my neck. One hand lifts to ghost over them, before he curls them around the back of my neck and leans down to give me a slow kiss.

"Son, there are plenty of words to be spoken before we get to that part," the priest sighs, shaking his balding head.

I can't help leaning in to take my own kiss in return, too darn happy to pay the priest much mind. The brothers whoop from behind us, and Ember knocks on my back as she laughs, "That's my girl!"

"Is this going to be a trend with the family now? I had thought you had more patience than the younger one," the priest sighs, raising a brow in mock annoyance.

Hand over Volodya's mouth, it takes a moment to control my giggles to give the priest a meaningful apology. "Forgive us father, we are just excited to begin."

Eyes softening, he pats my hand with a fatherly smile. "Everything in its own time child. God's timing is not our own, but it is perfect. Now if you are ready..."

Warm lips kiss my fingers, and we nod. "We're more than ready."

Step two to killing my past is firmly in my grasp. After nearly two decades, the man of my heart stands with me before the almighty to bind us together. The priest's words roll over me like a warm hug. He recites the many lines, all in Russian because this is how the silly man wanted things done. Something I easily gave into though I refused to allow Volodya to kidnap me before the wedding. There is only so much tradition that I could allow and knowing my past, he refused to do anything triggering to me.

I will have to get all the pranks from Dimitri when the show is done. While I've spent the last forty-eight hours being pampered, the wild cackling of the men tells me they went after him. Even being head of the family wasn't going to spare him today. Mikhail wouldn't have wasted the opportunity to get payback for what they did to him on his day. The smug look on his face tells me he's extremely satisfied with the outcome.

As for now, I have my wildest teenage dream before me. The man who is willing to give me the family that Frankie and I always wanted for ourselves after our parents died.

I love hearing his low rumbling voice as he gives his vows. The way his grip never falters on my hands.

My vows pour from my lips without trouble, because each syllable has his face softening more and more. Our eyes don't waver. Hands never lose their grip. It's like we're the only ones in the world. Making our vow to only God above and fuck the rest of the mortal world, because the world's laws and opinions don't mean a damn thing when we answer to a higher power and each other.

The cool slide of the steel bands slipping over our fingers has my breath catching while the priest pronounces us man and wife. I don't know who moves first. His hands frame my face, and I have his jacket gripped fast in my fingers, as I push flush to his chest to burrow into him for more.

Only the need to breathe has us pulling back enough for him to growl, "*mine!*"

"*Yours,*" I sigh and take his lips again.

Finally, *all mine*, my husband. A wild dream come true that I always wanted but never thought could ever happen in this lifetime.

I'm finally home.

Chapter 29

Vlad

Nevaeh cuddles into my chest, humming in quiet contentment as I play with one of the styled curls. She's tucked under my arm as we watch our family dance and act up. Damn, she's finally mine. After more than a decade of dark loneliness spent hunting the world's evil, I finally have my angel bound to me. A light that is entirely mine. Mine to spoil and keep safe for all time and no one can come between us.

Her head rests heavily in the hollow of my shoulder, after one too many toasts of vodka raised in our honor. I had to cut her off after the sixth shot, or she would have been on the floor hours ago instead of resting comfortably in the chair against mine. She's always had a hard time saying no out of sheer politeness, but she took to true vodka better than most newbies could have.

One of her hands absently drifts lightly back and forth over my abs. The monster in me lays belly up, content with the world for a time. The most dangerous part of me is complete putty in her hands. If I let her keep going, I run the risk of falling asleep as we are, and the night is not over yet. She's halfway there herself as it is already, and there is no way in hell I'm giving my brothers another chance to wreak havoc today. Her head tips lower, but doesn't jerk up with half the wakefulness of her last nod off.

Mother sits on my other side. A few soft words have her smiling and waving me away like a child. Several dirty teases that are more vulgar than I've ever heard slip past her lips, making my father burst out laughing before silencing her with a kiss. I don't have it in me to be even slightly annoyed at her as I stand and scoop my wife off her chair. They all deserve to have a good time tonight.

Her arms wrap around my neck to bury her laughter against my skin. Our guests cheer. Men call out suggestions, causing their women to slap them good naturedly. Their antics have my wife laughing more. The sound fills my heart. This is what she should have been doing instead of hiding in fear of a man that never should have looked at her.

Upstairs she leans over to open our door, so I don't have to set her down. Once the wood bounces off my foot back into place, I take us to the bed. I don't set her down. Don't hold her and sit myself. Instead, I set her gently on her feet, so she stands radiant before me. But only for a moment before she twirls to gaze out over the garden to stand in the soft light of the stars shining through the window.

Dear God, you truly made the most beautiful woman I've had the grace to claim as my own. The silk of my coat slides easily as I shrug out of it and the tie to toss both on the bed. Pulling my phone from my pocket, I set the music to play and toss it after my discarded clothes. Cuffs come undone before I roll the material past my elbows.

"Nevaeh, moya liliya." Hands out I wait for her to step into my arms just as the song starts. "Dance with me in the moonlight, moya lyubov'."

God, I could live on the smile she beams up at me for the simple request. She steps into my arms without a word, arms hanging loosely around my neck, and her head on my shoulder. A sigh leaves her as I wrap my arms loosely around her lower back, and lay my head over the woven weaves of her hair. Humming along to the lyrics as we move together.

Eventually, she lifts her lips, and I dip down to take them without being asked further. The front of her dress bunches into a bulge between us as she presses closer in a demand for more. Each taste becomes bolder, longer, more insistent. The sweetness of her cinnamon candy coating my tongue as I pull her flush to my hips. Holding her firmly to me as I taste deeper.

She gasps, pulls away and I curse myself for scarring her. Rushing her when she wasn't ready for more. My fists clench as I hold myself in place and apologize for the move, "I'm sorry, moya liliya. I didn't me-"

"Stop talking, Volodya," she demands, smile growing as my head jerks up to take her in. The silk and lace whisper against each other as she gives me her back. "Help me out of these ties."

Fuck, maybe I didn't mess up but if I don't get myself together, I'm about to. This is new. Something she's never allowed me before. Yes, she's let me share the bed. Hold her, kisses, and light touches but I've never ventured under her clothes or pushed. Not once since crashing her last date and setting her on the bathroom sink. I still dream about those stolen silky touches.

Hell, my hands are shaking like a green recruit as I reach for her. I'm not positive where to start other than untying the bow in the middle of the lacing. A few tries and the sides slowly part as I loosen each section. Her shoulders drop allowing the dress to slip from them and pool around her waist. Then she wiggles her hips and the whole thing on the floor so fast I swear I just swallowed my tongue. I've never seen something so gorgeous. The sight of my wife standing before me, unclothed down to the lack of underwear... Is perfection. Even if she still has her back facing me, the sight of her makes it hard for me to breathe properly.

Christ, did she go all day without them on? There were more than fifty of my men in attendance and some of our extended family. She'd interacted with most if not all of them after saying our vows. Fuck, how many do I have to kill for being around my wife in such a state of undress?

"Volodya, stop."

Her soft voice jolts me back to the present. Did I move or make a sound that upset her? I don't feel like I did but with how hard my fists are clenched I can't be sure. She never said what he did to her in this area and I'm not sure how much she wants or can take.

"Don't get lost in your head. Not tonight, please." One hand reaches for me, curling softly along my jaw as she moves closer. "Stay with me."

I can barely whisper the question to make sure this is what she wants right now. "Nevaeh- Are you sure?"

"Volodya, I need you," She whispers, stepping closer. Warm brown eyes gaze up at me, but she doesn't move any closer. "Please don't treat me like I'm going to break."

Jesus, she's going to test me to death but damn it if I haven't wanted her since I let her pour that damn tea over my head. She jolts under my fingers as they skim up the hard ridges of her spine with a feather-light touch. I reach the base of her neck, squeezing lightly until her head tilts back, baring her throat for me. I move them higher, taking her hair into my fist to drag her back so I can lean into her. My lips hover over the slim column of her neck before I kiss her pulse.

One slim hand lifts and tangles in the short strands of my hair as she arches, making more room for me. She moans with each new touch, while her other hand takes mine from her hip to lay over her bare breast, squeezing lightly until I take over the motion myself.

She's perfect in the palm of my hand. Perfect in my arms and under my tongue.

"Volodya," she pants, shivering and clawing at my hip. "*Please*... please kiss me."

Tucking her closer, I turn her so I can take her mouth. Groaning at the feel of her warm palms touching me. At the delicious slide of her touch over my sides, cupping my jaw, and dipping back down my ribs to settle on my hip.

I can't get the full grunt of surprise out as she tugs my shirt free and rips the fabric open. Her mouth is gone from mine and moving over my chest before I can stop her. The warm wetness jolts me so hard, I nearly grab her to shove her away, only to stop myself. It feels too good, but I don't want to upset her. Don't want to push for what she isn't ready for and I'm fighting to keep myself in control. But fuck, her aggressive touch has me near breaking.

Fuck, I don't ever want her to stop. I want her touch, and I want to touch her in return, but I don't want to scare her after everything he's done to her. I'm sure she won't be okay with me throwing her on the bed and fucking her senseless. In losing myself in her body and not allowing either of us to come up for days. Jesus, fuck I need to slow down!

She lifts to her toes, lips rise and tickle my ear as she whispers, "Get on the bed."

Her demand is bold and new but I'm not going to question my wife further on her wedding night. Reaching to lift her, I suddenly find myself bouncing on the mattress instead. I barely make it to my elbows when I feel her hands on me. Slim fingers gliding up my legs and stopping to knead at my thighs. Paying attention when they hit a knot and working the muscles, till they release with a groan I have no hope of keeping in.

I don't even realize I've closed my eyes. Not till my chest is heaving and I lift my head to take her in. Fuck! She's just smiling. Sitting on her knees between my legs, head resting on my thigh, hands digging flesh, and smiling up at me.

This woman literally takes my breath away and she's finally all mine, though I have no idea where to go from here.

While I love her smile, her stillness has me wondering what's going through her head. "Nevaeh, moya lyubov' what's wrong?"

A sharp red stains her cheeks as her head dips to hide in my pants and she peaks up at me through her lashes. "I'm just scared."

Her face is in my hands, and I'm leaning over her before she can say another word. Cupping her cheeks to wipe under her eyes, praying she doesn't start crying when we've had such a good day. Knowing that sooner or later we were going to hit a snag that would have her pausing.

"Tell me what you need," I whisper the demand, terrified she's going to tell me she regrets this. Regrets *us*.

At first, she says nothing which sets my nerves on end ready to defend her from some unseen threat. But she just looks at me with watery eyes and hesitation. And then the fear settles the moment she starts climbing into my lap. Taking my help as I wrap my arms around her and lift her to be crushed in my hold. Cradling her trembling form.

The monster raises its head, keen to know what's upset her and how much blood he needs to spill. "Tell me what's wrong, Neveah."

"I..," she stutters to a stop. Blush growing brighter as she buries her face against my shoulder, refusing to look at me. "I've never done this before."

Never done this before? I blink dumbly down at her head for several long minutes. "Never done what, moya liliya?"

"This," she whispers, so low I almost miss it.

"This what, moya lyubov'?"

"You're really going to make me say it?" She whines, pressing further into me. "I've never... ugh! I've never h ad...I've never had sex before."

The last of her statement is spoken in such a rush the words don't register at first. Even my training can't keep me from sputtering like a damn idiot. "You've..You're a ... So, he... Nevaeh?" Without thinking, I shove her back and take her face in my hands so she can't look away. The dots connect with lightning speed. "Are you saying he never-"

"No!" She hurriedly covers my mouth, cutting off my question. A shy smile curls her heated cheeks as she continues, "I've never done any of it. Not with anyone. He was obsessed with me staying pure till marriage."

Thank fuck. My lungs nearly collapse in relief that at least he spared her that abuse, not that all those others aren't bad enough. She's never been forced or had a bad experience that will mar our first time together. There has been no one before, and there such as hell won't be anyone after. I'm never letting this woman go.

But now, I'm left with a whole new problem I never thought I'd face. By the way she touched me and ordered me around I was sure she had some experience. "So, my shirt and the orders?"

Her tongue darts out to wet her lips as she heaves a sigh. "I got carried away, moved too fast, and scared myself."

Carried away? I can't help the laugh those words pull from me. "Moya milaya malen'kaya tigrovoya, don't stop on my account. I love your boldness and have plenty of shirts. I'm happy to let you rip as many as you like off me whenever you want."

"Shut up, Volodya," she pouts, looking back out the window entirely embarrassed by everything.

Damns, she's beautiful even pouting. A finger under her chin has her attention focused on me again. One soft kiss brings the smile back to her face. The next is deeper and has her eyes slipping closed. I take the chance just to sit here and watch her. Happy beyond relief that by God's grace and mercy, I have my most cherished gift returned to my arms.

When she finally opens her eyes, her smile is still in place. She blinks and shifts, fingers picking at the blanket. "Why are you looking at me like that?"

"Just counting my blessings," I chuckle, smoothing the hair out of her face. "He won't be brought up in our bed again, but I am beyond grateful I get to be the man to teach you. To hold you and love you from now until eternity."

"Oh stop, you weirdo," she demands, playfully pushing me back from her.

I let myself fall at her direction, but make sure she comes with me. Rolling to pin her hips to the bed and hover over her lips. Giving teasing touches just shy of kisses as I order, "Be a good girl and stay right here, moya liliya."

Those pretty brown eyes track every flex of my muscles as I pull away and stand at the foot of the bed. My gaze demands her complete attention. With deliberate slowness, I unbuckle my belt. Leaving it hanging in the loops as I pop the button and lower the zipper of my pants. Her eyes follow every move and track them down as I step out of them to stand over her with nothing on.

Fair is fair after all, and clothes aren't needed right now. Not when she's looking at me, eyes darkened with lust and that tongue darting out again. Hunger outweighs her inexperience with what is to come, and it's me that she's trusting to give it to her.

I give her one last chance to decide if she wants to continue. "Are you sure you're ready?"

That blush never goes away, but she also never takes her eyes off me. Never moves, except her breasts heaving as she crooks one finger at me in demand. Her words are bold as she says, "Come here."

Oh, so she's back to feeling sassy. We'll see how long that lasts for her in the weeks to come. First, I'm going to love her like the queen she is. There will be plenty of time to explore other-... things in our bedroom. I'm not a virgin, but I haven't even looked at another woman since my brothers blundered attempted to cheer me up a year after everything went down. It's been so long that I might as well be but I'm not going to blunder and hurt her from inexperience.

Eyes locked, she watches as I sink to the floor. Fingers skimming from her toes and up her creamy thighs to the flare of her hips. Giving her the same attention she gave me until she relaxes back onto the bed. Moaning with each stroke as I work her muscles and ease her mind. All while trailing feather light kisses over her lower limbs.

It's a struggle to curb my need to simply devour her. Each new taste is pure heaven, but the real treasure hasn't been reached yet. My palms glide down to brace over her inner thighs and hold her open for me to take what I want. At first just a breath and a small taste that has both of us groaning. Fuck, if I stay here for more than a few licks I'm not going to last.

"Volodya," she whimpers. Her hands tangle in my hair forcing me closer and lifting her hips as far as my hands will allow.

Chuckling, I give in and throw my concerns with scaring her to the wind. I suck her flesh into my mouth and ease a single finger into her slickening entrance. Working her looser with each flick of my tongue and plunge first one finger and then two until she disregards my instructions to yank at my hair. Dragging me closer, bucking, tugging my hair, and calling my name until she comes apart under me.

She's still arched in pleasure as I move above her to ease her shaking body to the mattress. Her eyes flutter open as I cup her cheek. Holding her gaze, I watch as she feels my cock settle against her and slowly inch inside. I watch as her eyes grow, her mouth opening in a stunned expression of pleasure. I stop, sliding up the bed and letting her see the proof that she's about to be utterly claimed in every way.

Understanding lights in her eyes up, plush lips rising to consume mine. "Volodya," she sighs, shifting slightly. Her legs part wider, arms curling over my shoulders as I settle against her, and grips the back of my head as I pull back ready to take everything. "Make me yours."

I'd laugh if I could around the breath she's stealing from me with a demanding kiss, but I nearly swallow my tongue as her hips tilt. Pulling me in and through the thin barrier.

"Fuck!" Everything in me stills in surprise and I force her hips into the mattress to keep her from moving but I don't pull out. A single tear trickles from her closed lids to crest her cheek and my heart stops. "Nevaeh! Did I hurt you, moya liliya?"

Choked laughter spills from her and she finally opens her eyes. They burn clear, bright, and full of wonder as she takes in my worried features. "No."

"Why-" Her kiss is so brutal in its demand that I stop talking. Fingers glide down my spine only to twist and roughly rake back up my ribs.

Words aren't needed. She isn't hurt and doesn't regret taking me in. My last fuck to be careful flies out the window and I start moving as she orders. Slow strokes that have me groaning but she still asks for more. I'm the first. The one she gave all of herself to. The one surrounded by the wet slide of her gripping wet pussy. *Mine*. She's all fucking mine.

The sound of flesh slapping fills the room but the only thing I make out are her pleading whimpers as we get lost in each other. For each thrust she lifts to meet me. Teeth dragging over skin and nipping at flesh. Nails digging in for a stronger grip taking everything I give. Heels tucking into my legs for more leverage when I shorten my thrusts to tease her.

I can't hold myself back any longer. The feel of her is too intense. More than I ever dreamed of. Muscles strain as I tuck her further under me to hit as deeply as possible, determined to finish with her this time. Fluttering walls squeeze me tighter. She's cumming again. This time sealed over my cock buried deeply in her.

The strangle hold has me shouting. Burying my face in her neck as my cock jolts in release within her, unwilling to let go of her for anything. Her scream follows mine drawing more from me until the both of us collapse to the side, so I don't crush her. It feels like my heart is going to pound out of my chest and I'm struggling to get my breath.

Smooth fingers brush damp hair from my face with contented hums as she cuddles close. Pressing a kiss over my heart before settling with sleepy eyes. "I love you, Volodya."

Chuckling takes most of my air, but I don't give a damn. My wife is in my arms drifting off to sleep without a care in the world. She's whole and safe and completely mine.

"And I love you Nevaeh, moya liliya."

Chapter 30

Nevaeh

Blank. Just a blinking cursor on the screen of a book I should be finishing the last ten chapters of by now, but I have absolutely nothing written. There should be a groove in my fingers from the number of times the pen has been flipped around my fingers as I hunt for the words. I've tried all of my usual tricks to break out of this, only to be met with silence.

Damn it, I'm so far behind on this project already. My editor is expecting the finished full draft before the end of June. I don't have the time to sit here staring. Not when the five weeks left are really two or I'll be taking time away from my husband during our trip to get this done.

"This is ridiculous," I groan, letting my head drop to the desk. Lifting myself up, I let my forehead thump off the wood another time before sitting back up again like one more knock would open the flood gate of words. "Why do you hate me now?"

The detailed outline stares up at me mockingly from beside my computer. Every act, each chapter, quotes that popped up for each one written and waiting for me to fill in the details. What I wanted to say with it all means nothing when the characters aren't talking to me.

This has never happened since I started writing in this room. The wide uncluttered desk, comfortable chair, lighting, and knowing that he's just on the other side of the door usually has me flying through my work. I don't want to call her and tell her I need an extension, but it's looking like I won't have a choice right now. Nothing is coming and staring at the screen is starting to make my eyes hurt. Maybe I should take a break.

My eyes flick to the doors separating the offices. The curtains are open giving me a perfect view of Volodya at his own work. Chin resting in the hole formed by his thumb and first two fingers as he leans closer to his own computer screen. The faint creases around his eyes, the twitch in his jaw, and pinched mouth. The littlest signs he probably doesn't realize he's showing his frustration. It makes me want to smooth the worry from him.

My poor husband has been at it since sunrise thanks to an angry call waking us up that set a tense mood for the rest of the day. Our first Saturday as a married couple was supposed to be calm and intimate spent in our bed.

After last night I just wanted to stay cuddled up to his warm body. Exploring each other, not him looking for more work.

"Fuck it," I whisper, closing the blank screen with a firm click. He's been at it long enough, and I want some attention.

If I can't write at the moment, I'm going to get some of his time before the men come back with another problem. Uncurling myself from the wide leather seat, the thick carpet sinks under the weight of my bare feet. Long blue cotton snapping around my ankles as I pad across my room and through the doors into his space before I can doubt myself.

The soft click of the lock and snap of the curtains have his head tilting my way. Tired frown deepening as he sits straighter to take me in. "What's wrong, moya liliya?"

I've never been this bold to come in here without being invited or knocking before. Sucking in a deep breath, I close the distance between us and cup his prickly jaw, leaning into his space before answering softly, "I need your help."

"Wha-"

I don't let him finish. Crushing his lips under mine and taking advantage of his shock to dip deeper into his mouth. Chocolate still strong on my tongue from the few pieces he had last night. Body halfway into his lap before his hands grip my hips to pull me the rest of the way. Purring at the low rumble from his groan as I push further into his firm hold.

Groaning as he pulls back to ease his way down my neck and I thread my fingers through his hair to keep him close as he moves. Latching onto the sensitive spot just under my jaw, fingers flexing to drop lower and grip the bottom of my ass to shift me into a better position. Teeth scraping lightly, before chasing the sting away with his tongue and a soft kiss. Teasing unendingly in the way he knows makes me squirm for more.

"Volodya," I pant, hissing when he stops to simply nuzzle at the base of my throat.

One hand slides up my back to twist into a fistful of my loose hair to keep me still while pulling away. A small smile replaces the frown now. "If you're going to barge in here, that best be the greeting I get every time."

Instead of answering, I just laugh and dive in for more. Enjoying the way his fingers flex over my hip while he opens to let me take control for just a moment. To think I'd fought so hard to stay away when I could have been enjoying life with him.

He pulls back again with a sad smile. "I'm afraid we won't have the time to finish this intriguing discussion when I need to get the crews' payrolls finalized. Not to mention my brothers are on the way back from their own meeting."

Damn it, I knew I wouldn't have him for long but I'm not giving him up until they walk through that door! If he thinks I'm going to quit that easily he's got another thing coming. I'm done being shy when I want something.

"So," I sigh, dragging my fingertips down the line of his throat and across quivering abs. "How long until they get here?"

"Nevaeh," he rumbles in warning, letting go of my hair to stop my hand. "You know I want nothing more than to take you back to bed but if I don't pay the men on time, I'll have less time for that tonight."

"Then you best get to it, Pakhan," I chuckle, enjoying his raised brow at my use of his title while I slide off his lap like I'm going to walk away. "I wouldn't dream of stopping you from finishing."

Whatever words are on the tip of his tongue turn into a long hiss, as I pull the baggy white turtleneck over my head and let it drop to the floor. Fingers bruise the leather armrests as the zipper comes undone to send the skirt slipping to pool at my feet. Dark hungry eyes burn, tracking me as I turn and make my way to the garden doors. Taking my time, gripping the long material before sliding them tightly closed just in case the kids are outside.

The storm in his eyes is raging so strongly, only his strict hold of self-control and the strangled grip is keeping him in his seat. Not so long ago the look would have sent me running. Now, standing in his space in only my bra and panties has my heart hammering for a whole different reason. It gives me the strength to slip the cloth down my thighs and unclip my bra. Heat burning low in my belly and growing with each dip of his gaze over my bare body.

Nostrils flare as he drags in a sharper breath, leaning into the high back of the chair with a thin dangerous smile that has my legs clenching. "Lock the door, Nevaeh."

Locking eyes, I back to the house door and twist the dead bolt into place. Shivers race through me at the finality of the click and the growing grin on my husband's face.

"Come here," he demands. "On your knees in front of me."

The same lush carpet, slightly more worn than mine, softens my position as I do as he says. Hands already moving, though he doesn't give me any more words or another direction. Pressing into his legs and wrinkling the fabric as I slide closer to the button hiding what I want. Refusing to look away as I take hold of it and slip it free before grabbing the zipper. One brow raised wondering if he's going to stop me at each tooth falling free, but he just copies me daring me to stop what I'm doing.

Once the zipper is undone, I stop. Head tilting, I smirk at his questioning look, smooth the flaps out of the road, take my hand from his pants, and sit back on my heels. "Unbutton your shirt... Slowly."

His brow rising with a devilish smirk. "Are you giving your Pakhan an order?"

"I'd never think about ordering my Pakhan around like some lowlife," I gasp, placing a hand over my heart in mock horror. "The only man I see in front of me is my husband and he's been ignoring his wife for hours now. "

"What kind of husband would ignore a wife like you?" He demands, pinching my chin to hold me in place as he steals a kiss.

Damn he tastes good but before I can fully appreciate it, I'm in the air. Barely a squeak and he sets me fully on the cool wood of the desk and steps back out of my reach. White shirt rolled up to his elbows, black slacks open, hanging off his hips, twisted smile, and the storm still raging in his eyes.

"Eyes on me, Nevaeh," he rumbles, sliding the first button free. "Don't look away."

For every inch of skin he reveals, I return the favor. Leaning back on one arm, and running the other over my abs while lifting my legs to give him a better view. I'm not ready to play with myself in front of him, but letting him see what's his? That I can do, even as I struggle to breath as he shrugs off the cotton.

Two steps have his hips notching flush between my legs. Arms bracing on either side of my ribs as he closes the distance. Stopping just shy of our lips touching to brush hair from my cheeks before cupping my jaw. Time seems to stop as our eyes lock, breathing in each other's air and silently reading the other's language.

"You are the most important thing in my world, moya liliya. Don't ever let me get away with making you feel like you aren't," he whispers, fingers feathering over my skin.

"You make me feel like the most loved woman in the world," I say, fighting back a round of tears with a smile.I lift my free hand, gripping the back of his head to pull him closer. "I want you. Here. Now. Forever. Now love me the way only you can, Volodya."

"Fuck, I love that mouth. You're even sexier when you get bossy," he chuckles. "Just remember this room isn't sound proofed well enough to keep your screams inside."

Is he really challenging me right now? Without thinking, my hand darts into his open pants and grips the hard length of his cock to give it a hard squeeze. The warm skin wrapped up under my fingers without a barrier.

"No boxers today, Vladimir Sokolov?" I sass, pulling him free. I tease the head through slick juices, nudging him up a fraction when his hips jerk, stretching to slide in. His frustrated growl when I keep him from his goal makes me feel powerful. Like I hold the keys to a weapon waiting to be unleashed.

"You've teased me enough, moya lyubov'. Please," he pants, pausing to shudder as my grip shifts to play with the tip, making him jerk for some sort of relief. "Bring me home, moya liliya. I need to feel you."

What can I say to that? Because this man is my home and I'm his in every way that there is. Each giving the other the peace we need from the world. No more playing when he says words like that. His next thrust slides home to the hilt in one motion so quickly my hips lift off the wood, forcing me to wrap my legs around him. Dragging him flush to me with a sharp cry. Arching back so far, he lays me on the desk and grips my hip harshly to hold me on the edge of the wooden surface.

Thankfully, he pauses with a grunt to let me adjust, relaxing to enjoy his heat inside and out. Firm lips crush over mine for the first several slow thrusts. His girth stretches me to the thin line of pain and pleasure that I'm still getting used to. While his mouth takes mine in hungry pulls, his cock glides in with an irritatingly deliberate slowness that sets my nerves on edge. Dragging out the pleasure with short strokes that leave me whining.

"Vol-" I start, gasping to demand more just as the door handle rattles. Fear streaks through me before I remember I locked it.

"Vlad?" Dimitri's voice floats hazily through the thick wood. "Why's the door locked?"

Fire flashes in his eyes as he stills above me, gaze locked on the door with a sneer. Voice hissing out as he growls just loud enough for me to hear, "Of course, the moment I have you they decide to be early. They can just fucking wait."

Another male joins Dimitri as he calls for his brother again just as Volodya picks up his pace. The force of it has him slapping a hand over my mouth to silence the moan when he hits the spot he knows makes my toes curl. His sharp smile is all I need to know that he did it on purpose. He loves playing with me, making me whine and cry in pleasure. If not for him knowing it would make me uncomfortable, he'd make sure the whole house heard us.

"Quiet, moya liliya," he whispers, nipping at my ear. "Or maybe you want them to hear you scream for me. Do you want me to take you harder Nevaeh? Do you want them to hear you?"

Right now, the way he's taking me I almost don't care if they do. I love the power behind each thrust, but I also know the kids are home and I don't want them to hear and think something is wrong. If he keeps this pace up, I will scream, but I don't want him to stop. Body parts will connect under my angry fists if he does.

An idea hits me like a train. It's bold. Crazy and something that's going to shock him. Strangely now that it's in my head I want it. I want him to do it and hold all the power. Refusing to allow myself second guess what I want, I grab the wrist from above my head and force his hand up and on my neck.

His entire body stills above me, only his chest heaving as his mind races to understand what I just did. Eyes wide, lips slack, unable to form words for several heartbeats. "Are you sure?"

Mikhail's voice joins the others. "Brat, why is the door locked... Are you okay?"

The door rattles behind me and I'm laid out on the Pakhan's desk without a stitch of clothing. Face flushed with desire, holding his hand to my throat asking him to tighten his grip. To thin my breath as he fucks me. To make me silently scream.

Tilting my hips pulls him deeper in my own unspoken demand. "Send them away and fuck me, Volodya."

Russian words thunder off the walls as he shouts at the ones outside the door. Telling them to leave which leads to more questions and an angrier man above me. The fury on his face when they keep talking would send even his brothers running if they could see it. His attention isn't where it needs to be.

Unhooking my feet, I let my legs fall, shifting my hips wider so it drops him deeper into me. When that doesn't bring his eyes back where they belong my free hand grips his jaw. Pinching the short hairs of his beard to pull him around. Smiling at the hard look now softening on me. My hand is still over his on my throat and without another word, I squeeze it again.

His right-hand flexes in question drawing a moan from me and I stretch my neck to give him more room. Left-hand slipping under my knee he pulls me further open with a nod and kisses me like this may be his only chance. We never break the kiss and he sets a brutal pace that has me seeing stars around the dimmed light above us. Hammering into me so long I have no idea how long he has me gasping for breath.

"Scream for me, moya liliya," he snarls, hitting harder, deeper, with only one purpose. "Give it all to me."

No need for him to give orders. I'm there, unable to catch my breath as the heat explodes and my mind blanks on the silent scream as I take him with me. Nail digging into skin, needing firm ground so I don't fly apart.

Chapter 31

Nevaeh

The school year is over. Kids are talking loudly in the halls about summer plans as I wave the last of my kids out for the end of the year assembly. Something I won't be going to this year. Getting everything packed up and cleaned is taking priority with the promise of my own trip. A honeymoon we've put off, because I wanted to get to the last day.

The wait hasn't hurt any of us. Though, I know the trip is to get me out of the city so they can find Chris. We haven't exactly been low key in public since the wedding. Holding hands, kissing, and hugs each time we part. Our leaving may draw him out faster for them to find him. I'm sure he isn't very happy now that he can't reach me.

I don't have to know the ins and outs of what the men do to keep the streets protected from others to know what will befall my ex. He got loose once, and all the ranks want his blood. For good reason too. You don't kill men tied to the family and think you can stay ahead of them forever. Hunting and threatening the Pakhan's wife is even worse and will never end well either. The whole family is out for blood including Ember. I think she's the most dangerous one of the bunch.

Not an ounce of compassion makes me sorry for the ending heading his way. An army of family and ex-military men looking to even the score for the death of two of their own and for what he's done to me. My husband won't be taking any more chances with my safety and has given large incentives for him to be found quickly. And honestly, I hope it's long and bloody. A taste of the horror he is so fond of sharing with others. They can keep him on death's door till we get home for me to watch.

I still have trouble believing just how much my life has changed since the day Katya's birth had him coming for the children. It's hard to believe the simple act of taking over the pick up that day to allow another to make an appointment would lead me back to the man I never thought to see again.

More astounding to believe. I've been married for a month already. Bound to my best friend, enfolded in a large family, happy, and free to be myself. I just wish he was free to help me pack up the room today, but such is the life of the Pakhan's wife. When the family has a problem, he has to deal with it, and I can't cry when he does. Not when I told him I didn't want him giving up everything he's built just for me.

He tries to keep all the bad from reaching my ears, but I know they are still looking for the ones who kidnapped Ember and Hunter last year. The same ones they believe are tied to Anya's murder. On top of all the legitimate businesses they run, I feel awful for adding on my own problems. The difference is I know that when he makes up his mind about something there is no changing it, and Vladimir Solokov has decided all my problems are also his.

"How much of these need to be taken down?" Dimitri asks, stepping into the room and pulling me from my thoughts as he eyes everything up with a disappointed frown.

"All of it," I giggle, watching his face drop from the corner of my eye as I reach for the boxes behind my desk. "We don't always get the same room every year, so everything goes."

"This will take us forever NayNay. Why did you not start before today?"

Glancing over, I have to bite my lips as I take him in. He looks ready to spend the night at his club, not get dirty helping me clean. "But I did. This is only half of what was up last week. It won't just be the two of us for long. As soon as Ember is done in the office she'll be here with the kids and Maskin."

"Oh, good the task master is on her way," he groans, slumping on the wall. "Where is all this going Nay? They look pretty damn advanced for elementary kids. At least better than mine at their age."

Chuckling at his pouting, I reach for the first piece above the window before answering. "The kids took all their work home last week. These are mine."

"What?" He stops with the bottom of one freed to level a serious look on me. "Between you and the kids there won't be a single free wall left in the house."

"Oh hush, before Josey comes in and thinks you don't like her drawings," I laugh, climbing on top of my desk for the next one that is a bit higher. "You're always the one fighting to keep her latest work."

His hands settle on my waist and spin me off and back to the floor just as I pull the painting free. One hand raising to wag a threatening finger in my face. "No climbing missy. I'll get the ones you can't reach. You're clumsy enough to fall and I won't have that on my head."

"Fine," I say, rolling my eyes. There's too much I'm looking forward to, to fight over such a silly issue. "Just don't rip the edges off, please."

His scoff has me grinning as I take the few already down from his hands and turn to put them in the first box. The door creaking has me looking up ready to greet Ember. My gaze locks with the twisted grey I prayed never to see again.

The true threat doesn't register until he grins. A black pistol is already raised and pointed at Dimitri's back. "Hello, Nevaeh."

My scream breaks free just as he fires. The bubbly grumbling of my brother is cut off as his body thuds to the floor behind me, and I turn fast enough to see him finish the fall. Blood soaks his dark hair and stains the floor under his still form. Horror turns my blood to ice. He killed him and I'm next.

I scream again, lunging for him with desperate hands. Whether he's still alive or dead at Chris's hand I know there is a gun tucked under his shirt. One way or the other I have to get it if I stand a chance of staying alive myself. Maskin will have heard the shot already. So will Ember. They will have called the team before heading for me themselves. I have to fight to buy my family time to reach us.

"Not so fast, little girl," Chris hisses in my ear as his hand tangles in my hair and jerks my head back. Pulling my head back until I can see him grinning down at me. "Where do you think you're going now?"

"Let go," I scream, praying Maskin is close. "Get the fuck off of me Chris. GET OFF!"

Pain explodes in my jaw and tears come to my eyes as he backhands me a second time. "We're going to have to work on that mouth of yours again baby. You know better than to talk back."

His grip tightens, dragging me further back pulling on Dimitri's shirt till it tears under my fingers, but I refuse to let go. The flash of black metal has my heart hammering, and I throw myself back into Chris's chest. It loosens his hold just a little, allowing me to lunge forward again and feel the heat of the gun's grip on my fingers. A blow to the back of my head drives me off course and I crash to the floor beside him. Dazed but already moving to collapse over my brother's back.

"I don't think so," Chris growls, landing a kick to my stomach and doubling me over, unable to breathe. "Get up, we have somewhere to be."

My lips part in a sickening wheeze as I stumble from his grip up to my feet. I can barely move but no matter how much I fall he keeps pulling and dragging me in his wake. Out into the halls that are empty of students thank God. No children for him to use against anyone trying to help.

He moves us towards the back door, away from all possible rescue. If we get out that door the path will be too narrow to fight in. He's pulling me so fast my mind hasn't quite caught up yet and all I can still focus on is my brother's body lying in a pool of blood. *Stall.* There has to be some way for me to stall him.

My ankle twists from the rushed steps and I don't try to catch myself this time. Letting my weight drop to slow him down. A sickening crack echoes in the hallway when my knees land and pain shoots through my legs with another cry of pain.

"Get the fuck up," Chris growls, yanking my head up by my hair. "I'm not in the mood to deal with your bullshit today."

My scalp burns as he rips some of the roots free. Feet slipping on the tiles as I grab above me to relieve the pressure. No matter how much I struggle, all he does is shake me harder.

"Stop," I scream, with what little breath I can draw in. "Let go, Chris. Let me the fuck go!"

"Shut up!" His hand slams into my head again with more force, knocking me to the floor. "You've caused enough problems for a lifetime, but we'll talk about that when we get home."

Ears ringing, I can't stop laughing. "I'm not going anywhere with you!"

"Of course you are," he sneers, reaching down and dragging me back to my feet to keep moving. "The bastard who took you from me is dead. That criminal will never hurt you again. I'm the only one allowed to make you cry."

I don't know if I want to laugh and cry more. He didn't shoot my husband but I'm not going to tell him that. If he successfully gets me out of here that thinking will make him feel safe. Make him boastful and cocky. Thinking that will buy me time to come up with something to get away.

"You'll never make it out of this alive," I whisper the truth before I can stop myself.

Brick bites into my back as he slams me into the wall and leans into my face. Eyes narrowed and the same nasty grin that never spells anything but pain for me. "What was that, Nevaeh?"

Stall, even if it makes him mad. Give them time. Chin raising in defiance I look him right in the eye. Something he never let me get away with before, but I'm not afraid of him anymore. "They'll kill you for touching me and it will be a long and bloody end that I will *enjoy* watching."

He reacts just as I knew he would. Straining against him does nothing but make him mad as he wraps his fingers around my neck and starts squeezing. "We'll just see about that won't we?"

Black dots swim in front of my eyes as I kick and claw at his arm. And then the pressure is gone but he doesn't let me fall thanks to the arm around my waist.

"Let go," I demand, still gasping. Stomping on his foot with little effect because I refuse to stop fighting.

Rough hands pull me back up so he can kiss my cheek. "Never."

"Get your hands off of her," Maskin's rough draw slices through the air with deadly authority.

Chris spins, keeping behind me so Maskin can't make a clean shot. The gun is hidden from view pressed into my kidneys hard enough to bruise. "This doesn't concern you, rent a cop so turn around and I'll let you walk away."

Oh my god! Has he lost his mind? Anyone with a brain can see the man advancing to save me is far more deadly. Trained beyond anything but what advanced military operations can achieve. I don't know how he hasn't reacted to the insult, but Maskin doesn't even twitch. Gun remaining level as he carefully creeps closer while Chris keeps backing us to the door. Slowed but not stopped by my stumbling steps that he forces me to try to match.

"Not happening," Maskin grunts. "Now let her go."

"I don't think so," he laughs, arm curling over my throat and jerking up so hard I choke, gasping for breath. "I'm taking back what's mine."

Black spots cloud my vision so fast all I can do is claw at his arm. My sandals scape the floor, desperate to get enough leverage to be able to breathe. I have to be able to breathe so I can get my brother help. There is no way I can let him lay in his own blood alone.

"Dii," I gasp out before he pulls me back further, cutting off the rest of my brother's name.

His pull has me off balance making me stumble sideways. It succeeds in letting air in my starving lungs, but he moves with me. Maskin barely moves his sights ready for a shot that doesn't come. He's holding me too close. Staying directly behind me so that any shot would hit both of us.

"Behave," Chirs hisses in my ear. "Don't make this worse for yourself than it already is."

"Don't look at him," Maskin demands in Russian. "Just stay with me."

"He shot him," I whimper, back in Russian. Tears building remembering the amount of red staining the floor under Dimitri's body. "He's-"

"I know." His hands flex on the grip as he nods at me. "She's with him."

"Shut up," Chris snarls.

The gun leaves my back. He shifts it to aim for the man holding my eyes. I can't let him hurt him. Red brick flashes in front of my eyes before blinding pain slams into my forehead. Gun fire explodes in the air over me as black clouds my eyes and my legs give out under me. My body slumps but I don't feel the fall or the cool tiles under my skin. Blood coats the inside of my mouth but I have no energy to clear it.

Through the ringing in my ears the sound of a baby crying has me pausing. I know that cry. What is Katya doing here? Why is Ember letting her cry?

Chapter 32
Vlad

The air is starting to reek down here. Stale blood and piss mixed with bone deep fear pour from the shivering body rocking like a child in the back of the cell. Funny how the table turns when one tries to overextend their hand and become greedy. How fast the ones who think they're untouchable topple with the smallest push.

He is no longer the polished figure of power he thought he was. His once perfectly styled hair hangs limply over his eyes full of dirt and grease. Scratches from his own nails line his skin in dried bloody gashes under the designer shirt he refuses to change from.

"Are you ready to talk or would you like more time to think?" I question, arms crossed as I lean against the wall at the base of the steps.

Shoulders flinch as if I'd struck him and he huddles further into himself. "I had nothing to do with the kidnappings."

I can't stop the eyeroll. Damn, the kids and Nevaeh are rubbing off on me. I detest such childish actions when dealing with work. "That may be, but the millions of dollars funneled from going to the right places is no less a crime and against the oath and contract you agreed to. By allowing drugs to be run on my streets and sending countless citizens to the hospital. The people unable to get the help they needed are no less hurt by your actions."

"Then turn me in or kill me," he shouts, stumbling to his feet only to fall to his face. Lips pulled back in an animalistic snarl as he keeps going. "Why not just end this? You've already found everything and made up your mind. Stop toying with me like a rat."

"Are you not?" Mikhail snorts next to me, twirling the blade around his fingers. "Leaving you down here is the least you deserve for breaking your word. However, we have plans, and I want loose ends handled before we leave."

"Patience brat, he still hasn't told us who is paying him to lie to us."

He isn't the only one anxious to find answers so we can enjoy a few weeks of peace with our women. As much as I want to rush things, this needs to be handled the right way. There are many things I would rather be doing, but we are almost done. The cracks in his armor are barely holding on. He's about to cave and then I can kidnap my wife for a few weeks in the sun with no one to trouble us.

"I told you I don't know." His bravado is gone, and the fear is back causing him to make himself as small as possible before us. Head bowed to the ground and tone broken as he says, "Never any names. Never the same contact and always untraceable cash. They came to me. I don't know who they are."

My brother and I share a look with a sigh when his phone goes off. Shrugging, he pulls it out, a soft goofy smile pulling his lips as he answers it. "Moya Pl-"

His body snaps straight, hand clenching the plastic with wild eyes. "Hunter slow down, I cannot understand you ...."

Cold fear slams into my heart from nowhere as he calms the boy down. Fear grows to a near terror as his face goes from dark to white in less than a second. Something is wrong and the roaring in my guts has me whipping out my own phone to call Nevaeh. It rings through and goes to voicemail as does Dimitri's.

His gaze lifts to mine mid reach for the pistol at his back. The safety clicks off before he speaks again. "Where is your mother?... Do not move, we are on our way... I know-don't take pressure off the wound and keep him talking."

I give him the nod he's asking for and take the stairs at a run. The phone is back at my ear ringing a third time. Benson is ended before I make it more than a few steps and then my brother's bulk is running at my back. When Max answers a snarled code word has him rallying the men even before I end the call and snap it back into my pocket.

Neither of us speak on our way out of the warehouse nor when we throw ourselves into my car. Rubber squeals and an acidic burn left behind us as I race for the school. The normal hum of the engine drowned out with the roar of the pistons rapid firing.

"Tell me," I growl, as we fly from our shipping district and onto the main road.

"Dimitri and Maskin are shot. Ember is working to slow the bleeding," he chokes out, slamming his fist into the dash several times. "He shot our brother in the head."

He doesn't have to say more. Both of us knew before the call was finished that we'd failed her. That she was back in the hands of that bastard. Hot rage burns through me so strongly I want to roar in fury. But I can't let it out to control me right now. Can't afford to let the monster take control when so much lies in the balance.

First order of business is making sure Ember, and the others are safe. He may have her now but not for long. He thinks he's safe from me, that he can just disappear without a trace with MY wife. What utter bullshit. I'm not as foolish as I was in my youth. She is never out of my reach for long. I'll have their location shortly and then the monster can unleash hell for the disrespect done to my innocent wife.

***

By the time we skid into the parking lot, it's filled with police. The extra guards assigned to our women are surrounding the kids. Viktor's hulking body cradles Katya's small form to his chest with one arm and a crying Josey with the other. Hunter stands, leaning into Ilya's side watching his mother.

"Mikhail," Hunter shouts, breaking into a run.

He jumps into my brother's arms before he can get ten feet from the car. His blood stained arms clutching around his neck as Mikhail drags him closer. Hand cupping the back of the boy's head and whispering in his ear as he continues moving for his wife.

Josey's head snaps our way, and she isn't far behind her brother. Only she doesn't run for Mikhail. Her slim little arms reach for me ahead of her tear-stained cheeks and gut-wrenching sobs as I drop down sweeping her into my hold glad to have someone to focus on so the monster stays back. Someone who can calm the monster long enough to go in with a clear head.

"Hush, moya milaya hush," I whisper, kissing her head as she, like her brother, tries to strangle me. My heart beats a little more regularly knowing the kids are safe at least. But they're still upset that they were subjected to witnessing their uncle and Maskin fall. "I am here, moya plemyannitsa."

Ember is busy talking to the cops, but the moment Hunter's shout reaches her, she turns. Hazel eyes widening in relief at seeing us. Feet eating up the ground as she runs to fling herself into her husband's free arm. A shiver just visible as she allows herself to relax into him.

"Sastra," I demand as gently as possible. "Are you alright?"

"I'm sorry Vlad." Her hazel eyes shimmer full of worry as they swirl a deeper green. "We had just left the office when we heard the shot. The office staff kept the kids and the two of us ran. I went to Dimitri because Maskin was the only one with a gun. There was so much blood... I couldn't leave him."

"You have done nothing wrong, sastra," I quickly say, sparing a hand to grip her shoulder in reassurance.

"She kept fighting. I'm sure Maskin hit him but...," Ember says, shuddering under our hold. Troubled eyes tremble as they lock with mine. "He knocked her out on the bricks. If I had moved faster."

Knowing my wife is hurt nearly unleashes the monster in me, but Josey's scared whimper keeps me in check. Barely, but enough to keep me from simply running after the bastard. I know Ember would have charged in and fought for Nevaeh just as she would for her own children. "I would be much angrier had any of you three been hurt as well. You did exactly what you should have. How are they?"

"Maskin was still conscious when they loaded him but just barely. Dimitri..." One second more of vulnerability and she's standing straight again. "He's fighting. Groaned and muttered but never truly woke up or spoke. They rushed him away."

"Are Dyadya Maskin and Dimitri going to be okay?" Josey whimpers.

"Vlad!" My mother's shout stops any of us from answering her. Her feet rush our way, pushing past the cops with single minded determination that has them parting like the red sea.

Josey squirms in my arms, new tears falling as she reaches for her. "Babushka!"

"Oh, my little one come here," mother urges, nearly taking me with in the process of stealing Josey from my arms. Her normally collected hair slightly lopsided like she was in the middle of getting ready when she got the call. "It is alright now, I have you."

Mikhail looks as if his eyes are going to pop out of his head as he turns to take in her less than perfect appearance. "What are you doing here?"

One dainty hand shoots out, and the slap echoes off his arm. Normally soft eyes blaze when she lifts them from Josey, straightens her shoulders, and stares him down. "I came to get the children so you and the men can bring our Nevaeh home."

"Mat-"

"No," mother snaps, cutting off Mikhail's objection, pulling Hunter from his arms and into her side. Her free hand runs over his jaw gently, but her eyes are full of steel as she looks at both Mikhail and Ember. Her gaze flickers to me before returning to the pair. "You help your brat bring your sastra home."

Chapter 33

Nevaeh

It's raining outside. A light cold spring shower that leaves dampness in its wake and has Chris building a fire too big to make things comfortable. The hot humid air inside the lake house is making my lungs ache, though I much prefer that to the thick coil of rope chaffing my wrists.

Nature can't be changed. It is constant and ever changing at the same time. Rain will give way to the sun just as night gives way to the day. A cycle that repeats without end. Able to be predicted with each season unlike the demon muttering over something in the next room.

At least the view from the large bay windows is enough to lighten the darkness of the situation I find myself in. One way or the other I won't have to wait for an end. Volodya will not let this stand. He'll be coming with an army of men Chris is completely unprepared for. I just wish that I could know for certain whether Dimitri and Maskin were stubborn enough to pull through.

How far he's managed to get us in the time I was knocked out, I can't be sure of. All I'm certain of is that when I finally came too, I was laying in the back of his car, seat belted in and hands tied behind my back. I'm not the tallest woman, but there was little room for my legs and by then I couldn't feel them. Not with how tightly they were tucked into my chest.

The warm weight of the five beaded bracelets Josey made for me roll under the tip of my finger, offering a small bit of comfort. Each an array of mismatched colors, though they all contain one bright bead. A glittery orange with a tiny lily inside. Volodya must have had them specially made, but I'm grateful to have these small pieces of him, since Chris tossed my wedding necklace somewhere along the way here. I miss the slight weight of the jewels at my neck.

Chris's steps echo off the wooden floors well before he takes to his knees in front of me. "Why so sad, Nevaeh our time has come at last. We're finally getting married."

What a fool. I'll never marry him regardless of the time or place. He could be the last man on earth, and I'd light myself on fire and fling myself off a cliff rather than choose him. While I fought Volodya's pull, he was the only one I have ever wanted. The only one I would ever willingly give myself to in this world.

Fingers grip my chin, but I feel nothing. No fear, disgust, or anger at his touch. He has no power over me any longer. All I feel is a soul deep longing for my husband's hold. To hear the throaty rumble of his off key singing, and the thud of his heartbeat under my ear as we lay in our bed. Feel the solid strength of him against me and the gentle carding of his fingers through my hair. The whispered exchange of plot ideas for my latest book.

His hold bites in more harshly as he forces my head up and shakes me till my eyes lift to his. "Do not ignore your husband, Nevaeh."

Disbelieving laughter spills free before I can stop myself, but I find that I don't care. Not anymore. He can harm my body, but he will never have my heart or soul. Those are already claimed and well taken care of by my husband. Because Volodya just wants to hold me close, hear my laugh, and see me smile.

Smiling, I tilt my head and meet his eyes calmly. "You have never been, nor will you ever be my husband. Nothing about you can compare to the man I already have."

I'm facing the lake, blinking tears from my eyes before the sharp pain of the slap registers in my mind. Hands tear at my hair as he forces me back around. "Watch your mouth, baby."

"Enjoy hitting me while you can." I glare, refusing to back down. "Volodya won't make your death quick."

Red faced, he slaps me again. Twisting a chunk of my hair till I think he's going to rip the entire thing out. "That bastard is dead. You are mine and mine alone Nevaeh!"

"Never," I say, lifting my chin in defiance.

Another slap. This time harder before he gently runs his fingers over the reddening skin. "Don't make me hit you anymore, baby. Not on our wedding day."

"Even if he was dead, I'd never marry you," I vow around the taste of copper trickling past my lips. It may not be wise to taunt him, but I can't keep the words in. "He's better than you in every way including the perfect way he fills me."

Another hit stops mid swing. Hand trembling in midair, nostrils flaring, eyes bulging as he stares at me. Eerily silent, the hand slowly lowers, and his face goes completely blank. Looking at me but more through me. Like he can't see me any longer.

His shoulders heave deeply for several breathes then one tear falls and he cups my face like I'm made of glass. "He made you. He made you do it and say such cruel things.

Don't worry baby, I'm going to make everything better again."

Uneasy cold terror curls down my spine. I don't like this tone, nor the way he's looking and touching me like I'm fragile. Denial sits heavy on my tongue, but I bite it back. This isn't him, and I'm becoming truly scared for the first time since he shot Dimitri and dragged me out. Whatever he's planning now is going to be so much worse than what he's put me through before. That I can live through again, but this new gentlemanly behavior reminds me of a venomous snake ready to strike.

God, *please* bring Volodya to me soon. Please don't let him find me like Anya. He won't live through that again. It will be the final straw that breaks him.

"Let me finish getting our clothes ready and then I'll help you get to the shower before getting dressed." He kisses my brow, humming as he goes back into the other room.

Damn it, I have to get out of here. Volodya is coming. I can feel it in my bones but staying here isn't safe. Waiting for him isn't an option when everything in me is screaming at me to run. Run and hide. If I sit here and wait it will mean certain death.

Eyes remaining glued to his form, I desperately start working on my escape. Coarse rope digs harshly into my skin, releasing small streams of trickling blood with each new twist to get just a fraction of space to slip free. I don't need much. My wrists are slim, and I've learned how to disjoint them over the years. I just have to find the right spot.

THERE! The pop is loud in my ears, but Chris doesn't seem to hear it over the roar of the starting shower. Keeping the rope in hand is a welcome discomfort compared to being unable to move within their restrictions. Caution has me holding still just to be safe and thank God I do. Chris turns back to me with a smile growing as he comes closer.

"Let me get myself cleaned up quick and I'll be right with you baby," he says, still humming as he cups my face for another kiss. "Won't be long."

Waiting has my nerves on edge, but I hold myself from bolting just yet. Endure the wink he sends my way when he glances back and sees me watch him undress. Don't twitch as the curtain is pulled between us, and the crack of a shampoo bottle fills the air. Just a moment longer, knowing he'll wash his hair three times.

After a count of ten, I toss the rope off and creep the ten feet to reach the door. Lifting the older latch and pushing it open is surprisingly soundless, but I don't rush. Can't afford to make any noise. Moving slowly, I squeeze through the opening and ease the door closed. Inwardly jerking as lightly warped boards creak under my sandals before sinking into the spongy ground.

Time is of the essence. The moment my toes sink into the dirt, I take off to the right and run for the tree line. The only available cover between the mountains and the lake. One hundred yards on my left are his car and the road he brought us in on.

I'm not stupid enough to go that way. The keys are in his jeans and Dimitri never got around to showing me how to hotwire a car. Soon as I get out of this mess, I'll be damned if one of the men doesn't teach me. I'll learn all the dirty tricks they know to keep myself and the others alive. If Volodya doesn't like it, *too bad.* I'll have back up and an alibi, should he start asking questions.

I need to get lost in the pines so I can hide. Let him get ahead of me, and then follow him out when he realizes I'm gone. Make him show me the way and pray to God Volodya is on my path. Needles scratch my cheeks and catch in my hair as I break through the fringes. Branches slapping off me, roots twisting around my ankles trying to trip me, but I don't stop. Can't when Chris's shout sounds from behind. If he catches me, I'm done.

***

Mud is caked on every part of me and most of my dress. I gave up on my shoes hours ago. Took them off and tossed them down a ravine maybe about five miles back... I think. Measuring distance in the woods is Ember's field, not mine. All I know is that I've been playing cat and mouse with Chris for hours now and it's fully dark. Has been for some time.

Exhaustion is pulling heavily at me in the dark starless night. The shivers started an hour ago. It may be spring, but the nights are still cold. Especially out here in the mountains where there are no towering buildings to block the wind. Being near the lake hasn't helped either, given I've fallen countless times and can't stay dry. While rolling in the mud blotted out the white to help hide me, it also left me wet and chilled.

Glancing up, I wonder where he is. How close we are to each other. I sorely miss the never-ending warmth of my husband's arms. *Soon*. Soon, I'll be back at his side where nothing can hurt me, and Chris will be a long-forgotten memory. A soundless whisper of my husband's name on the wind has me fighting to hold back my tears. I want him so damn bad right now I could curl up and cry.

"Nevaeh, come out," Chris shouts, breaking the quiet with the efficiency of a gunshot.

Everything in me wants to scream in fear and I only just keep the sound in. The smallest gasp could lead him straight to me. Staying silent and praying is all I can do to stay out of sight. Hours of cat and mouse. Numerous slip-ups that nearly had him discovering me. Stopping just short of stepping out into his view. I can't continue like this much longer.

Smooth wood slides under my tightening fingers long since debarked by my hold on the four-foot-long branch I found when I dropped into the mass of roots. It isn't much, but it's a better weapon than my hands.

His tone is smooth as silk as he tries to coax me out. "I know you can hear me, baby. Just come out and we can forget this little chase ever happened."

Feet crunch carelessly off the years of brittle leaves and dead branches littering the forest floor. From the sound of the impacts, it seems like he's nearly on top of me. Nerves nearly desert me, but I fight them and keep still. Refusing to allow myself to twitch with the need to run or curl into a tighter ball. Only the thick tangle of roots above cover me. Maybe I should have tried to flag the helicopter down that flew over the lake half an hour ago.

"Damn it! Where the hell did she go?" He snarls to himself, stopping right above me.

By the time he turns and walks away, black dots are dancing in my eyes from holding my breath so long. An unexpected sob nearly bursts from me, but I choke it back down with a whimper. Now isn't the time. Once I'm out of here, I can allow myself to dive into Volodya's arms and really break down.

First, survive this. Second, find my husband so we can both come to terms with what has happened. Third, find out if Dimitri and Maskin are still alive and maybe have another breakdown. And finally at long last watch Chris draw his last miserable breath.

The chill is sinking deeper into my bones. I need to move to get some warmth though I'm not sure how good an idea that is. Not without knowing where Chris is, so I don't walk into him. But I'm not sure how much longer I can just sit here. There's no way I can curl into myself any tighter and my teeth though clenched are about to rattle my whole jaw. The pale almost blue tips of my toes can't be a good sign either.

Inch by slow inch, I creep out. Eyes darting over every shadow and darkened tree, terrified Chris is sitting out here waiting for me to show myself. Phantom pain prickles along my scalp like he already has me. A large chunk of my hair wrapped around his fist as he dragged me around.

Shaking me for some slight, I have no hope of understanding.

"Stop it," I hiss, and mentally give myself a slap to snap out of it. Now isn't the time for these flashbacks and panic. I can doubt myself later. "Just keep moving."

The night remains calm with the gentle hum of insects, small waves lapping on the shore of the lake, and the light breeze blowing through the pines. No sign of Chris makes me bolder. Feet moving faster down the path closer to the lake hoping to get around him and make for the road. The heavy storm clouds are slowly moving away, allowing the first rays of moonlight to peek through the clouds.

Here I move with more caution. One wrong move can have me slipping, falling ten feet to the rocky shore or into the water. I desperately don't want to get any wetter. Not only that but depending on the spot there's no telling how deep that water is. A fall would most certainly mean injury or even death. The cold still clings to me and refuses to let go though I've been walking for ten minutes.

The soft crack of wood breaking off to my right has me diving into the larger rocks. Curling into the small space wishing it was deeper than the scant foot of shadow allowed by the cleft. Fear skitters over my skin. The sensation of being watched has me wanting to break out into a reckless run just to get away from the feeling.

Something is moving in the darkness. There's a monster close. One that is hunting and intent on spilling blood. Dear God, please that it be my protective monster and not the one intent on ending my life.

Chapter 34
Vlad

The smallest flash of movement has my attention snapping towards the rocky drop off while I mentally curse myself for a careless step. A body disappears before I can get a definitive look at it, but it was for sure human. Without the night vision, the others have I can't be sure if it's one of ours or the ones we're hunting for.

"Movement in the rocks, anyone get a look at it?" Mikhail whispers over the comms.

Fifteen men and Ember voice low mutters of negative before I speak meaning one of the ones we're hunting is right there. My confirmation comes in a low hiss, "Too fast but human. I'm moving in."

"I'm right behind you," Ember says, easing from a thicket of pines from my right without a sound.

Mikhail emerges less than a step behind her, equipment covered eyes sweeping the area for any threat to his wife. I've never known him to allow another to lead him in the field but knowing the woman the way I do, I'm not surprised. These may not be her home grounds, but she moves with the same quiet deadly purpose only an expert hunter is capable of. Still doesn't make me feel better about having her out here. I'd rather she was safe at home with the children, but I'm not stupid enough to say that to her face. Her knowledge is too valuable to leave behind tonight.

Both flank me before I can take a step closer to investigate the new presence, and Ember's sharp uncovered eyes cut up to my own. "How close is she?"

Pulling my phone from my pocket, they move closer to shield the screens glow from any prying eyes. My thumb unlocks it, and the tracking screen zooms in on our position. The bright red dot of my wife's marker blinks so close to us we could be right on top of her.

Fuck, the movement could have been her! Her marker has been back tracking on itself for the last four hours over the same four-square miles. She'd gotten away from him somehow and has been on the run. She could be a mere six hundred feet from me.

I knew the asshole would take the necklace from her at some point if only it was because another man gave it to her. I wasn't fool enough to let that be my only means of keeping tabs on her. The special beads cost me but not nearly as much if I didn't have a way to keep track of her. The added bonus of spending time with a giggling Josey is something I will never turn down either. History wouldn't be repeated a second time. Everyone in the family has a tracker whether they know it or not.

Ember slides into my space and looks for herself. A bright grin pulls her lips up, and she sends me a wink. "Told you she is a fighter. Not enough cover for either of you down there, let me get her."

Swift arguments rise only to be silenced by Nevaeh's scream, "Let go!"

Mikhail's hand stops me from blindly running for her. "Let go of me," I snarl.

"Stop," he growls, shaking the arm he refuses to let go of. "Rushing in won't do her or us any favors. Hell, it could get her killed! He still doesn't know we're here. Trust me brat, let us use the advantage we have."

Fuck, he's right and I hate it. This type of hunting is his world while mine is in the business rooms. Hell, even Ember outpaces me here. I don't have a choice but to follow their lead and take care of my wife as soon as she's in my arms. Once we get both of them home, the monster will have his fun with the bastard before I allow my wife to get the closure she so desperately needs.

"Be smart Ember," Viking crackles, over the line. "We're a thousand yards to the north and moving your way."

My sister snorts and moves toward the rocks with fast strides, rifle held low but at the ready without answering her brother. "Let's go boys."

Mikhail simply shrugs at me with a grin before following her with a quick chuckle thrown back at me, "When she says move out here, you move."

Moving without making noise has me going more carefully than the two in front of me, but the growing argument covers my clumsy steps. It doesn't take long for me to lose sight of her and if Mikhail wasn't staying back, I'd have no idea where she was. She can't be more than twenty feet from me, but I can't spot her. She's like a damn ghost.

Step by step, we close the distance along the bank toward the north. Pinching the bastard in between the teams without him knowing. Finally, through the swaying branches the glint of the rolling waves reveals the struggling shadows of the bastard dragging my wife along.

Four hundred feet from them I watch as she breaks free and runs five steps before he tackles her. Pinning her too briefly for us to take a shot without touching her. A sharp Russian curse flies from her lips as they struggle. He pulls her up and all she can do is stumble. She snaps another curse at him, but he just starts dragging her again by the arm. The fucker tied her hands.

"Three hundred yards off them," Joker growls, through the comms. "Shot lined up, but she's moving too much."

"Hold," Viking hisses. "We want him alive."

"Net's closed," Viktor rumbles with iron control restrained fury.

The confirmation that everyone's in place has me moving to take the lead. Mikhail wisely reaches for his wife and steps aside. Nevaeh isn't going to see the others before she knows I'm here. By the time I break through the last of the tree line, he's got her to the edge of a long wooden dock and there's only forty feet separating us. Raising the pistol, the safety clicking off echoes loudly in the quiet air and I let myself be seen.

Forcing the monster to stay back so I sound like it's just another day in the office. "You have ten seconds to get your filthy hands off my wife."

My name gets cut off before she can fully form it as he spins them around to face me. The white summer dress she was so proud of finding at the thrift store last week is ruined. The one she'd bought especially to wear on the plane today because I turned into a fool as soon as she tried it on to show me. Nearly every inch of the once pristine white lace is covered in mud with dozens of haphazard rips and ribbon strips, leaving it hanging off her shoulders.

Her normally pale skin is even paler. Eyes shimmering with relief and guilt as she takes me in. Trembling lips cracked and bleeding from the cold, her own teeth, or his hits I'm not sure of yet, but the sight has the monster snarling. No matter how she got the wounds, they are ultimately his fault. He's the one who took her, so he will be the one to pay for each precious drop of blood she's lost.

"Don't come any closer," Chris shouts, a blade suddenly appearing to land across Nevaeh's throat in a clear warning.

But I do step closer. Moving into the dim light enough for him to see my face and the deadly grin pulling at my lips. Eyes flashing in stormy joy, eager to see this man beg as he makes the connection. I stand before him in my normal clothes, pistol raised, and body covered with no protection unlike the rest of the team. A blatant dare to take a shot at me while he thinks that I'm the only one he has to worry about.

If this was a time for laughter, I'd let it out right now as his eyes bulge so large they nearly jump from their sockets as he stutters, "*I killed you.*"

"No, it was my brother you shot earlier today." I say, tone bordering on friendly while my smile turns sharp and deadly. "We've never had the pleasure of meeting until now, but don't worry we'll get to know each other quite well as soon as you hand my wife back to me."

The change has me on edge, though I don't show it. I knew the man was evil just from reading what he's done to my wife but now watching the normal looking blond-haired man in his thirties as his face twists, the truth is shocking. Even with what we do and the number of evil men we've put down this one is different. Darker and fouler than the normal trash. A darkness that lays in wait just under the surface for the perfect opportunity to strike.

"I said stay back," he shouts, angling them onto the dock as Viking steps into view with the rest of the team. They cut him off from moving anywhere else. The hand holding her bound wrists lets go, to grip her neck, jerking her back up as her bare feet slip on the wet surface.

The choked gasp leaving her lips has the monster coiling tighter. Demanding to be released to end the threat to what is ours. But not yet. For every step he takes I shadow him clocking his every move to time my own. With how tightly he's holding her, we'll only have one chance at this. It's too risky to steal a glance to reassure her. He's waiting for me to mess up and look away from him.

"One last chance to do this the easy way," I calmly speak, while I match his steps unto the flexing wood. I know that he won't back down even before I finish speaking. "Or... do you prefer the hard way?"

"Stop," he demands, pressing the blade against her skin.

Like hell. He touched what he had no right to. What he never should have and now he's going to pay. The monster sharpens my grin. "You played a dangerous game. A stupid one you never stood a chance of winning."

"She's mine," he snarls, pulling her closer.

"You never had her to begin with," I laugh, taking another step. "She is and has always been *mine*."

His eyes dart to the multiple bodies stepping from the darkness, the murky waters at his sides, me, and the woman in his arms. Cold, calculating, and knowing that he's outmatched with no easy way out. When they bolt my way with my next step, I know he's going to do something bad before he does it.

"You want her back?" Nevaeh gasps on a choke as he lifts his arm and kisses her cheek as if she's fragile. Like she's something he can touch without a care. His eyes lift back to mine as he starts cackling. "If I can't have her, no one else will either."

Before any of us can speak, he picks her up and throws her. Terror flashes through her eyes in silent pleading before her body tips mid fall, and she loses sight of me. Her startled scream silenced as she sinks below the surface. The sound of a gunshot echoes in my ears, but I don't know who shot nor do I care. I barely notice him drop to the dock gripping his leg as I sprint across the distance.

Fuck the bastard, my only concern is getting to her as fast as possible so when there isn't another step, I dive into the water. It's too dark to see anything but I can feel the disturbance in the current, so I aim for it. Pushing myself further down the small bubble trail coming from below. Praying to find her blindly before it's too late. If I don't have much air left, she's got to be nearly out. Even on a good day she can't swim well and now her hands are tied behind her back. She has no way to get loose or help herself. She needs me.

Something soft brushes the very tip of my fingers before the current pulls it away. Lace- it feels like lace. Her dress. My hand stretches, floundering in the water until I feel the brush again and latch onto the small piece and kick harder. A foot drifts into my arm, and my hands drag her closer until her waist is anchored against my hips. Her small body hangs limp in my hold.

Lungs burning and crying for air I shove the creeping horror to the back of my mind and work overtime to get us to the surface. Ignoring the straining in my lungs, the tiredness in my limbs, my only focus is getting her out. By the time we break back into breathable air, it isn't the dark water that has me seeing black. Another second and I would have lost the fight myself.

"Here," Viking shouts, just as a hand grips the back of my shirt and pulls me backwards. "We've got you."

Multiple sets of hands grab Nevaeh's limp form, pulling her out of my arm and onto the dock to lay motionless. Her head rolls with the motion but not even a finger twitches otherwise. Mikhail and Viking lift me between them, and I move to grab her again before they even let go of me.

"Nevaeh," I call, rushing to crawl over to her as Axel works. Pumping her heart while Viktor forces air into her lungs every few beats.

My fingers don't get to make contact before I'm pulled back and held tightly. Mikhail's gruff voice whispers in my ear as I start fighting. "Calm down, brat. Let them work without you getting in their way."

"Let me go," I snarl, ready to turn on him when two soft hands grip my face and pull me around. "I have to get to her!"

Hazel eyes blaze down at me as Ember sinks to her knees in front of me. "Calm down Vlad, none of us are giving up on her. Let them help her."

My lips part ready to scream, when coughing and then vomiting shut me up as I watch them turn her on her side.

Firm hands continue slapping and rubbing on her back as she brings up more water. Painful seconds crawl by as I watch her struggle to get it all out, but Ember still doesn't let go and the men don't back away. If anything, they draw in closer, each gripping the chain around their neck or laying hands on the shoulder next to them. Even Viking's team step forward, eyes sober as they watch, muttering prayers of their own.

Ember presses closer and pulls me into a hug that keeps me in place as I watch my wife's body listlessly shift under the men's hands. Vaguely, I hear Ember muttering her own prayers next to my ear while the men keep moving with grim faces. Mikhail keeps his grip on my arms as if I'm going to fight them.

My mind goes blank with raw terror as Nevaeh flops limply between them when they try to lift her up. Dear God, don't take her like this! I can't lose her. Not like this. Another hard blow finally has her giving a wheezing gasp of breath cut off by hacking coughs that nearly fold her body. She just hangs there limply moaning with each movement until they lay her back down.

"She needs oxygen," Axel growls, without looking away from her as he turns her head to keep her breathing easier. "You got her out quickly, but she swallowed a lot of water too."

“Irish is on his way,” Joker says, kneeling next to the group.

“Good,” Axel grunts, ripping out supplies from his pocket. “Vlad, I need you to hold her still and talk to her. Give her something to focus on and fight for.”

“Come on, Nevaeh,” I plead, rushing over the distance and lifting her into my lap. Hand shaking violently as I brush wet hair from her face shocked by the chilled flesh under my touch. “Moya liliya, I’m right here. Open your eyes for me.”

A choked whimper passes her blue lips, but she hears me. Turns her head to the sound of my voice as she starts shivering. Two emergency blankets are tucked around her and bodies crowd in to block the wind from the helicopter as Irish lowers to land.

Axel grabs one of her hands, inserts a needle with quick fingers, checks her breathing, and moves to reach under her legs. Once ready he gives me a sharp nod. “Let’s move.”

Together we get to our feet and gently carry her over the rocks to the chopper. The medics both join me and start hooking her up to IVs and placing the oxygen mask over her mouth while I hold her in my arms.

Someone wraps a blanket around my shoulders and lands a heavy pat to my back, not that I care until they speak. "You worry about her for now and leave the rest to us."

I glance up long enough to see Viking. "You've done plenty just helping get her back where she belongs. Mikhail will handle him."

The big man grins and shakes his head. One hand drapes lazily over his gear and the other adjusting his collar as he shoots a quick look back at Chris hogtied on the ground. "Now see that's where you're wrong. You're family which makes her family." He nods at Nevah with a softer smile. "And that prick thought he could touch her without dealing with us. My men and I plan to see this all the way through."

Those words have caught my attention. Though, I never expected them to come from Viking. Sure, he sends messages to check in, but he still keeps a careful distance with the work he does. It's a good but strange feeling to know how much he's with us. "I promised her."

"Don't worry we'll make sure he gets all the help he needs to be a well-cared for guest as long as needed." That big grin is back, but the light burning in his eyes is the exact same as Ember when she's promising a brutal retaliation. "We won't do more than keep him company for now. The honor of the final blow is hers."

Chapter 35
Nevaeh

I don't need to open my eyes to know I'm in a hospital. The smell and sound of machines along with the thin blankets covering me are all the clues I need. Though the air is oddly silent. No nurses talking at the desk, no patients' voices drifting in, or rapid footsteps in the halls. The contrast is unsettling to say the least.

I don't hear anyone though the warmth on my left side lets me know I'm not alone. There's at least one other person in the room sleeping from the sound of their breathing. Someone I know at least since we're the only two in here. And being here means that I'm safe.

Volodya saved me somehow, though the last thing I remember is being thrown into the lake. Hands tied behind my back, unable to do anything about what was happening, as I sank under the water and the desperate tightening of my lungs from lack of air. Wanting to thrash and free myself, but knowing that it would use what little air was in my lungs.

Remembering the flash of terror in his eyes as I went airborne has me shuddering under the thin blanket. Breath stalling in my lungs as the scene plays on repeat in my head.

"What's wrong, Nay?" A raspy male voice filters through the air behind a pained groan but I can't shake loose of the memories.

My lungs are burning but if I try to breathe, I'll drown. I have to hold on just a little longer. Volodya is coming. He won't let me die like this. He's right there, just hold on!

"Naveah," he whispers, closer this time. Warm fingers slide over my forehead before dropping to my cheeks and wiping away the tears. "It's okay, just open your eyes. Come on sastra, calm down and look at me."

Oh my God! My eyes fly open on another sob while I take in the smiling form of my brother. His skin is pale and there is a bandage wrapped around his head and over his right ear, but he's alive. Chris didn't take him from me too. It's hard to talk but I stutter the words out, "You're alive!"

"Of course I am," he laughs, but sways mid chuckle and drops a shade paler.

I grab his arm and pull before I can think better of it. My hands tugging him onto the bed next to me as he turns another lighter shade of white. "Sit before you fall. I won't be able to get you off the floor by myself."

The mattress shifts though not enough to bounce as he settles next to me. After a moment he takes a breath and looks a touch healthier. His eyes are full of laughter when they lift to meet mine. "Are you calling me fat, sastra?"

"Well, if the shoe fits," I can't help but giggle though he probably doesn't have an ounce of fat on him. Volodya certainly doesn't have any extra flesh on him, and I know Dimitri is far more active than his twin. The humor is gone as fast as it came as I gently touch the gauze ready to cry again. "I'm so sorry."

"I'm fine," he promises, taking my fingers for a kiss.

"It's all my fault," I choke out, unable to keep looking at his eyes. "He nearly killed you. I nearly took everyone from Volodya again."

"But he didn't because your scream had me turning." He grips my cheeks between his hands. A crocked little smile twists his lip when he gets my eyes back up. "Everyone is safe because you fought for us."

Did Chris really fail? Was everyone still breathing? "Everyone?"

"Everyone," Mikhail chuckles, walking through the door with Ember behind him. "Even Maskin's grumpy ass. He'll be out of the game for a while, but we aren't digging a hole for him right now which I'm thankful for. Can't say he's fully of the same opinion with all the death glares he's passing out, but he'll get over it and take some much needed time off."

Relief floods me until the door closes behind them and my husband hasn't followed them in. He isn't here. Panic flares brightly as I jolt up in the bed and throw the covers away ready to find him myself. "Volodya... Where is he? Why isn't he here!"

"Nay stop," Dimitri demands, planting his hands on my shoulders and shoving me down to pin me to the bed as I start fighting. "He's fine, Nevaeh, I promise."

"Where is he?" I cry, unable to stop the deep aching need to disappear into my husband's arms. "Where is HE?"

Ember steps forward ready to step in. "Dimitri I wouldn't do-"

"Enough!" The voice I need booms like a gunshot off the walls of the room making me cry more as I reach for him.

Mikhail grabs his wife and steps out of the way, unwilling to get in the middle of the twins. "Let it go, moya plamya."

"You shouldn't be out of bed yet, you fool," Volodya growls, eyes locking on his brother. Long legs have him within reach to toss his brother back to his own bed with a careful shove before taking his spot and pulling me into his lap. “I’m here moya liliya, calm down and breathe for me.”

Safe. He’s safe and whole under me as I burrow further into him. “Volodya!”

“I am here,” he whispers, arms pulling me closer as I sob into his chest. “I’m right here. You are safe moya liliya.”

The overwhelming relief of being in his hold doesn’t stop the tears. Only the fear of never seeing him again is banished as his warm heat chases the chill from my body. In his arms nothing in the world can hurt me. Nothing exists but the two of us.

When I can finally breathe, my head lifts, eyes searching for his. “Is he...?”

“Not yet,” he promises, pinching my chin in his fingers before giving me a brief kiss. “The men have him hanging around waiting for us. I vowed to allow you to be there for his end and I always keep my word.”

“Yes. You are very persistent with your vows,” I laugh. I can’t help it. He hates what I forced him to agree to, but he’s going to see it through anyhow.

“Are you teasing your husband, Mrs. Sokolov?”

“Never,” I promise, my hands moving to frame the prickly edges of his jaws as I lift myself around to lean our foreheads together. I smile, lips hovering just over his as I whisper, "It's one of the things I love most about you."

Chapter 36

Nevaeh

"You don't have to do this right now," Ember sighs, stopping next to me eyeing up the area we're heading to. "No one is going to say anything if you just let the fucker rot down there."

Sucking in a deep breath, I try to shake the edge of fear from my veins. The glow of the hallway behind me calls like a warm friend begging me to give in and back away from the darkness on the other side of the oak door. "I want to end this so we can move on."

Wrapping an arm over my shoulders, we stand at the top of the darkened stairs no one but the men have ever been allowed down. "You know he isn't going to look good after two weeks of the guys taking turns with him."

"I'm aware," I say, smiling at her words as I face her. "Volodya doesn't have to say anything when he comes back every night, knuckles and clothes covered in blood and bruises. I know who I married. He may be a monster but he's *my* monster and Chris was stupid enough to wake him up."

While I hate that he is locked within the walls of my sanctuary, this is the way it has to be. He's gotten away and killed two of our own before. This time he wouldn't get the chance. Not in the maze of cells and gates now surrounding him. Every man living on these grounds wants a piece of him for what he's done to the family. He's taken more than his share from us and now it's time to even the score.

Her rough fingers slide into my own with a dark chuckle as she leans close. "Then let's go show him what a queen you are."

God, I want to snort at her words because I'm definitely not a queen in any way, shape, or form. A queen wouldn't worry about all the self-doubt that's spinning in my mind. Hell, there's days Volodya refuses to let me out of bed until I believe the way he sees me. I don't even have to say anything or open my eyes, and he already knows. Not a queen, just a woman blooming under the care of her personal protective monster husband.

I grip her in return as we start the long climb down the stairs. The further we go the more chilled and damp the air is. Dark stone walls of the same big stones that make up the rest of the house. Viktor stands at the bottom of the steps across from Maskin's straight form. One leg kicked up on the wall behind him as he leans against the stone with his arms crossed glaring at the tunnel leading further in.

"Really boys, waiting for us isn't the end of the world you know?" Ember sighs, shaking her head.

"Not mad," Maskin scoffs, eyes still locked on the next gate.

Hazel eyes roll without a word. Shaking her head, she lets go of me to pat the big man's arm like he's one of the kids. "Don't worry Mass, I'm sure Nevaeh will let you get a few more shots in before it ends."

His gaze finally snaps to look at her for a second and then raises to mine. Some of the hardness leaves his features, and I swear guilt flashes before he nods. "Let's go."

My fingers tangle in his sleeve to pull him up short. His sharp eyes snapping back to mine so fast I nearly lose my nerve. "Maskin... Thank you."

He literally jolts, taking a step back with wide eyes. Head shaking, he pulls from my hold and mutters, "I nearly got you killed. It was you who saved me."

"What?"

"You fought Nevaeh," Ember murmurs, a soft smile I've only ever seen her use on the kids greets me as she hugs my shoulders.

"He shoved me into the brick," I whisper, shifting uncomfortably while racking my brain for what happened in the standoff. "He-"

The feel of Chris's arm around my neck, unforgiving metal digging harshly into my side, his excitement over having me back in his power. The knowledge that he'd hurt more than just me if he got out of there. What did I do besides stand there before everything went dark? "I don't remember anything else until I woke up in the car."

Maskin nods, his good hand raising to squeeze my fingers. "He didn't throw you. You broke free just as he pulled the trigger. If not for you he'd have hit me in the heart, but you knocked his arm up enough to take my collarbone."

"Sastra." Dimitri steps out of the door and walks our way wearing a grim smile. He still wears a bandage on his head, but it's smaller, just covering the wound that doesn't appear to affect him any longer. His hug is fast, hard, and full of protective guilt as he keeps me close longer than needed. "Are you sure you want to do this?"

I can't help the chuckle from working its way up at the reluctance in his stance. All these big scary men bent on coddling me from a little blood and death not knowing that I've already witnessed it. Seen it, watched it happen, and felt the blood on my hands as I pulled the paring knife free of a pale neck. Felt the muscle give as I stabbed again. Death's final gurgle in my ears and pulsing under my fingers before I was pulled away and checked for injuries. A dark secret kept quiet between my husband and myself.

"I'm not afraid of him brat," I say, smiling up at him and tap his nose to lighten his mood. "I've only stayed away this long because of Volodya. He needed to feel like he handed out enough justice for me with his own hands before he could be satisfied with the end."

Viktor snorts, pushing away from the wall. His dark eyes meet mine over a predator's smile before he heads for the door with a wave for us to follow. The air vibrating with his smokey rumble as he speaks, "Two weeks is not long enough to right those wrongs. It wouldn't be long enough for me if he touched my woman like that, but he wants things wrapped up so you can move on."

Chapter 37
Vlad

"Are you sure about letting her in to see all this?" Max rumbles, next to me in Russian while keeping an unnerving smile on his face.

All I can do is nod and growl, "I promised."

Honestly, if I hadn't made that promise she wouldn't know he was even down here and still alive. Hell, no matter how late I tried to sneak back into our room she was always still awake. Calmly curled up on the couch under a blanket reading or working on another book. Only looking up to give me a soft smile but not moving until after I finish showering. Then, meeting me at the door with a deep kiss before pulling me into bed. Her soft fingers mapping the spilt skin and bruises before thanking me and drifting off to sleep.

"It's what she needs," I say after a moment, continuing in Russian. "She needs to know he's truly gone for good."

"She wants to see him cut up like this?" He raises a brow at me, before tossing his own suggestion into the mix of laughing men.

As strange as it seems to the men she does, and I can't fault her for it. But more than anything, she wants to close the last horrible chapter of her life on her own terms. Look him in the eyes and deny him the same way he denied her. To send him off with the knowledge that he failed.

Chris's eyes haven't left me since I walked in and while I hate to give him any credit, at least he knows who's in charge. He still starts each day with self-righteous demands but they're getting quieter and less sure that he'll get out. Which he won't. Not after everything he's done. Even if he hadn't taken Nevaeh again, his life was forfeit for killing two of my men and bringing his drug obsession to my streets. Every man in the room has heard the truth and taken blood in repayment. Ember and Mikhail have taken part together, with the skillset of artists in carving into his flesh. They'd turned it into a game to see who could make him scream the most. Now not a single inch of his skin is free of the payment for his crimes except for his face. We've been careful to avoid messing up his vision, so he sees his end coming clearly.

The brief surge of defiance in his eyes as the men clean up the mess quickly hardens when Mikhail and Viking decide to play with him. I could stop them, but I don't. I let the fucker hang from the chains, squirming, barely able to touch the floor with his toes. All the while the men trade bloody stories of what they'd do to him if it was their wife he touched. How long they'd drag it out and how they'd take care of the body, so no one would even know. How they'd scatter the small chunks of him but all anyone would know was that he was a missing person.

A casual grin on his lips, Mikhail pulls out his big blade and sits to start sharpening it right in front of Chris's widening bloodshot eyes. Drawing out the motions and sound while joking with Viking seated on a chair on my other side. The rest of their teams save for Maskin and Viktor stand back silently watching with large grins. A few offer grisly techniques to draw it all out.

Each painting a bloodier picture with each offense they tick off the list that all of us have memorized. It isn't all that he's done to her. I wouldn't hurt her by airing everything, but they know enough that Viking and his team are in agreement to look the other way as we deal with this piss ant. Working in the dark where the government can't be seen going has its bright spots.

There's still blood on the floor that hasn't been washed down the drain, but that can't be helped any longer as the door clicks to let the others in. The hardness I've worn since stepping into the cell softens as I watch her walk in tucked under Dimitri's arm. His eyes darken as soon as he steps in to see the hanging man's gaze lock on my wife.

Fuck, she changed into the new teal sundress I bought for her the other day. I knew she would look beautiful in it, but seeing it in person? It's taking all my strength not to toss her over my shoulder and running back to our bedroom. Or even falling to my knees at her feet. Her hair hangs loose and wild, shifting like waves with each step she takes. The necklace fully repaired of the light damage sits boldly at the base of her throat. She's utterly stunning as she walks into the bloody room. A queen. My queen.

Nevaeh doesn't even glance at him as her eyes find me. She pulls from my brother's arm before he can speak, rushes to jump into my arms, and drags me into a kiss. The old me wouldn't take more than what she gave, but I do. I drag her so there isn't an inch of space between us and dip far deeper than is appropriate in view of the men. Pulling away I bury my nose in her neck, pleased that she smells like her favorite flower in this dark place.

"You don't have to do this, moya liliya," I whisper, cupping her head closer. "But I know you won't let me take you back upstairs yet."

A breathless giggle shakes her form. "Not yet."

I'm reluctant to let her go, but I let her back away to meet my gaze. Though I know she can do this, the protector in me wants to take her far away. To shield her from all the evil. The tilt of her chin and glint in her eye tells me she won't back down till this is done. The monster resting just under the surface approves of her bravery to avenge herself. Teeth bared in a feral grin as his queen takes her place next to us.

Forcing myself to breathe, I give her a smile and nod. "As soon as you're ready."

She lifts and takes my lips in a long slow kiss that has me dragging her closer. A few moments where it's just the two of us. When she spins and leans back into my arms, I lift my head to look at the others. Mikhail stands gripping Ember's hips. Dimitri, Maskin, and Viktor stand guard at the door glaring at the breathing corpse. Viking and the rest of the team step closer, eyes watching to see how things play out.

Chris quickly covers the rage in his features as he looks at my wife. The trembling in his limbs can't be hidden even by his pitiful whimper. "Nevaeh... Baby, please help me."

Her shiver is small. Barely noticeable but every man in the room is trained to see it though she doesn't back down. Straightening her spine, head shaking, she gives a little laugh. “Do you think I didn’t know what they were doing down here? Who do you think told them to do this?”

His face falls like he can't believe her words. “Why?”

“A better question is after the hell you put her through why wouldn’t she?” Dimitri snorts, lowering himself into the only chair in the room next to me. His skin is slightly paler than normal.

“You’re mine, Nevaeh!” His breath stutters, like he can’t believe that she isn’t helping him.

“Oh *please*, not this again,” Nevaeh grumbles, shoving my hands down and stepping forward to lean closer to his face with a sassy grin. “You could never be a fraction of the man my husband is.”

“Stop playing Nevaeh, you'll always be mine in the end. He’s just playing a game with you. He doesn’t truly love you, not like I do. Don’t let him come between us like this.”

My nails dig painfully into my palms, so I don’t close the distance and start beating on him. I have to stay where I am. If I move, I’ll kill him and take the ending Nevaeh deserves from her. The rest of the others don’t bother masking how they feel over his word. Only a simple wave from my wife keeps us all in place.

“So, all the slaps, punches, kicks, the nasty degrading words... that was you loving me?” Her lips twist in disgust as he blinks at her dumbly. Like he can't believe she doesn't understand. "I'd rather spend the rest of my life in a nunnery than live with that form of love but guess what-"

"You needed to be taught," he spits. "I had to break you down to make you perfect. To make you see that our life was the only way."

"Enough," I snap, stepping forward, unwilling to hear more. It's taking everything in me not to bloody the fool again with the way he's talking about what he did to her. "You will not talk to my wife like she is worthless when you aren't worthy to be in the same time zone as her."

One soft hand on my chest halts my movement. Her arm wraps around the back of my waist, and she cuddles into me under my arm as I lift it to draw her closer. Her warmth soothing the anger just slightly. "Don't waste your breath Volodya. He'll never understand how a man is supposed to truly love his wife. All he's ever done is make women scream in fear unlike you."

The men chuckle around him as the mask falls again. His eyes narrowing into slits, blazing in rage as she relaxes into my arms finally cracking his pleading play as he spits, "You whored yourself out to the devils you stupid bitch!"

Viking, moves faster. The force of his hand's strike echoing loudly in the air first. A strangled grunt follows as Maskin buries his fist so far into the bastard's guts it lifts him and folds him in half. Knuckles pop around the room but no one else moves, not even me. Nevaeh stands calmly in my hold seemingly unbothered by the violence with her head over my heart and fingers playing with mine.

Maskin grips his hair and forces his head back as Viking leans forward. A grin eerily similar to his sister's that spells nothing but trouble grows as he cracks his neck. "I'd watch the way you talk to my sister Christopher, or my brothers and I are going to take it personally. You think what's happened already was bad?"

"Speak of our Pakhan's wife so disrespectfully again," Maskin growls, pulling harder. "And we'll make things for you much worse. Much longer than the short two weeks of fun we've had."

"I'm sure Kenna wouldn't mind me waking her up to tell me how to castrate this trash," Ember purrs, digging into Mikhail's pocket for his phone with eager an glee burning brightly in her eyes at the new idea.

"Leave Kenna alone. Let her sleep sastra," I chuckle, speaking up before she can unlock the phone screen.

Nevaeh steps to the end of my hold only stopping when my fingers flex in resistance of letting go. "Ember."

She glances up at me for permission, and I just nod at her unspoken question. Her bright smile is all the reward I need. Whatever she wants to do is fine by me and I'll help her anyway I can. I don't like him being so close to her but there's nothing he can do to her besides scream and rant.

Blonde braid swinging sharply, Ember turns to her in interest as Mikhail takes his phone back. "What do you need Nevaeh?"

Licking her lip, she takes a breath, raises her chin, and makes her request. "May I borrow your knife?"

"No ma'am," Ember laughs, reaching behind her back and drawing something from under her shirt. "As much as I love you, I'm not dealing with the tantrum your husband is going to throw when you cut yourself on it. The blade's far too big for you, but you can use your own."

She steps forward, out of my arms and reaches for the blade, fingers curled around the sheath carefully. She freezes, registering Ember's words. Her wide brown eyes lift to meet Ember's amused gaze. "Mine?"

Chuckling, Mikhail pulls his wife back for a kiss. "That little blade had her from our bed far longer than its size should have warranted."

Laughing, she kisses his chin and tucks herself closer. "Oh hush, you know I can't sleep until I get it out once it hits me."

"Yes, and you always make it up to me so sweetly," he says, giving her a kiss before tuning back to the rest of the room. "It's sharp and ready to be used. Show us what you have in mind, sastra."

Humming Nevaeh raises her new knife to study for a moment before pulling it from its leather housing. The polished antler handle fits into her palm perfectly with a small guard protecting her from the six inches of sharp steel. The lone light bulb catches the edge revealing the detail of the Damascus.

"Thank you, Ember," she whispers, voice warbling over the emotions rushing through her. "This is perfect."

"I know," Ember grins as Mikhail rolls his eyes at her. "Dream blades are meant for only one person so they're always what their person needs."

I watch my wife's shoulders lift in a deep shuddering breath before she lifts her eyes to Chris. "I've been dreaming of this end for a very long time. How I'd drag it out and make you feel everything you did to me."

Chris opens his mouth to argue but Maskin jerks harder, silencing him before he can speak. His growl is harsher this time, vibrating the air with an electric chill. "She isn't finished speaking, boy."

"Thank you, Maskin," she says, smiling sweetly at the quiet sniper before facing her ex. "You didn't just hurt me but my whole family."

Her words are low, just an octave above a whisper though the whole room hears them. Watching as she twists the knife between her fingers while she decides what she wants to do. The rawness has my feet moving before I give them the command. Her tone, her stillness, the way she stands has my guts churning. Something pivotal is about to happen and I need to be there to help her with it though at this moment I have no idea how. Just the overwhelming need to be right next to her in the moment.

A smile tips her lips up as she continues. “But more than anything, I want peace. You’ve controlled enough of my life as it stands, and I won’t give you any more of my time.”

One arm moves my way, takes my hand, pulling me flush to her back, and pressing our laced fingers over her heart. Her soft lips ghosting over our fingers for a brief second. The other moves at the same time, arching through the space filling the air with the bloody gurgle of a dying man.

A fall of hot blood runs in a thick stream over the lower portion of his throat and down his chest. Flowing faster at the angle Maskin holds his shuddering, dying body in. Chains rattle with each spasm until the light fades from his eyes.

“I’m giving you more mercy than you ever gave me.”

Chapter 38
Nevaeh

He doesn't let go of me. Doesn't say a single word. Not once since I pulled him to me as I killed my past. Warm fingers play in feathery strokes on the bare skin under my arm as he leads us out of the darkened hallways into the brightness of our home. Light burning off the last hints of darkness being cleaned up below.

The men left on duty track the splatter on my clothes and nod at us as we walk by. Murmurs of approval, respect, and praise follow us up the steps until our door closes us from the world. Stopping only long enough to kick our shoes off before he keeps us moving without saying anything.

Walking us into the bathroom he finally let's go to turn on the water of the walk-in shower. On a normal day, I'd spend time taking in the warm marble floor and brass finishes. Today none of those things hold my interest. My eyes don't stray from Volodya's silent form. The smooth flow of his movements as he checks that the water is the right temperature.

We reach for each other at the same time. Fingers popping buttons, pushing clothes out of the way. Not that it's very fair given that I have half the items he does. He has me bare while I still have his pants. He stands still, allowing me to finish without interference.

Then once I stand from dragging his pants off, he pulls me with him into the steaming spray. Fingers tangle in my hair, tilting my head back so that the water soaks into every strand. Lathering up my hair with deep slow kneads that have my eyes rolling in pleasure. He soaps me up from head to toe, rinsing the suds from my body with gentle strokes.

His hands frame my face so tenderly, I'm on the verge of crying as he leans down. Lips barely brushing over my forehead before dropping to hover over my ear whispering, "I'm so proud of you, moya liliya."

"I killed a man," I say hoarsely, playing with the panel of muscles over his abs."Looked him in the eyes and felt... nothing. After it was done I was numb and relieved at the same time as I watched his life fade."

"Moya liliya." He gently tips my chin up, understanding burning in his gaze as he strokes wet hair back. "His fate was his own design. Death was the only way to stop him.

Whether it came from our hands or not, he was not going to live. Viking and the men would not have allowed it. "

Tears cloud my eyes as I whisper,"I should have felt something other than numb and grateful."

"You are," he sighs, pulling me close. "Here and now where he can't hurt you any longer, you are feeling. Your heart is acknowledging the feelings it hid to protect you during the act. You did what had to be done with the emotion that was needed. A goodness and mercy I don't have in me to extend to his type of trash."

Oh lord, now I really am going to cry. Why does this man have to be so sweet all the time? I just killed a man while holding his hand and he's proud of me. "I didn't do anything extraordinary."

His husky chuckle bounces off the walls as he tips my chin to meet my eyes. "Everyone else in the world doesn't see it and they don't have to. But everything..."

"Volodya," I say, trying to cut him off because I know the rest of his words are going to make me cry.

He pulls me closer, tucking me into his hard chest. "Everything about you is brilliant in my eyes. You are the light of my world, always pulling me back from the darkness before I lose myself."

Fuck, I'm not crying right now. He's seen me at my lowest and never made me feel less than real in his eyes.

I have just enough strength to speak as I burrow into his hold. "The way you talk I seem perfect but I'm not."

"No, not perfect," he whispers. "Real. The only woman I don't have to hide myself from."

Real...Turning my head to press my ear over his heart, I roll the words over in my mind until the only thing I can do is smile at the truth. The past is behind us and with him by my side all I want is to move forward. To take my dreams and make them come true with this man by my side.

Shifting away, I give him a long, slow kiss that leaves me seeing stars and in danger of passing out from lack of air. Our panting breath mingles as I cup the back of his head and stare into his eyes.

"Take me to bed, Volodya," I demand, playing with his hair. "I'm tired of dreaming. Help me build our future."

Glossary

Pakhan- the boss or leader of the Bratva

moya plamya- my flame

moya lyubov'- my love

moya liliya- my lily

moya tigrovaya liliya- my tiger lily

moya milaya malen'kaya tigrovaya liliya- my sweet little tiger liliy

moya milaya- my precious

sastra- sister

mladshaya sastra- younger sister

plemyannitsa- niece

plemyannik- nephew

brat- brother

mat- mother

otets- father

doch'- daughter

babushka- grandmother

YA vsegda budu zashchischat' tebya, take zhe kak ty vsegda budesh' oberegat moyu dushu. – I will always protect you, just like you will always shelter my soul.

M.A. is your average small town tomboy, trucker's wife, boy mom, and feral horse girl from Central Pa with a love for a way of life most think outdated. Yes she cooks with cast iron. -if you know you know ;)- If she isn't at the keyboard disappearing into her own worlds she is outside and most likely in the barn. She loves spreading time in the wilds- hunting, tracking, hiking, riding, and exploring places most wouldn't try.

www.ingramcontent.com/pod-product-compliance
Lightning Source LLC
LaVergne TN
LVHW100504110826
845146LV00002B/514

* 9 7 9 8 9 9 0 7 4 9 8 7 0 *